PRAISE FOR TJ NICHOLS

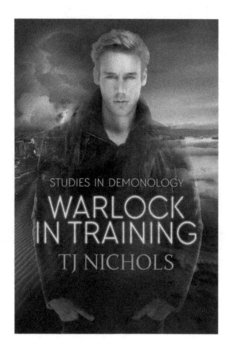

"This fantasy story is truly brilliant."

— GAY BOOK REVIEWS

"A book that provokes thought as it entertains."

— BINGE ON BOOKS

"Engaging characters, interesting and compelling world, and outstanding story telling. I wholeheartedly recommend this book to any fantasy lovers out there."

— JOYFULLY JAY

"WOW! The world building and emotion in this book bowled me over!"

"We're completely hooked into the story, wanting to know more..."

"...if you're looking for a suspenseful adventure full of surprises, twists and turns, and more than one revelation, then you will probably like this novel as much as I do. I can't wait for the final installment!"

"I was so excited to see Angus and Saka again and I wasn't disappointed. This story was just as in depth and thought out as the last one."

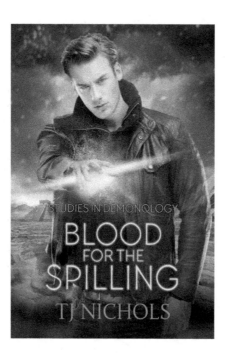

"...a fun, exciting finish to Nichols's trilogy."

"I would highly recommend them if you like epic fantasy/erotic romance with graphic violence."

"...both met and exceeded my expectations."

WARLOCK IN TRAINING

STUDIES IN DEMONOLGY

TJ NICHOLS

WARLOCK IN TRAINING

Angus Donohue doesn't want to be a warlock. He believes draining demons for magic is evil, but it's a dangerous opinion to have—his father is a powerful and well-connected warlock, and Angus is expected to follow the family tradition.

His only way out is to fail the demon summoning class. Failure means expulsion from the Warlock College. Despite Angus's best efforts to fumble the summoning, it works. Although not the way anyone expects.

Angus's demon, Saka, is a powerful mage with his own need for a warlock.

Saka wants to use Angus in a ritual to rebalance the magic that is being stripped from Demonside by warlocks. If Angus survives his demon's desires and the perils of Demonside, he'll have to face the Warlock College and their demands.

Angus must choose: obey the College and forget about Demonside or trust Saka and try to fix the damage before it's too late. Whatever he does, he is in the middle of a war he isn't qualified to fight.

CHAPTER ONE

It wasn't that Angus Donohue couldn't summon a demon; it was that he didn't want to. He didn't even want to be here. A cool breeze brushed against his skin, and the trees around him rattled like a closet full of old bones. Maybe if he didn't put enough will into the spell the whole thing would fall apart.

If he couldn't summon a demon, he'd fail the class and get kicked out of the exclusive Warlock College his father had forced him to attend. While there was a certain prestige in being a warlock, it wasn't what Angus wanted to do with his life. He certainly didn't want a demon to draw magic from. He had to fail this class. His father would be horrified, but Angus would be free from all things magical.

"*Widdershins*, three times," the lecturer commanded.

All the college students of Demonology 102 started walking anti-clockwise around the circles they had carefully constructed out of will. Angus suppressed the shiver. He wasn't afraid of demons. Okay, maybe just a little. What if his demon was something truly monstrous?

Last semester they'd been learning about the different types of demons and the theory behind drawing magic from one. This semester was about putting that knowledge into practice. Those people with magic who didn't draw on demons were called wizards and usually sold their services cheaply in the local paper. Angus didn't want to be a practicing wizard either. Just because he had magic didn't mean he needed to make a career out of it, and telling his father that hadn't been a wise move. His father had spent three hours railing about why wizards were dangerous and should be banned from practicing magic.

So here he was, trying to summon a demon that he didn't want, to give himself more of the magic that he didn't want either. He let his circle weaken and his attention drift. He would not summon a demon.

He'd have rather been a vet.

Maybe studied medicine.

Although the rich, these days, saw specialist warlock healers who had demons. Though his father sneered at them too. He sneered at anything that didn't increase his power and standing. That he was on the board of the East Vinland Warlock College did not make life easier for Angus.

Angus tried not to focus on the spell, but it was hard not to think about the demons on the other side of the void. Whatever demon popped into the circle would be his personal demon to summon at will. He'd be able to control it. And when it was no longer of use, or drained of magic, kill it and move on to another demon. It all sounded perfectly safe as long as he followed the rules.

Still, none of the rules he'd learned about dealing with demons had worked to assuage Angus's fears or doubts. It was safer not to summon one.

After all, if humans could summon demons across the void, what was to stop demons from summoning humans across the void? No one ever talked about that. Not in public anyway, though wizards and warlocks occasionally went missing. Those who had been found and brought back from Demonside never spoke publically. What had happened to them in Demonside?

There were groups, websites that suggested that demons were no different than humans. They looked nothing like humans. The college reminded students at every opportunity that demons were lesser beings.

Cold balled in Angus's gut as he made his third turn around the circle. He cleared his mind of demons and did everything short of dropping his carefully made circle.

His skin prickled as the circle went pop. The power was there, a breach in the void between the worlds now existed in his circle. *Damn it.* He hadn't even meant to get that far. The lecturer looked at him, his face fixed in a mask of expectation. They all knew who he was. His father was too well known, and his family had attended this college for generations.

Angus couldn't shut the tear in the void without the lecturer noticing. Maybe he could avoid calling a demon through. If he didn't call, surely there would be no answer. Maybe he didn't have a demon waiting for him.

Around him other students held their circles, the forest now full of little tears in the void. What if they ripped and joined up...?

"Now call your demon to you. Feel the energy. There is a link between the worlds, a demon that wants to rush to your side and act as a magical conduit for you." The lecturer's voice rung out, bouncing off the trees. "Your demon that will give you the power you need. This is a very important moment. The kind of demon you call will say a lot about your magical skills and your warlock potential."

Angus wished that his parents hadn't insisted on him going to Warlock College. He really just wanted to be a normal nineteen-year-old guy who was nothing like his father. Not everyone who could control magic should.

The air in his circle shimmered as something came across the void. *Oh, crap.*

This wasn't supposed to happen. He was supposed to fail and be kicked out of college. Failing demonology was an automatic out. There was nothing his father could do. Angus would've been free.

He risked a glance around. Demons were popping into existence in the circles of the other students. A cat-like thing with a scorpion-like tail, that was a scarlips. A hulking purple saber-toothed gorilla. A white-skinned woman with blood red lips and talons to match—a vampry—powerful and dangerous.

Angus snapped his attention back to his circle. A tall mannish creature with elegant black horns and a tail stood there. His demon. He was now officially a warlock. All his hopes of failing and leaving the college fell apart. He closed his eyes for a moment. He needed a new plan. He didn't have one. He'd pinned all of his hopes on not getting a demon.

Now that he had one, he was going to have to deal with it. He opened his eyes to study what he had summoned.

In his circle was a typical black-horn demon. A garden-variety demon, nothing too horrendous or dangerous, nothing his father could boast about. While its chest was bare, the demon was wearing black pants and carrying a rather ferocious looking machete. It was also smiling.

That was disconcerting, as though the demon wanted to be there. Maybe his lecturer hadn't lied about demons wanting to serve. The longer Angus looked at the demon, the broader its—his—smile became.

The demon was supposed to be anathema to him. He wasn't. Intrigue fluttered in Angus's chest. Then he remembered that he was in class, and he was supposed to be exerting control over his demon.

"I am your earthbound master," Angus said, echoing several other students.

The demon laughed, dark and rich. "And I am your Demonside master."

No one else's demon was answering back. They were all waiting for orders.

"That's not the way this works." Why did he have to get the smartass demon? Why did he have to get one that could talk?

The one that looked almost friendly in a dangerous kind of way.

The lecturer was still speaking. Angus struggled to tear his gaze away from the demon. A warm breeze brushed against his skin. Summer had just finished, not that it had ever really begun. There was talk they were heading for an ice age. No one could agree on why, but the top warlocks were working on it. The heat was tempting, and he took a step closer to the circle and the demon. Until one of them died, he was stuck with this demon.

"Right, now everyone has their demon, let's try a simple gathering of energy before we send them home." The lecturer sounded pleased with his class. That everyone had a demon meant that he'd got a 100 percent pass rate. No doubt he'd won a bet or would get a bonus. Not every student was successful.

Angus had screwed up failing the class.

He returned his attention to his demon. The demon stared at him. Angus was sure the demon was creating the warm air but he didn't know how. He had a bad feeling about drawing some power from the demon since his demon was smiling and looking entirely too comfortable. In the fading light, his skin had lost its reddish gleam. For a demon he was attractive in a dangerous kind of way.

Angus pushed aside the thought. He should not be admiring the creature in the circle. Or the way it was so calm. Other demons were obviously agitated, thrashing their tails and snarling. The vampry was picking her at her nails as though bored. Angus shuddered; she was creepy. At least his wasn't creepy.

All he had to do was draw some magic, and then he could get rid of the demon that he hadn't wanted to summon in the first place, until the next class when he'd have to see him again. Now whenever Angus needed power, all he had to do was summon him and tap into his demon. He'd spend the rest of the semester, his life, being entirely too close to the horned creature.

Angus closed his eyes and tried to feel the magic flowing from Demonside. It was soft and spicy like a freshly baked treat that was begging to be eaten. He wanted to reach for the magic and sample its delights.

His demon laughed.

Magic swelled, but it wasn't Angus's doing.

"I want to see what lies within your heart." The demon broke the circle. Before Angus could protect himself—the first thing every warlock learned—the demon grabbed Angus by the wrist and pulled him through the void.

Heat slammed into Angus and then sank into his skin. He stumbled on the uneven ground, the demon's grip on his wrist tightened to prevent him from falling. The air was hot and thick and heavily scented. He wasn't in the cold forest of Vinland anymore. He knew where he was, but he hoped he was wrong.

Angus squinted and blinked against the bright sun. Around him the conversation quieted and then became appreciative murmurs. Someone clapped and a few others joined in.

"Thank you. I was prepared. If a mage of my level cannot snare a young warlock, then something is amiss," the demon Angus had summoned said.

Angus looked around, his eyes dazzled by the glare coming off the sand. Everything was too bright. He blinked a few times. He seemed to be in some kind of market.

In a shimmery blue circle with his demon.

With a small gesture, the circle shattered like crystal, leaving a sharp tang on the air.

Wait…. Magic was visible here? He had seen the circle. Had anyone else?

"Don't try to run, there is no settlement for several days and the scarlips will find you most tasty… assuming another demon doesn't get hold of you first." His demon's voice was smooth and too close. He was still holding Angus's wrist as though he expected him to flee.

Angus lifted a hand to shield his eyes. Beyond the mats of wares, there were colorful tents, beyond them miles and miles of red sand. Red, not yellow. He glanced up. Above him in a slightly more purple sky than he was used to was a fat orange sun that seemed too big and too close.

He knew the answer, but he still had to ask. "Where am I?"

"What you call Demonside. We call it Arlyxia. It is one of the dimensions closest to yours, thus the bleed through."

"What?" Only the first part of that sentence made sense. He knew where Demonside was, and he hoped that he wasn't there. All the talk about demons summoning their warlocks had suddenly become truth. Some of those missing warlocks were never heard from again.

Angus felt that he should be panicking or crying or begging or something, but all he could muster was a kind of numb shock.

The demon stared at him. His skin was a dark reddish brown and glittered as though covered in metallic dust. His eyes were black, as black as his horns. The typical black-horn demon was considered relatively harmless. They had no sharp teeth, or claws. If anything, aside from the horns and tail, they looked fairly human. There was no glory in having a common black-horn demon. His father would be disappointed. No, his father was going to be infuriated that a demon had dragged him across the void to Demonside.

"Aren't you supposed to be an all-knowledgeable warlock? Hmm?" The demon lifted a brow ridge. He had no eyebrows or any hair on his head. "Did your classes not give you the whole truth?"

"Um... no?" None of his teachers had ever mentioned what to do if taken. Not in ethics, spell casting or the theory of summoning, or even the history of demons and their use throughout ancient and classical history. Modern history and the demon wars of the early twentieth century were well known.

Had he read something about horned demons being tricky and debauched? Gaining mastery over your demon was so important so they didn't act up. *Oops.* He obviously hadn't succeeded, that or his demon was trickier than usual.

Nice work, Angus. He could hear his father's disappointment already. Did this count as a fail? He hoped so.

"I should be getting home. My parents will be worried." How hard could it be? Make a circle and open up the void. Easy. Demons crossed the void all the time and ran wild through cities until the college stopped them. He started to imagine a circle. It formed, and shimmered around him, then shattered.

Angus gasped. That was twice in one day this demon had brought down his circle. Had the demon called himself a mage? What was that exactly? Was it like a warlock? If it was, he was in trouble. More trouble.

The demon shook his head. "I don't think you understand your situation. I told you I am your Demonside master and I meant it."

Angus blinked at the shimmery, handsome demon. "You can't be my master. That's not the way it works." He needed to get home. "I am going home."

He cast another circle only to have it pulled apart again.

The demon laughed. "Humans. You have such a limited understanding of magic. You think you can pull us through the void and tap us for power whenever you want. Where do you think that magic comes from?" The demon stalked closer.

"Here." Everyone knew that magic flowed cross the void from Demonside, but only some humans could use it.

"We call it alchemy; I believe you call it physics. Energy cannot be created or destroyed, yes?"

Angus nodded, suddenly aware that there were still people, demons, watching them.

"So where do you think the magic comes from, and where do you think it goes?" The demon crossed his arms over his bare chest. "What happens when the two worlds become unbalanced?"

"I haven't studied that yet."

"I don't think you will. It isn't in the syllabus." He turned away. "Follow." Then he glanced over his shoulder with a grin, his teeth were a little too pointy for it to be reassuring. "Or not."

Angus did a quick assessment of the market full of demons and decided that, in this situation, it was most definitely better to go with the demon he knew if he wanted to get home.

CHAPTER TWO

Saka waited for a moment to make sure that the human warlock, warlock-in-training he corrected, was indeed following. While the unwritten rules forbade kidnapping humans, anyone who opened up a portal was considered fair game. After all they had invited the connection, and one didn't accidentally open up a portal to another dimension. That took effort and will and an ability to use magic.

If a human could use magic, it meant they could also then abuse it and the demon they took it from. Saka pressed his lips together. He hoped his lover was still alive, but he knew in his heart that Kitu was gone. Waiting for a fresh connection with a new warlock had been torturous. But today there had been a crackle in the air. He knew the scent and the feel on his skin.

Arlyxia might be full of magic, but the tears to Humanside couldn't be opened from here. Which, while annoying, made sense. After all magic, like any power, would rush to equalize across the dimensions. The universe could implode. He shuddered despite the heat. At least humans knew how to contain the small tears they made, even if they didn't understand what sucking too much magic out of Arlyxia did to his world.

He would be able to rebalance some of that magic now that he had a human. But the blood of one warlock wouldn't be enough to stop the desert from spreading. One drop on dry sand quickly evaporated.

"Um... where are we going?" the warlock asked. His long legs eating up the distance Saka had put between them.

He bit back a grin. At least the human wasn't crying. He'd caught one with some courage. He might prove to be useful for more than rebalancing. "I have to report your capture to the leader. It is a formality."

It had better be a formality. He didn't want Miniti to eat the warlock; he was not an offering. One could never tell how she was feeling, though.

"Capture?"

Saka glanced at the human, this time he let the grin form. "You are my captive."

The warlock's eyes widened. They were a curious shade of blue. Like the Humanside sky. It wasn't just the blue that was odd, there were also white and black parts. Humans had very strange eyes. It was surprising they could see at all. White eyes usually signified blindness —not that blindness had ever stopped riverwyrms from finding prey when they came to the surface to hunt. A riverwyrm didn't need eyes to hear the heartbeats of prey.

"Can't I just go home? I'm not supposed to be here." There was a hint of fear starting to edge into the warlock's words.

"No. I have need of you for a time... surely the notion doesn't offend you? You were going to use me after all."

"Um." The warlock fell out of step.

"I shall call you Um. You say it a lot."

"My name is Angus," he said with bite.

"I am Saka." He stopped in front of a tent painted in varying shades of green. "When we go in, drop to your knees and stay there and keep your mouth shut unless spoken to."

Saka didn't give Angus a chance to disagree. He pushed open the tent flap and walked into Miniti's tent. It was only because of his standing as tribe mage that Saka didn't need permission or an invitation.

He acknowledged the guards and kept going. Miniti was reclining on cushions, reading a map and cross-checking with other papers. Trade? Water? A small gathering before the main one that was coming? Saka didn't know, and he didn't care. It wasn't his job to lead their tribe.

"You finally came to show me the human specimen?" She didn't look up.

Had she really expected him to rush here? Yes. Someone had already brought her the news, so it was clear he had walked too slowly.

Behind him Saka heard Angus drop to his knees. Miniti gave a small nod as though pleased. Her skin was as white as chalk and her lips were red. Her mouth was wide enough to swallow a soul whole. Her lack of teeth was more than made up for by talons as long as her fingers. Many considered her beautiful. Saka wasn't one of them.

"Time well spent educating him. What do you want to do with your pet, or is he for me?" She looked at Saka and then Angus. Her mouth opened and her black tongue flicked over her lower lip.

"With respect. I would like to keep him and see if he can be taught." Saka paused, then lowered his voice. "It isn't often that a mage gets a warlock."

Kitu wasn't the only demon to be taken, never to return. Saka had seen all the demons pulled through in the class. He'd taken note of the different types. Many had been animals, but some had been sentient. The young warlocks would return them all to Demonside. Older warlocks, who had burned out one demon and wanted more power, were the dangerous ones. They had the knowledge and the ability to trap a demon on Humanside where he'd run out of magic that much faster.

The loss of magic was bleeding Arlyxia dry. It had to stop, or soon there would be no demons in Arlyxia, only endless sand.

"Hmm. I do remember something about more mages being asked to make a bond with a warlock. You have excelled again."

Saka inclined his head at the compliment. It wasn't actually hard to get a warlock, but few mages were willing to take the risk. He didn't tell her that in case she took Angus and gobbled his soul before Saka could learn anything from the warlock. He waited for her decision; hurrying her would do no good.

"You may take him away. Report to me in the morning after I have communicated with the other leaders. Then we shall decide if I get him or you get him."

"May I use him to rebalance the magic?" He needed to know how far he could take Angus's lesson in alchemy. Although there was little point in schooling the warlock if Miniti was going to devour him.

She laughed. "I only care about his soul. You may do whatever you want with his flesh."

CHAPTER THREE

ANGUS FLINCHED AND LOOKED UP. The white demon wasn't even looking at him as she tossed his fate around. She wanted his soul and Saka wanted his body? What was going on? Did they regularly divide humans between them? Was this what happened to missing warlocks and wizards? They got eaten?

He closed his eyes, wanting to wake up and find himself in bed. This was just a nightmare brought on by his fear of summoning a demon in a class, which would happen later today.

Wake up.

But the air was hot in his lungs. Outside the tent demons were talking and singing as though there was nothing strange about having a human around. He opened his eyes. He was still in the tent with the demons. His stomach sank, nausea clawed up his throat. This was so not good.

Saka inclined his head and turned. He flicked his hand, indicating for Angus to get up and follow. Given the choice between Saka and her, Saka seemed less likely to kill him... at least until morning.

He needed to find a way to get home, tonight. If he could get a few minutes alone, so Saka couldn't break his circle, then he could escape back across the void.

13

Uncertainty and confusion had given way to fear and tension. His gut clenched, and sweat rolled down his back. It was hot in the tent, but at least it was shady. Now he was going to have to leave the lovely shade.

He followed Saka outside. The brightness of the sun hurt his eyes and struck his skin. He was already burning; suddenly the cold of home didn't seem so bad. Saka's skin shimmered like metal as though he reflected the sun's rays. He seemed unbothered by the heat. Even the sand beneath Angus's sneakers was hot and sucked at his shoes, finding a way through his socks to rub against his skin.

Few of the demons wore shoes. Those who did were wearing sandal-like things. Adults watched him either openly or subtly. There were even little demons, children. He hadn't thought about how demons were made. Or how they lived. He'd thought, he'd been told, they were little more than animals. Angus slowed so he could take in more of the market. It seemed to be laid out in a cross. At the center was the tent they had just been in. This was the work of a civilized people. While he'd seen pictures of the different demons, there had been no mentions of thriving towns.

Not all the demons he'd seen pictures of were here. Maybe some were animals. Again he cursed his luck at getting one that talked, a mage and a demon with obvious standing in his town.

Saka led them down a leg of the cross, away from the market.

"Where are we going?"

"My tent." Saka paused to speak to another man. Most of the demons seemed to be either the vampry or black-horned, but there were a couple of other types that Angus couldn't remember the name of.

Every so often there would be a crackle of magic. Something sparked between Saka and his friend. A flash of purple, then the other demon handed Saka something that looked like food. Angus hoped it was food. He was hungry and thirsty, and he'd really like some answers. However, after kneeling in front of the demon in charge, he didn't want to ask anything in public that might draw attention to himself—extra attention.

They moved on, ducking down the side of some tents before stopping. Saka pulled open the flap. "My home."

The maze of tents had led here. Even if he had wanted to run away, he had no idea where he was going and there were demons everywhere, and he suspected some might gobble him up without thinking twice. Then there were the creatures. He was sure some were pets, running around freely, and others were food, but they all looked dangerous to him.

Plus, if he went into the tent, at least he'd be out of the sun.

The inside of the tent was mostly cream. Shear white panels of cloth divided what could be rooms. Gold lettering adorned other walls. Saka put his purchase on a small low table, then poured two cups of something.

The table looked as though it was made of a smoky gray glass. The jug and cups out of gold. It looked expensive, but Angus couldn't be sure of anything.

"Sit. Eat. Drink." Saka waved his hand over the offerings.

Fattening me up for tomorrow?

After a moment of hesitation, he drank—he was so thirsty—what tasted like sweetened water. "Is it always this hot here?"

"This is cool. The hot, rainy season won't start for another couple of lunar cycles. Before then we will gather at Lifeblood Mountain to trade and have face-to-face talks."

"This town moves?"

Saka nodded. "We are not here to talk about the customs and lifestyles of greater continental Arlyxia. You're a warlock, I'm a mage. We are going to talk magic."

"It's visible here." That was the first thing he'd noticed about magic here. It was about all he could say about magic. He was a wizard, someone who could use magic, with a bit of warlock training.

Saka considered him for a moment. "You really have no idea, do you?"

"I haven't known anything since you pulled me through the void." That had to have been less than an hour ago. He'd been a warlock for less than an hour. Were people already looking for him? He couldn't rely on help, he had to try to escape, but he was interested in what Saka had to say about magic. The theory had always fascinated him. It was his father who had put him off using magic by pushing him into the college to become a warlock. *No son of mine will be a wizard.*

"Magic is visible. Most of us here have it to some degree. Some of us train to use it and it becomes our job." Saka sipped his drink and smiled. "My world runs on magic. But all the magic you take from here, from your demon, has to be replenished. Magic, energy, cannot be destroyed or created."

Angus nodded. "If we pull it through to our side...." He looked at Saka. "Then somehow it has to get back here."

Saka didn't take his gaze off him. His eyes were unreadable pools of ink. "Do you want to know what happens?"

Not really. He was sure he wasn't going to like the answer. "You capture and kill humans?"

"Crude, but effective. Blood magic is one of the three ways. It usually involves a lot of ritual cuts and gets quite messy." He flicked his fingers as if dismissing the notion. "Miniti devours souls. Soul magic is another way of reclaiming some of the magic back. Blood and soul usually work together to maximize the gain."

Angus flinched. He didn't want to end up as some kind of ritual sacrifice. But he'd heard of warlocks sacrificing demons for big workings. Was it any different?

"Don't worry. We don't go around snatching just anyone. We only take those that offer themselves as a conduit. Like you."

"I didn't offer. It was part of the class, and I didn't even want to be there." He'd never wanted to be a warlock. "My father made me go to Warlock College. I'd have rather been a doctor or vet or something." He looked away to the gentle flapping of the white cloth. It was almost soothing. Somewhere in the town, there was music and laughing. If he closed his eyes, it could be Vinland, but the music was alien and the air had a taste that he couldn't quite place. Well, maybe not Vinland, but it could be somewhere on Earth.

"You would've still been able to use magic."

16

"Yes, but no demon. I didn't want a demon." He glanced back at Saka. Was what he'd said incredibly rude? "No offense intended."

Saka broke off some of the food. It looked a little like flaky bread stuffed with something. The demon ate and stared at Angus.

Angus tried not to fidget. His cheeks burned. His father was never going to let him forget this failure, assuming he got home. Hopefully his father would let him walk away from being a warlock. He wasn't warlock material. That was painfully obvious.

Saka finally spoke. "Why didn't you want a demon?"

"It never seemed right. I've read underground theories about magic and demons and what happens to missing people... guess they were right." Some made it home. But not all. How many had been sacrificed, their souls eaten?

"We take some. We have to balance the magic between the worlds. Too much is going through to your world. If my world collapses, what would that do to your world?" He tapped his cup. "I forgot to tell you the third way magic is balanced."

Great. Blood and souls. The third option was probably worse.

"Maybe I'll just cast a circle and go home." Angus crossed his arms.

"Be my guest." Saka indicated the central floor space.

Angus stood, but that bad feeling was growing in his stomach. Why was Saka letting him try now? Didn't he need to rebalance the magic? Angus's head spun with what that meant.

Too much magic was going across the void. How did Saka know too much was being taken?

In the middle of the floor space, Angus closed his eyes. He breathed and tried to find that place within him. There was magic all around. He could feel it, and it was nothing like the weak currents of home. If he opened his eyes, he'd be able to see it as he created a circle around him. He kept them closed. He needed to focus.

When summoning a demon, the circle was to keep them in until the warlock gained control over them. Now he had to put himself in a circle and tear open the void. It should be easier here. He was in a world where magic was everywhere, talking to a demon and learning new things. He wanted to learn more about magic and how to use it as a wizard, not as a warlock. The circle snapped around him. For a heartbeat he expected Saka to tear it down. He didn't.

Angus reached out to feel the void, to send himself across.

Nothing happened.

Of course. If it were that easy, the other humans that had been taken would've all come home straight away. That didn't stop him from trying again.

And again.

The void was there, but he couldn't tear it. It was as smooth and strong as diamond.

There was a rustle of cloth as Saka got up. Angus opened his eyes and stared at the demon through the shimmer of his circle. "Why doesn't it work?"

"Because it doesn't. No demon can get through to your world without someone opening the way from the other side."

Angus shook his head. "No. That's a lie. Demons get through and go on rampages all the time. It's why there is a warlock strike force."

"I haven't told you a lie yet, Angus. If a demon is rampaging, it is because someone wanted it to. You lump every being from this world into one basket, but just as there are humans and animals so there are demons and animals. Sure the animals look different than yours and they have magic in their bodies, but they are dumb beasts. Most warlocks get a beast, something to match their ability—at least that's what we theorize here."

"I'm not very good at magic." But then he had been busy trying to fail.

"You connected to me. Your innate talent must be vast."

Angus laughed. Was Saka flattering him or himself? "You lucked out with me."

"I don't think I did. You aren't my first warlock."

Angus cut the circle. There was no point in keeping it there when he could do nothing with it and Saka could break it anytime he wanted. It broke apart with a tinkle like a wind chime. Little flakes of blue crystal spiraled away on the breeze.

"What happened to your first warlock?" The words tumbled out before he could think if he even wanted to know the answer.

"He was killed by humans. It was most unfortunate."

"I'm sure he felt the same way." Angus frowned, remembering the conversation with Miniti. "Why do you need a warlock?"

"There is a growing imbalance between our worlds. The mage council is concerned. Those without a human were told to snatch one if they got the chance. I did. And here you are." Saka grinned in a way that was most unsettling. "Before tomorrow's fate decider, you owe Arlyxia some magic."

Angus went to raise the circle, not wanting to part with blood or soul in a hurry, but Saka was faster, grabbing Angus's wrist. The circle reformed around them both. He swallowed and looked Saka in the eye.

The demon's bare chest lifted with each breath, his nostrils flared.

That twinge of lust that had hit Angus when he first saw Saka returned. Maybe it was the lazy smile, or the way he was half-dressed. Angus had always let his head be turned by a half-naked man. Saka might be a demon, but he was also male.

The demon's grip gentled. His fingers caressed the soft skin on the inside of Angus's wrist. His touch was hot, as though his body temperature was naturally warmer, and his skin felt nothing like human skin. It wasn't soft or smooth.

Saka stepped closer. "Don't you want to know the third way to rebalance?"

Angus was getting a good idea what it was, and as long as it meant no ritual cutting or eating of his soul, he was tempted. Very tempted.

He shouldn't be. He should be running fast and far. Curiosity was stronger than fear, at least for Angus. It was curiosity that had led him to reading the underground theories. To preferring to study unofficially rather than officially. His father had banned that, but by then it was too late. The seeds of doubt had already been cast, and now Saka was watering them.

Here... here was an opportunity to learn more about magic than he ever could at home. Unless Saka was lying. Warlocks lied, wizards lied. Did anyone tell the truth about magic? However, if Angus could see it, there would be no hiding what was happening.

Angus stared at Saka. If Angus couldn't open the void, he was waiting for rescue. He didn't let himself wonder what would happen if there was no rescue. "When they come for me, will you let me go?"

"If it was my choice, yes. I would rather have a warlock that I can work with than one who sees me as inferior and wants to drain me. I think we could work well together." His fingers hadn't stopped moving on Angus's skin, and he had stepped closer. Again.

The blue magic of the circle shimmered around them, casting its own soft light and blurring the world on the other side.

"Did you *work* with your previous warlock?"

Saka smiled. "He was never here the way you are now." His hand lifted to cup Angus's jaw. "But he was interested in how magic is balanced. He also preferred women, so it was all theory. I could show you the third way magic is restored to my world from yours."

Angus stared into the bottomless black eyes. They weren't empty or soulless the way he'd been told. Saka was smart and dangerous. Angus wasn't going to be tricked into anything, or agree to anything blindly.

"What is it?"

"Sex magic."

CHAPTER FOUR

SAKA WAITED for Angus to say something. Anything. Instead the human man stood there as if magically silenced. There had been no magic involved in Saka's statement. From the moment he'd felt the tug across the void and readied himself to capture a warlock, Saka had known that there would be rebalancing.

However, on seeing Angus for the first time and watching him fumble the spell and blush, there had been only one way Saka had wanted to create balance. The red-gold hair and blue eyes made Angus seem delicate. But that wasn't the case. He couldn't forget that this was no innocent human. No, Angus had enough innate talent to bridge the void even though he didn't want to, and enough magical ability for Saka to make the connection.

Angus could be dangerous.

However, unlike other warlocks, he hadn't ignored what Saka had said about the worlds being unbalanced. He'd seemed almost interested. That was an improvement over his last warlock, who'd listened but had done nothing. Too afraid of the other warlocks. Saka didn't know the details about his death, only that no demon had been involved.

For years the demon mages had been trying to share knowledge across the void. There had to be balance, but warlocks didn't seem to care about anything but personal power. Angus's underground was all that had been achieved. A small step, but better than nothing.

"Blood, souls, and sex," Angus said finally.

Saka's tail flicked in agreement. "Energy is available from all three."

"Two require death."

"No, only one does. Blood magic just requires sacrifice."

"And you use humans." Angus made it sound like a bad thing.

He who would've been happy to use a demon for magic. The nerve. Saka had to remind himself that Angus didn't know better. Humans had to pay for the magic they used. It couldn't remain on their side of the void. Too much had already been taken, and Arlyxia was suffering, drying.

"Only those who have bridged the void."

"Those missing warlocks died here to rebalance the magic."

Saka shook his head. "No, not all. But most. Those that might be useful are returned if people look for them. Most don't get looked for. Why could that be?" It was a question he already knew the answer to.

Angus swallowed and glanced away. "Because the warlocks in charge know about the rebalancing. They know some have to die." His gaze refixed on Saka. The brilliant blue of his eyes made brighter by the circle shimmering around them. "If they know, why aren't they saying something?"

"I am hoping they'll look for you, and that you can find the answer to that question. If they do not look and you do not agree to help, then Miniti will take you from me." And Saka would have to wait for another warlock and try again. Maybe another mage would have more luck. Many mages preferred blood and souls. Sex required more from them. Saka liked the challenge. There was also a bigger reward at the end. Blood and souls only had a finite amount of magic. Sex magic, though, could be repeated again and again and again without killing or maiming the human.

Perhaps he was too kind, too greedy, and too much of a perfectionist to expect anything but the best. However, that was the reason he was Miniti's favorite mage, a position he'd like to keep.

To do that he needed to get some magic out of Angus.

Angus frowned. "That's not much of a choice."

"I didn't get one when you summoned me. I am being more than generous." Saka let the circle fracture and scatter. The scent of the magic was cold and sharp.

"They will look for me." But he didn't sound sure.

"Good." He meant that. Angus was more use to him alive and on the other side of the void than here and waiting to die—which would happen eventually. Demons couldn't live on Humanside, and humans couldn't live in Demonside. They would weaken and eventually die even if a mage wasn't using them to rebalance. "Then we can work together to find out who is killing demons." Kitu was dead, he was sure of it. He had mourned and now just wanted to work out what was going on and how to stop his world from dying.

Angus drew in a breath, his shirt clinging to his chest. "And why the truth is being suppressed."

"The answer to that is always for power. If we do not find a way to stop them and fix the balance, both worlds could die. The balance must be maintained."

"How do you know the balance is off?"

"The desert is spreading. Each year there is less rain. There must be changes in your world from excess magic." Or was it just his world dying? Perhaps Humanside would be fine.

"My world is getting colder, but the warlocks are working on it."

"By using more magic?" Which would only make the problem worse.

"It may not be connected." Angus didn't seem convinced. Confusion pulled at his features as if he was trying to make sense of two different worlds.

"Do you really believe that?"

Angus stood still for a moment, then shook his head. "Our worlds are connected; no one disputes that."

"So if something is happening in one world, there must be an effect in the other." Perhaps this warlock could understand. "How will you rebalance the magic you have used?"

Angus's gaze focused. He swallowed. "I want to keep my soul in one piece."

"A wise choice, I don't want to kill you—though you can lose small pieces at a time."

"I haven't used that much magic."

Saka shrugged. "No, but your kind has. Is a little blood too much to ask?"

"It won't be enough, will it?"

"No, but it is better than nothing, and I need to show Miniti something to convince her not to eat your soul."

Angus considered for a moment. "A little blood... only a little."

Saka smiled. "I do not want you dead. It will be no more than you can safely give up." He'd been hoping that Angus would want sex; that was far more satisfying and gave far more energy. He picked up his set of knives. "You know all magic has intent? That the emotion behind it strengthens it?" He pulled a small knife free and examined the blade. It was clean and sharp. He kept his tools immaculate and always ready, but he wanted Angus to see it. "Do you prefer pleasure or pain?"

"What?" Angus stepped back, but his gaze never left the knife.

"You want to see some magic, some rebalancing? For the most effect, there needs to be an underlying emotion. Fear isn't my favorite, but being afraid the first time is normal."

Angus straightened his back and tore his gaze off the knife. "Pleasure."

He didn't sound revolted by the idea, nor did he sound thrilled. Resigned with a touch of curiosity, but it was tempered with caution. That Saka could respect—along with the way the young warlock was making decisions and thinking of the future. There was still the very real chance that Angus would attempt to kill him once he was back on Humanside.

But he could worry about that in the morning.

There would be no attempted rescue for twenty-four hours—if the warlocks even bothered with a rescue. The warlocks in charge knew some rebalancing would be done in that time, and they were happy for someone else to pay for their magic use. It was one of the unwritten rules. Not killing demons was another unwritten rule. One the warlocks were now breaking.

Perhaps the time of smiles and handshakes was over.

Once demons had been respected, worshipped, or feared. Now many warlocks treated them as chattel and slaves. But not all.

"Really?" As much as Saka would like to indulge, Angus was still too uncertain. "I don't think so. I think if I kissed you or touched you while holding a knife to your skin, your fear would only get stronger. Sit." He pointed at the cushions by the table.

"Why ask if you don't care what I say?" Angus sat, but his gaze never left Saka.

"I do care what you say, because I want to learn more about you. Don't you want to know about me?" Saka picked up a small vial for collecting the blood.

"What do you prefer?" Angus countered.

"Pleasure." He smiled as he sat next to Angus and then extended Angus's arm over the table, exposing the soft underside. He ran his finger down the pale blue vein. "But there will be later for that if you change your mind."

"You just said no to pleasure."

"You are not ready. You are thinking of the knife, not the magic. Humans don't practice sex magic, do they?"

Angus's cheeks turned pink, and he stared at the table. "We aren't supposed to."

And yet it was clear that at some point Angus had broken the rules. This warlock became more interesting by the moment. "It can raise a lot of power. Your college should be encouraging warlocks to use it... if they want to stop the drain of magic from here."

"Only wizards draw up magic from themselves. Warlocks have demons."

"I know." He rubbed his thumb up Angus's arm. His skin was so soft. "You have a choice to make, Angus. You follow your college and shun me, or I can teach you the magic they don't want you to know about."

CHAPTER FIVE

ANGUS LIFTED his gaze from his arm where Saka was paying far too much attention to the blue vein that ran its length. Had his veins always been so noticeable, or was he being paranoid now he knew what Saka wanted from him, and it wasn't just his blood.

There was a certain seductiveness about his touch. If Saka was human and they had met in a bar, Angus would be thinking about going home with him or taking him home. But Saka was a demon and Angus was a long way from home.

He could be home tomorrow.

"How can you teach me when I go home?" Why was he even asking? He didn't want to be a magic-using warlock. Yet he was. He had a demon and not any old demon but a mage. Saka knew magic.

There was a glint in the demon's eyes. "You will summon me for class and in private. You will need to pay for the magic you take from me, but I will teach you how to draw it up from what is around you."

"I could get a wizard to teach me that." Jim and he had experimented with all kinds of wizard magic before Angus's father had put a stop to it. They had broken up when Angus had been accepted into Warlock College. Jim couldn't afford college, and he didn't like warlocks.

Angus had to agree with Jim for the most part. He didn't trust his teachers, and when some piece of theory didn't feel right, he went looking for other answers. He tried to imagine another three years of disbelieving and looking for his own answers. Would he eventually fall into line, or would he get caught out?

"You could, but they are untrained. I know about your world, Angus. Your college keeps knowledge locked away for only a few, and those few are carefully selected so they don't challenge the rules. How did you get in?" Saka's fingers trailed over Angus's palm.

He kept expecting to feel the bite of the knife with every touch, but he was enjoying being touched. He shouldn't like it, but no one was here to judge him and no one would ever know what he did.

No one might come for him either. He might have to find a way to live in Demonside. Miniti's extra wide mouth for swallowing souls lingered in his mind.

No, someone would, because his father wouldn't want to live with the knowledge that his son had been taken. He'd pull favors to make sure Angus came back across the void, if only to have the opportunity to berate him for being so careless.

What would he say about Angus offering his blood? Nothing good. Personal sacrifice was beneath warlocks.

Well, he'd never wanted to be a warlock. "I got in because of my father. I come from a long line of warlocks." Men who hadn't cared about anything but what they could get. "I want to learn."

"You agree to the terms?"

Angus nodded. "I will pay for the magic that I use… is that all?"

Saka inclined his head. "That is all. The balancing of magic is a very simple concept. One that has been forgotten by many in Humanside."

All the magic used in every class, in every Warlock College was being drawn from here and not returned. While Saka's world got drier, his world was getting colder and wetter. The warlocks weren't working on the problem. They were causing it.

If Saka was telling the truth about magic and the need for it to be rebalanced. It could be tricky demon lies. But Angus had no idea what

Saka had to gain by lying. If the demon wanted him dead, it would've happened already. While he had no idea if Demonside was actually getting drier, he knew his world was in trouble, and Saka's explanation was as good as any he'd heard. "Rebalance, then."

A circle snapped closed around them. Saka hadn't even moved. The shimmery blue made Angus's skin look paler. Saka gleamed.

Angus wanted to reach out and touch him the way the demon was stroking him. His fingers curled by his side, but he didn't reach out. "How does this work?"

"We sit here until I think there is enough energy to make it worthwhile."

Angus frowned.

Saka picked up the knife and nicked Angus's arm. Blood welled, and for a moment, Angus thought he saw a shimmer as his blood spilled, and then there was nothing. Saka swept his thumb over the cut, and it stopped bleeding immediately. There had definitely been something that time, a golden heat that spread beneath his skin.

"What was that?"

"It's rude to leave someone bleeding from multiple cuts so I healed it. It will be gone completely by morning. Did you see how little magic was released?"

"I think so." That had been the faint shimmer. "Then what is the point? There must be a more effective way."

Saka laughed. It wasn't mocking. It was a dark and dangerous sound. "There is."

Angus waited for him to continue, but he didn't. "I thought you were going to teach me."

"I am. The higher the emotion, the more magic that is released. Fear is often used. Humans who come here are usually terrified." Saka's dark eyes held him captive.

"I'm good at hiding it."

"No one is that good. You're sitting with a demon who wants to cut you, and you aren't trembling. You haven't once begged for your life."

"Are you disappointed?" So far there hadn't been a need for him to beg for his life. Even in Miniti's tent, when he'd been kneeling and listening to them talk about him, it had been clear Saka wanted him alive.

"No, quite the opposite, but it means I need to find something else."

"You could make me afraid." It wouldn't take that much. The fear he might never get home was lurking, but worrying about it wouldn't help him. This wasn't like any lesson he'd ever had.

"I could, but that wouldn't be as much fun. Tell me about the time you did sex magic."

Angus looked away. His cheeks heated even though he tried to ignore the embarrassment. He could feel Saka's gaze on him. The demon's grip on his arm. He wanted to pull away and end this, whatever this was.

Couldn't he take the blood and be done with it?

But Angus had seen the barely there shimmer. There was no point in bleeding when there was so little magic being released and rebalanced. He drew in a breath. Of course a demon wasn't going to teach like a warlock.

"I had a boyfriend, and we experimented with some of the stuff we'd read about. He was the one who introduced me to the underground. He accused me of falling into step when I went to college." Angus closed his eyes. The breakup had hurt. He hadn't dated anyone over the last four months. Hadn't even picked up.

"And? Did it work?"

Angus shook his head. The memory of that night was clear in his mind. They'd started so seriously. Marking out the circle and lighting candles. Even though the breakup had hurt, that memory was one of his favorites to relive when alone. He remembered the heat, the lust winding through his body and making it hard to breathe. But it hadn't mattered because his body had been so far away. Then before they could do anything with the magic they'd been raising, they had fallen, crashed into their bodies, and all pretense of magic had been dropped. He had never wanted, needed, anything so badly. They had screwed themselves senseless. A shiver ran through him, and he was aware that his body had responded.

The sting of the knife brought him back to the moment.

This time his blood was shimmered more; there was more magic. He watched as it flowed over his arm and into the vial. "Why the change?"

That he could see it, instead of just having to sense it was amazing. He wanted to practice all of the basic things he'd been taught in theory just to see what they looked like.

"You were aroused."

Angus snapped his gaze up. "Pleasure."

What would sex magic look like?

Saka hadn't spoken. He didn't need to. It was clear from the curve of his lip and the tilt of his head what he wanted.

Temptation slid through Angus's body. He shouldn't want that. He shouldn't be thinking of a demon that way. But he already was. What would it be like to kiss Saka? What would the magic look like?

Angus reached out to brush his fingertips over the back of Saka's hand. His skin was warm and not quite smooth.

Saka drew in a breath, and when he exhaled, the circle expanded to the walls of the tent. That was a very big circle to hold. Angus knew he couldn't do that even if he could see what he was doing.

"Shall we progress?"

Angus nodded even though he wasn't sure what he was getting himself into. If this was his only chance to see magic forming and being used, he didn't want to waste it. At least at home, he'd be able to remember the feel and hope for the best.

Saka put the knife down, then slid his hand up Angus's thigh. "I don't want you to get scared and run away."

"I have nowhere to run to." He had never been keen on outdoor activities, and fleeing a perfectly good tent town to run around the desert did not seem like a good plan.

Saka's hand slid higher, then eased away. Angus found himself inching closer. There must be something in the air, or maybe it was because he hadn't had sex for months, because the last thing he wanted to do was run. He wanted to lie down and drag Saka with him. That Saka was a demon didn't seem to matter at the moment.

The demon's tail traced up Angus's arm. "Don't fight the lust. Let it bubble and rise. I'll let you know when it's time to spill."

Angus refocused his attention. His breath was catching, and he was hard. His erection pressed against his jeans, and he was uncomfortable kneeling. Was he allowed to move?

"What are the rules?"

"There are no rules. This is just a little something to raise the heat in your blood so when it is spilled it is full of magic."

"A game, then."

"No, a ritual."

It didn't feel like any ritual Angus had done. Not even when he'd tried this with Jim.

"You can do what you need to, but you must listen to me since I'm the one who knows what to do."

Angus unfolded his legs and rearranged his jeans.

"You can take your clothes off if you want."

Angus lifted an eyebrow. His clothes would be staying on. But even as he thought it, he wondered what it would be like to sit naked and feel the warm breeze on his skin instead of sitting there sweating in his long-sleeved shirt and undershirt. He'd come from a cold, autumn evening to this place.

He pushed off his shoes and took off his socks, then pulled off his shirt—but only because it was hot, not because he wanted to be naked. Parts of his body disagreed and thought taking what was on offer would be a great idea and that he should take off all his clothes.

Somehow he'd ended up closer to the demon. The warnings the lecturer had drilled into him about the dangers of not controlling his demon properly seemed like lies. He was sure that some of the bigger, badder looking demons would eat him, but so would a tiger.

No one had warned him that a demon could be attractive, or seductive. Maybe that said more about him than the demon. He must be broken.

Saka's hand cupped Angus's jaw. "You are thinking too much."

His lips were only millimeters away, but there was no kiss. Angus closed the gap and took one. He couldn't wait; the need was eating him up from the inside.

There was a crackle in the air like a coming storm as their lips met. Heat rolled down Angus's spine. He hadn't realized how long it had been and how much he wanted to get laid. A small part of him was a little concerned about what would happen when he went home, but no one needed to know about what happened across the void.

Saka's tail wrapped around his wrist, while a hand slid under his shirt. Saka's chest was bare, and Angus made the most of it, running his hand over the demon's skin. When Saka's tongue flicked against his lip, Angus opened his mouth. His eyes closed as he sank into the moment.

The hairs on his arms plucked to attention. He forced his eyes open to see the magic that was building. The air seemed to be alive. There was more magic in a kiss with Saka than there had been in bed with Jim. But magic was common here.

"Stop thinking." Saka's voice was soft in his ear as the demon pulled off Angus's T-shirt.

He didn't resist. He had far too many clothes on, and his skin was hot. He wanted to be touched everywhere. Saka brushed a thumb over one of Angus's nipples, before reclaiming his mouth.

A hand or a tail traced over his hard-on. Angus was barely breathing, waiting for Saka to open his jeans.

The cool edge of the knife sliced into his skin, but instead of a rush of pain, there was a sense of relief, as if the pressure had been building inside him. He drew back to look at the wound. His blood didn't look like blood at that moment. It looked like liquid metal, or liquid jewels, as it trickled into the vial.

For a moment he was disconnected from what was happening, and then, just as he was about to say something about how much blood Saka was taking, the demon placed a thumb over the cut. There was a pulling sensation as the wound closed.

"Is that enough?" Was it too much? Would he faint if he stood? He did feel a little lightheaded. His body wasn't sure what was going on because he was still painfully hard.

"It is a start."

"A start?"

"This is a token of your willingness to rebalance."

"And if I hadn't been willing?"

Saka's gaze became hard. "I would have handed you off to the other mage to die."

Angus rocked back. He had not realized that his situation was so precarious. "I thought you had to keep me alive for twenty-four hours."

Saka dismissed the circle. Glass orbs around the roof glowed faintly. With another wave of his hand, the lights dimmed. Angus hadn't even noticed them before.

"Technically yes, but warlocks are killing demons when they aren't supposed to."

"Only the ones that break through." As the words tumbled out, Angus knew that was wrong. He couldn't escape Demonside. No one could. Demons couldn't be breaking through and rampaging. Why lie?

A headache started to form as he tried to work out what was truth and what was lies. He shouldn't believe a word a demon said, and yet what Saka said made sense. How many demons had been killed?

How many warlocks had died here?

Saka pressed a cup of the sweet water into his hand. He wrinkled his nose at the taste. It was too strong, but there didn't seem to be anything else to drink.

"Do you need time alone?" Saka gave a pointed look at Angus's groin.

"No," he said too fast. He did want to be alone. He wanted to be home, but he had to get through the night first. And every time he looked at Saka, his body got entirely the wrong idea. "Is there something in the water?"

Saka shook his head. "But I could put something in there, something that would amplify the magic."

"Drugs? Warlocks don't use drugs." Wizards did. Some thought it helped them connect with the magic.

"You use demons instead." There was an edge in Saka's voice. "Eat, take care of yourself, have a rest. We will do more later."

More later....

Angus looked at his arm. There were two faint lines where Saka had cut him. The wounds had continued their rapid healing as they talked. "I don't think I like being cut."

"You will." Saka brought over the bread-like food. He offered it to Angus first.

"I don't want to like it."

"It's delicious. Pastry filled with dried fruit. Breakfast fare but my favorite to eat after working magic. Very grounding."

"You know what I meant."

Saka regarded him for a moment. "Sometimes we all do things we don't like. I will do what is required to save my world and yours too. What are you willing to do?" He picked up the knife. "Blood, sex, and soul, Angus. The worlds need to be balanced."

"I cannot bleed enough for that."

How much magic had he just returned? One simple finding spell? A healing spell? Or maybe an hour's worth of security for one of the big banks? He had no idea. But if the warlocks didn't pay for the magic they used, the burden fell on someone else.

Someone like him.

CHAPTER SIX

SAKA LEFT Angus sitting in his tent. People watched as he walked away. They nodded or smiled their gratitude. While they might not have known exactly what was going on, they knew that he was taking magic from the human, and that was a good thing.

He didn't go far, though, and he wouldn't leave Angus long, just long enough that he had time to breathe, take away the edge of lust, and think about what the warlocks had told him about magic.

Saka knew that they lied; he'd learned that from his last warlock. The man had lived in fear of being discovered as a demon sympathizer. Turned out that fear had been well placed. Saka gritted his teeth. It wasn't teaching when half the information was lies and the other half was hidden away. How could they call themselves a college?

Perhaps not all colleges were bad—he didn't know enough about the human world to be sure—but there had been an increase in magic use over the last few decades and less and less being returned.

Angus was right. The blood of one warlock wasn't going to be enough. Everyone here knew, no matter how much they were smiling.

Slowly Saka turned around. He wove his way through the tents. He needed more from Angus but didn't want to push too hard. They had to work together. Angus could get into places in the human world that he couldn't, or Angus could report Saka to his teachers and Saka would find himself the next to be sacrificed for some magical working.

Even alive Saka was the conduit for Angus to draw magic from Demonside. He hated the damage that would cause, but he had to believe that his sacrifice would be worth it. He drew in a breath. People were starting to cook their evening meal.

If he stayed out of his tent, he'd get plenty of invitations. He never had to cook for himself. But tonight he didn't want company and he didn't want to drag Angus out. He wasn't part of the tribe and didn't deserve to be treated like a mage.

Saka pushed open the tent flap. Angus wasn't sitting by the table anymore.

If he had run....

Saka created a ball of light in his palm to look around the dim interior. Angus was lying back on the cushions, his arm over his face and his hand down his pants. Saka watched for a moment.

A part of him was glad he'd caused such a powerful reaction. Kissing Angus had been pleasant, and it was nice to be able to enjoy his work. Rituals were so much easier when the attraction didn't have to be forced.

Saka cleared his throat and noisily poured himself a drink.

Angus startled like he'd had hot coals dropped down his pants. "I didn't hear you come in."

Saka bit back the smile. He hadn't been meant to. He'd wanted to see what the young warlock had got up to. "Did you need a little more time alone?"

"No, I'm fine." Angus did up his pants.

Liar.

"Sometimes if a satisfying conclusion hasn't been reached during ritual, the body can struggle to let it happen." He'd chosen the end point of the ritual to leave Angus waiting.

Angus sat up and pushed his fingers through his hair. He looked like he wanted to say something but couldn't find the words. It would do him good to think before speaking.

"I'm not going to be able to sleep like this."

It was too early to sleep. Saka sipped his water and watched the human as he struggled to come up with the right words. He'd looked very appealing lying back on the cushions feeling himself. Freckles decorated his shoulders, and red-blond hair dusted his chest. His legs had been stretched out, and his features had lost their worried pinch. It had been a very nice sight in his tent.

"I wasn't getting anywhere. Are you sure you didn't put something in the water?" Angus's frown was back.

"Your body is reacting to the ritual. That is all."

In the shadows created by the ball of light, Angus's eyes were dark. He kept glancing at the light as if expecting it to do something. It wouldn't do anything.

Angus winced and lay back. "I'm tired."

Not so exhausted that the arousal had faded. Saka inhaled and swore he could taste it on the air. "You could ask for help."

Angus's head jerked up so he could stare at Saka like his horns had fallen off.

"That would be another ritual." His words were slow and carefully formed.

"Yes. But you don't jump straight into having sex. It's too easy to lose focus." It was a progression, and Saka already knew that Angus was willing to try, and wanting to learn. They were the two biggest hurdles.

"What am I signing up for this time?"

Saka considered the human for a couple of heartbeats. "You don't like getting cut, so no knife—though I should warn you there will be times when it has to happen." Angus flinched. It was a quick method for rebalancing, one those who paid for their magic used if they couldn't handle the thought of having ritual sex. It wasn't for every-one. "So that leaves sex magic."

Angus bit his lip and nodded. "How?"

"You start by taking off the rest of your clothes."

"And you?"

"I will be staying fully dressed this time."

Saka could almost see the wheels turning in Angus's mind as he weighed what he was willing to do. Would he back out and go for the familiar knife? If he did, Saka would let him come this time. He wasn't cruel. He wasn't doing anything that hadn't been done to him as part of his training. It was all a test to find limits and to learn to work within them—and sometimes push them.

Slowly Angus stood. He undid his pants and pushed them over his hips. "No knife, and I get to come?"

"Yes."

A smile formed on the warlock's lips, and then he took his pants off.

CHAPTER SEVEN

TOTALLY NAKED, the breeze caressed Angus's skin, and for the first time since arriving in Demonside, his eyeballs stopped feeling like they were sweating. It was still hot; the floor of the tent was warm beneath his feet from the sand. Spices scented the air as people cooked their meals. He was hungry. However, there would be no food now until afterward, to ground them after the working of magic.

Angus used his hands to cover himself. The idea of getting with a demon shouldn't be making him hard. But it had and he hadn't been able to get close to getting off on his own.

Saka walked around him. His fingers traced Angus's spine to his tailbone. Angus drew in a breath. Warm fingers traced over one hip, and then Saka was in front of him. "Uncover yourself."

Angus did as he was asked. The air was too thick and hot to breathe, and they hadn't even started yet.

Saka ran two fingers along Angus's hard length. "I am glad you want this."

He couldn't lie and deny it, but he didn't want to admit that he found the demon intriguing either.

Saka brought both hands to Angus's face. He rested his forehead against Angus's, the base of his horns also touching Angus's skin. The horns were cool. For a moment they stood there. Angus wanted to move, to fidget. He was too naked and vulnerable, but his magical training kept him still and his breathing even.

After a while, he couldn't say how long, they were breathing in sync. The magic around them pulsed in time with his heart.

They had started.

They had started before their lips had touched.

Saka was actually getting ready for the ritual. This wasn't what Angus had done with Jim. They'd simply made a circle and had sex.

"You are distracted." Saka's voice was low. There was a hum of power beneath the words.

Angus's father had always raised his voice when working magic. Most wizards and warlocks did, as though noise gave them strength. The quietness was infinitely more powerful.

Saka's voice seemed to reach into him. "Breathe."

Angus closed his eyes and obeyed. Their breathing fell into sync again. Saka's thumbs brushed his cheeks, and then his mouth was covering Angus's. Saka's lips moved, demanding a kiss.

Angus let his lips part as Saka's pointed tongue sought entrance. The heat of his hands, his mouth, and tongue was a constant reminder that his lover for tonight was a demon. There were names for warlocks who got too close to their demon, who let the demon take control. None of them were nice, and he'd never thought that they'd ever apply to him.

No one needed to know.

They would suspect. Those in power would know the magic had been rebalanced, and they would ask how. Angus flinched.

"Focus," Saka murmured.

Angus dragged his attention back to Saka and the way his lips moved, the way his mouth tasted hot and like burned honey. For a few moments, nothing else existed except the two of them. He was aware as Saka created a circle and then pushed it out. In his mind Angus felt it become one with the walls of the tent and solidify. He wouldn't be able to escape Saka's circle while Saka lived.

He drew in a heavy breath and opened his eyes. Soft light seemed to be coming from their skin as though they were glowing with magic. Around them the white walls of the tent shimmered with the blue of the circle that had been cast. He was starting to love visible magic.

Saka took his hand and led him back to the cushions. He indicated for Angus to make himself comfortable. The rapid beat of Angus's heart suggested that wouldn't be possible. However, it was entirely possible to be aroused and yet full of nerves at the same time. This was all too different. A part of him wanted to hide until he was rescued—they would retrieve him, they had to—the rest of him wanted to take this opportunity.

This was more magic than he'd done in college, more than the basics all wizard kids learned. He wanted to revel in it. Experiment with it. Magic pulsed with every beat of his heart.

He took a step, then dropped to his knees not sure what to do.

Saka kissed the back of his neck. "Stay like that. I like it."

Saka murmured something, and the soft glow that had enveloped their skin went out. Suddenly lights appeared around the room. The glass orbs filled with light, and the gold writing on the walls came alive.

Saka had not been joking about being a mage of some skill. Angus realized that he was completely outclassed. How had he ever thought to control such a magnificent being?

Saka's fingers brushed Angus's cheek. Angus turned into the touch. Saka's thumb brushed over Angus's lower lip. Lust filled his veins in the place of blood.

With that simple touch, the glass orbs burned brighter—fed by magic.

He didn't want to be the only one naked. He wanted Saka naked. He wanted to have sex. "What about you? Are you sure you don't want to...?"

"No. This is ritual, not fun. I have trained for the difference. You have not, but that will just make this more interesting. As a warlock in training, I am sure you will not embarrass yourself." There was a hint of a smile on Saka's lips.

Lust tightened and knotted in Angus's belly. This wasn't just about sex; this was a magical challenge. And oh so different than what he'd done previously.

The demon knelt behind him, his hands trailing over Angus's shoulders and down his arms. Saka pulled Angus's wrists behind his back. For a moment Angus resisted, but the demon was strong.

"I would prefer that you obey, but I can make you. Here you do not have the power. On Humanside you would, but this is not your world."

Angus bit back a laugh as he imagined himself getting busy with Saka in class to draw up power. He wouldn't need to do that. The demon would be there, acting as a channel for the magic. He frowned. Death magic was forbidden, but he knew wizards without demons used blood and sex.

"Sex with a demon on my side would raise more magic than just channeling."

Saka nodded. His hand slid around to close around Angus's shaft.

Angus tipped his head back against the demon's shoulder. His touch felt so good.

"Tomorrow there will be time for unraveling. When you return there will be time for seeking the truth. Tonight you are mine." Saka moved closer. The length of his cock pressed against the crease of Angus's ass. There was cloth between them, but the promise of more was there.

Angus struggled to keep breathing.

With his hands behind his back, all Angus could do was absorb each sensation. Each kiss. Each lick. Each touch. Each stroke of his length.

The demon's thumb swept over the head and then slicked its way down. If he kept going, it would be all over. He didn't stop. Angus's balls tightened. He thrust into Saka's grip, well aware that precome was smoothing each stroke. So close…. He had to regain control.

Didn't he?

He struggled for a moment, and then Saka released him. The demon's hand traveled over his body. He nipped Angus's neck and pinched one nipple. Each sensation drawing a gasp. It was like spinning one way only to be turned around and sent in the other direction.

The room got brighter as magic gathered in the glass orbs.

Beyond the cloth walls demons were talking or singing. There was music filling the air and being carried on the breeze.

Just as Angus felt he had gathered up control, Saka wrapped his hand around his shaft again. Angus groaned. His hips moved even though he wanted to be still. Heat enveloped him.

He turned his head and tried to free his hands to push away. He wanted to come. Saka stopped stroking and squeezed just below the glans of Angus's cock. Angus sucked in several breaths. His skin was too tight. He wanted to grab his own dick to finish.

His cock was throbbing and his balls heavy. The entire tent had taken on that soft glow. The gold symbols shimmered and danced as the breeze buffeted the cloth. He watched them as he steadied his breathing and tamped down on the need coursing through him.

There was a peace in the movement of the gold sigils, a calming.

Saka ground against him, and Angus pushed back. He wanted more. He was struggling to remember this wasn't about the sex, but about the emotion and the magic.

There was plenty of magic. It was everywhere.

The tent was glowing.

The demon's tail was between his legs, teasing. Then Saka was stroking, his grip firm.

"When I say." His voice was soft in Angus's ear.

Angus closed his eyes. He gritted his teeth, torn by the need not to screw up the ritual and the need to come. He had to focus on his breathing, not on every sensation. Heat raced down his spine, lodged in his hips, and spread. His stomach muscles contracted.

"Now."

He was already there and unable to stop. His hips jerked, and he thrust into the demon's hand, his climax tearing through him. He swore he could feel the magic flowing out. Static energy moved across his skin, and the room brightened as though he was under the midday sun.

He leaned his head back against Saka's shoulder and sucked in great lungfuls of the warm air. All the tension that had been in his body was gone. He half expected Saka to push him away, but the demon held him in his arms as though they were lovers.

Angus didn't fight. No one had held him like this since Jim.

Gradually he opened his eyes. His heartbeat had settled, but he couldn't stay like this. Saka wasn't his lover; he was his demon, which made Angus his human. In that moment he glimpsed what the demon-human relationship should be. The use of magic, then its return. All balances kept.

Somewhere along the way that had been twisted by those in charge.

Saka broke the circle, and the glass orbs winked out.

"What are they?" Angus pointed. The orbs hung all around the tent.

"Collectors. Without them there would be magic whipping around and making a mess." Saka eased away. There was a smile on his face as he looked at Angus. "Every time you have sex here, a little magic is restored."

It was infinitely better than getting cut. He didn't want to think about how much he had enjoyed it—too much.

"You didn't...."

"Someone had to be in control. You don't know what you are doing. Yet. You could learn. The better you get, the more magic would be returned." Saka rocked back on his heels, then stood. "We should eat."

Angus nodded. He glanced at the cushions. While it was too dark to see, he knew there would be a mess. "Um, what about the—"

Saka pointed at a vial to the side. "Two hands and a tail."

That Saka was taking little pieces of him, first blood and now come, was unsettling. There were too many things a magic user could do with them. "Why did you collect that?"

Saka broke off a piece of the bread-like food and passed it over. "It is a gift for Miniti so she will see you have more value alive."

"What will she do with them?" Angus hoped it wasn't what he thought she was going to do.

"Eat them in lieu of your soul."

Angus shuddered.

He didn't feel like eating after hearing that but knew he had to. He was disconnected from his body after being involved in two rituals. He shoved a piece of the flaky bread into his mouth. It was surprisingly nice. Somewhere between a dessert pastry and fruit bread. He swallowed and took a drink. The small amount of food had grounded him so he didn't feel so fragmented. He wasn't used to working such big magic.

It was odd, but he didn't feel as though he'd lost anything in returning the magic. He was more concerned about Miniti. It must have shown on his face.

"Do not worry. There will be no lasting effect. We do not use body parts in magic here. That is considered distasteful and unethical."

"You took without asking."

Saka sipped his water. "Not true. You agreed to participate."

"You didn't explain the fine print." He would've liked to know in advance what would happen to what Saka collected.

"Perhaps eat is not correct. Miniti will absorb some of the energy that you returned to Demonside. A gift to Miniti is required. She is our leader. It isn't something I have a choice in. Nor will I have a choice if you summon me to Humanside... demons summoned have no choice but to obey. You have your rules, and I have mine." Saka drained his cup and got up. "Follow."

"You could ask, instead of ordering." The moment of intimacy that they'd shared had evaporated. Saka was back to being the distant, bossy demon—not unlike many of his lecturers—he much preferred the demon who'd held him and kissed him. But it had been an illusion. All Saka had wanted was the magic, and any human would have done. That distasteful feeling of being used crawled over his skin, but Saka was right. He had agreed. And he had enjoyed it at the time.

Saka considered Angus for a moment. "I could, but I want you to know how it feels so when you summon me, you think twice before you speak."

CHAPTER EIGHT

ANGUS LOWERED HIS GAZE. Saka considered the human for a moment. He seemed to have found a little fight. Saka liked that. He didn't want to crush the warlock, only to open his eyes to the reality of life on Demonside. He might be the head mage, but he wasn't free to do as he pleased.

Not all the time anyway.

He picked up two cloths. He handed one to Angus who held it in front of himself as though he had only just remembered he was naked, and then Saka took off his pants and wrapped one around his waist. He noted that Angus had looked even though he had made a show of not looking.

Humans were so strange about nudity.

"Where are we going?"

"To bathe." Saka didn't wait to see if Angus was following him to the baths.

The night air was cool on his skin, but the sand still held the heat of the day. He glanced up to the inky sky to see how late it really was. The town was mostly silent. A couple of pet ghirns woke as he walked past but then laid their scaly heads down on their hooves. Saka walked to the edge of the town.

He waited by the doors of the latrine. "Throw sand over when you are done and then refill the bucket." He pointed to the pile of sand that had been made when the holes had been dug. Whenever the town moved, facilities had to be set up. Latrines and baths. It was the mage's job to make the location habitable by making sure there was water.

Then Saka went through one of the flaps. He was aware of the growing distance between them. They didn't need to be friends, but they needed to be able to work together. They were stuck together until one of them died.

He finished, then filled the sand bucket and waited.

Maybe he was being too harsh on Angus. He was young; he had talent but not the experience or knowledge. He should've been more careful. And run the risk of Miniti devouring Angus? No.

Someone would open the void and retrieve Angus once the twenty-four hours were up. Then things would really get interesting. For both of them. Would Angus be as willing when he was back on his side of the void, or was this simply for survival?

Angus came out and filled the bucket of sand. "I'm guessing water is a limited resource."

"Was it the endless sand that gave you that impression?"

"Are there oceans or rivers or forests?"

"Not here. Not within walking distance." Not like there used to be. Even when he'd been born, forests had been something that someone else had seen. He'd never been to the ocean either. Rivers could be raised, but he remembered when they had snaked across the landscape and there had been grasses and great herds of animals.

"What is walking distance?"

"Anywhere that can be walked to before the water that you carry runs out. Only mages have the power to tap into the underground rivers and draw them to the surface." They walked back through the town and stopped at a tent decorated with depictions of water. It was hard to miss.

On the outside was a pump and tap for filling jugs and urns. On the inside was the shower. The tent was divided into six big wedges.

People usually went with their friends. Showers were quick, but the preparation wasn't.

Angus looked at the combs and pots on the bench.

Saka hung up the wrap he had worn. Its soft, thick weave made it ideal for drying. He had no hair to comb through, but he liked to use the paste to rub himself down. He was aware as Angus watched him pour a little water into a bowl and then select a pot full of salt and ground fruit seeds. He added enough to make the paste, then started rubbing it all over his skin, scouring away dirt and sweat.

"Comb through your hair. Scrub yourself, then shower."

Angus picked up a comb. "Everyone uses this?"

Saka nodded. "There are people who restock and clean the baths. However, it is bad manners to leave a mess. When we rinse in the shower we also wash out the bowl before stacking it in the pile to be reused."

He knew enough about humans from his previous warlock to know that humans didn't bathe like this. He also knew that, while they lived together, they lived apart as though what they did didn't affect anyone else. Here everything was interwoven.

Saka stopped his own preparation. He offered Angus different pots to smell. "Which one do you like?"

"I don't know." He shrugged.

"There is no right or wrong choice. People like different things. I like the salt and tang of the seeds. Others prefer something a little subtler." Saka handed Angus one that was slightly green. "This one has the bark of the darrinka tree."

"You have trees?" Angus gave it a sniff. "Smells kind or sweet... a little like cinnamon?"

"Of course we have trees. But not at this site." Saka mixed up the paste. "Maybe they are the same tree, or were the same tree thousands of years ago when there was more free interaction across the void." He handed over the palm-sized bowl. "Now you scrub."

"Then I shower."

"Yes. Then you finish off with something to moisturize."

Angus lifted an eyebrow. "You moisturize?"

"Everyone does. The desert is drying." Saka went back to scrubbing himself. When he was covered head to toe in paste, he walked under a spout, gave the handle a couple of pumps and let the cold ground water sluice over him. He tipped his face to the stream. The river below them was strong and fast. It was the one they wanted to follow to Lifeblood Mountain. It was his job to make sure that when they moved they didn't wander away from water. As long as the hunters were bringing home meat, they wouldn't have to move too soon. Being able to tap into the river also meant that they didn't have to live close to a watering hole. That was dangerous.

The stream became a trickle. Then stopped. That was it. He was cool and clean, and tired. He watched Angus shower. While there was hesitation, Angus wasn't running or whining. He was getting on with what needed to be done. Even if Angus didn't see it in himself, there was strength of will many warlocks lacked. When trained he would be powerful, and hopefully not dangerous to Demonside.

Saka rubbed in the moisturizer. If showering with friends, they would help each other. Scrub the places that were hard to reach. He and Angus weren't friends, and he suspected that if he offered, Angus would pull away. Angus went through the same process of sniffing before selecting what to use. His skin was pink from being scrubbed.

Saka caught him glancing his way.

"Would you have... been intimate... with whomever you pulled through?"

Saka considered him for a moment. What was the answer that Angus was looking for? Did he want to be special or know that it was just magic? "No. If I didn't like the warlock's attitude, I'd have been more than happy to use my knives more ruthlessly."

Angus took half a step back. "You said blood and souls went together."

"They do, and they can all be used together. So can sex and blood, or even sex and soul. Most mages have a preference. I prefer inflicting pleasure over pain, although there is a fine line." He ran slick hands over his horns. There was nothing worse than dry, cracked horns.

"You have taken other warlocks."

"No. I have been gifted other humans to rebalance the magic. Some were wizards or warlocks who weren't retrieved and taken back to Humanside." Saka put his wrap on. His skin was cool and damp. It was a nice way to end a very long day. He would sleep well for what was left of tonight.

"What happened to the others?"

Saka drew in a breath, then sighed. He looked Angus in the eye. "If no one comes for them, they become ours."

"What happened to them?"

"They died eventually." Mages kept humans who had bridged the void without proper precautions. Another unwritten rule. They kept whomever wasn't retrieved. Only those who were specifically asked for had to be returned. Most were left in Demonside. Some humans were deliberately sent across the void, criminals that the humans thought nothing of. The warlocks in charge knew the cost of magic but didn't share the truth.

"If no one comes for me tomorrow...." Angus swallowed, his Adam's apple bouncing.

"Then I will not trade you on or gift you to another mage. You have my word." But that didn't mean that Miniti couldn't order Angus away or decide that the warlock's death would serve a greater purpose. If Angus wasn't his warlock, then Saka would be free to take another. There would be a lot of magic to be regained from taking warlocks and keeping them for ritual. Not all would be retrieved.

CHAPTER NINE

IN THE DARK Angus lay awake on the mattress, naked except for the sheet that covered him and Saka. Saka was sleeping. He should be sleeping, but he was sharing a bed with a demon. His skin smelled of strange herbs and lotions, and his body ached from the magic and the sex—how could a simple hand job have felt so good?

His mind kept skipping to tomorrow. What if no one came? He would be stuck there with Saka to rebalance magic. His fingers brushed the almost fully healed cuts on his arm.

How easy would it be to raise magic on his own at home? He'd have to look up some of the wizard practices—not at the college, though. That could get him thrown out. As much as he didn't want to be a warlock, he wanted to be a rogue warlock even less. He sighed. There he was assuming that he would be going home.

He glanced at the demon next to him.

Several flaps of the tent were now open, and a cool breeze swept through, but it was too hot to sleep and he couldn't get up and start wandering around. He'd seen the animals around the tents, and he had no idea if they ate meat or plants, and he didn't want to find out by getting bitten. He didn't want any demon to bite him.

Angus turned onto his back and folded his hands on his stomach.

He closed his eyes, determined to find sleep even if it took the rest of the night. Saka reached out and put his hand over Angus's. A feeling of heaviness followed. He wanted to ask if Saka was doing something to him, but the next thing he knew, he was waking and soft morning light was bathing the tent.

Talking and the sounds of cooking dragged him further out of sleep. Was it morning already? His dreams had been full of things that could have happened last night and the way Saka had felt pressed against him. Angus blinked a few times. His eyes were gritty. He threw his arm over his face. He wasn't ready to face the day or the demon.

"It has been a long time since I have woken up with a man in my bed," Saka said.

Angus glanced at Saka from beneath his arm, but Saka's eyes were half-closed.

"Same." Too long. The demon's dick was lifting the sheet. Angus closed his eyes. He should not want sex with a demon. But lust was waking up and his body was remembering how good Saka had been with just his hand.

His dreams of doing more than that resurfaced and added to the heat in his blood.

He'd already broken all the college rules; what did it matter if he broke them more than once? He opened his eyes, his gaze on the demon. He'd glimpsed the demon's penis last night while they were showering. It had looked surprisingly normal.

Everything here was normal. Demons weren't the bloodthirsty beasts the college claimed they were. Saka probably knew more about magic than some of his lecturers. He would be a fool to waste what time they had.

"What would you normally do with the man in your bed?" He hoped that he didn't sound lame, or desperate. But he was.

Saka's warm fingers trailed over Angus's stomach, down to his very awake dick.

As Saka's hand gripped and stroked, Angus let himself sink into the rhythm. Saka took the arm that was covering Angus's eyes away and pinned the hand above his head. The demon's body was pressed close. He kissed Angus, his tongue thrusting deep.

A circle went up around them, and Angus groaned. Couldn't they do anything without magic?

"Shh. Enjoy." Saka's voice was soft in his ear, his hand firm on Angus's shaft.

Angus gave a halfhearted attempt to break free, but the kisses and the caress felt too good. Besides he'd been dreaming of it all night. He reached for Saka with his free hand.

"No. You will get your turn later. Put it behind your head." The strokes slowed.

Angus hesitated then obeyed, and Saka placed his hand over both. If he really wanted, he could probably slide them free, but why would he? It felt too good... and he was doing his bit for Demonside. He closed his eyes as the burn of lust consumed him.

"You make this easy," Saka murmured, his thumb rubbing over the glans with each stroke.

Angus thrust into Saka's hand, expecting the demon to stop him at exactly the wrong moment. The strokes became slick. Angus's breath caught and his back arched as he came. Saka stole his moan of pleasure with a kiss. The rush of instant release instead of the delayed gratification of last night made his skin break out in gooseflesh. He shivered, despite the heat of the demon's body against him.

As he drew in a couple of breaths, he became aware of Saka's thick cock pressed against his thigh. Angus opened his eyes. Saka's metallic-looking skin gleamed in the magic. Saka released Angus's hands, then rolled onto his back. His fingers ruffled Angus's hair, then drew him down, leaving no doubt about what he was expecting.

Angus licked his lower lip. Saka's other hand was already holding his cock and stroking. Not wanting to be caught in an awkward position, Angus moved between the demon's legs. As he moved willingly, the pressure on his hair decreased.

He licked the demon's smooth skin, paying close attention to the ridge around the base of the head. He took the time to learn the shape and taste of the demon. After not getting any release last night, Saka was probably eager to get some pleasure for himself. Angus took Saka into his mouth. Saka's fingers moved through his hair in a caress as Angus worked his mouth over the demon's length. He took him a little deeper each time. The heat of the cock filling his mouth. Would he have to swallow?

He wanted to. He liked to.

Saka's chest lifted with each quick breath. His hips started rocking in time. The pressure on his head increased as Saka thrust up, deep into his mouth. The demon growled, and come filled Angus's mouth. He swallowed, and swallowed again.

"All of it." Saka thrust again, deeper.

The sweet come slid down Angus's throat, leaving that burned sugar taste. Saka lay down, finally spent. Angus pulled back. He wiped his mouth just in case; there had been more than he'd expected. Next time Saka was going to suck his dick and swallow. But he couldn't imagine Saka on his knees in front of him.

Saka spread his hands and drew in a breath. Angus looked up. The glass orbs were glowing softly, filled with magic that they had created. Then they went out, and the circle came down.

"We need to get ready to see Miniti." Saka got up in one smooth motion.

Angus sat back on his heels.

Saka's tail flicked his cheek in a caress. "Try to obey and not ask questions in front of Miniti. It would be better if it looked as though I have you firmly in hand."

Exactly what he was supposed to do to his demon on the human side of the void.

Saka tossed him a damp cloth. "Don't put your shirt on."

Angus wiped himself, stood, and handed the cloth back. He walked through the tent to where he'd left his clothes on the floor the night before. That seemed like so long ago. Now that he was no longer distracted, the fear came back. If no one came for him, it was very clear what his life would be like. He would be Saka's.

That was infinitely better than being Miniti's—although he

wouldn't live long enough to regret it. He shivered and pulled on yesterday's briefs and jeans, then shoved his feet into his shoes.

"Take them off." Saka pointed at the shoes.

His shoulders dropped, and he took them off again. "Why?" They were his favorite sneakers, and he didn't want them lost in Demonside forever. "She can't kill me before the time is up? Can she?"

From the look on Saka's face, she could. Saka picked up the small vials that Angus had seen last night. "Hopefully not. But it would not be wise to keep her waiting, so eat and then we will go. She will not appreciate being rushed as she will know exactly when the minimum time you are to remain here is up."

Angus ate half of what was left of the bread. It was drier this morning. And while he wasn't hungry now, he would be later, and whatever happened he'd rather have food in his stomach.

Saka put on his machete, then put on a black arm guard. Angus stared at it for a moment before he realized what he was seeing. Small ceremonial blades. Four of them.

He choked down the food in his mouth. "What do you need them for?"

"Precautionary."

"Against what?"

"The demand for blood. Better me than another mage." Saka's head tilted, and his brow ridge rose.

"The rules keep changing."

"The rules have stayed the same; you just aren't well versed in them. There are etiquette and demands to be met the same as on Humanside. Remember what happens here when you go back. Remember that I could have handed you to her yesterday—you wouldn't be the first to die *accidentally* during the twenty-four-hour wait—eventually another warlock would've tried to summon a demon and I would try again."

"Why didn't you?"

"Instinct... so far it hasn't led me astray." Saka ate quickly.

Angus's stomach was made of lead and sinking. He had no doubt that he would feel the bite of Saka's knives again before he went home.

He *was* going home.

Too soon he was following Saka to that central tent. The sand burned the soles of his feet, and it wasn't even midday yet. The sun struck his bare shoulders, and he was sure he was burning already. This time as they walked through the market where he had appeared —there was a demon on a mat in that spot and people walked around it—people looked at Angus and spoke softly. A few made some kind of gesture.

Saka dropped Angus's shirt and shoes on the mat and kept going.

Someone at home would be using something of his to locate him across the void. He glanced back, the mat was the location and his clothes an anchor. It was deliberate and everyone knew that. No one wanted to be standing there when the void opened.

He returned his gaze to Saka's back. Saka seemed to know everyone, from the other metallic-skinned black-horned demons to the white-as-a-ghost vamprys, and every other demon in between. The men mostly just wore pants; some of the women wore little more, just a band around their breasts. Other demons wore what seemed to be a sundress, for men and women. No one was worried about being burned to a cinder except him.

As the patterned tent got closer, Angus thought blistering would be a safer option than going in. The guards let Saka in immediately. As before Miniti was reclining by a table. This time instead of being covered in papers, there was a selection of food. There were a couple of other demons also in attendance.

Angus knelt behind Saka, the same as yesterday. It rankled. He didn't want to be kneeling, but if Miniti was something like a queen and Saka a high-level lord, then perhaps it made sense. It also made him the human captive. The reality of his situation hit home. That was exactly what he was.

Saka walked up to the table and placed the vial down. "A gift from last night."

"I have been looking forward to it. There was quite a release I am informed."

Every inch of Angus blushed. He knew it wasn't sunburn. Hopefully no one else would notice the difference.

Saka inclined his head. "A modest first try."

Miniti laughed. "You have always liked to play."

"You have always enjoyed my games."

She removed the stopper and drank the contents. Angus winced at the idea of her getting a taste for him.

"Very pleasing." She got up. Her pink dress trailed behind her as she moved around the table and stopped in front of him. She cupped Angus's chin and forced his head up. "You think they will come for him?"

"Yes. From what I have learned, his father is high ranking."

She nodded and stared into him. Angus tried to clear his thoughts, but they scattered and memories of last night tumbled to the surface clearer and sharper than he could recall them on his own. She released his jaw and walked around him.

"His flesh is too unmarked. I don't want them knowing how much he enjoyed his time here." She leaned down. "And I know exactly how much you did. You even went back for more. Tough soldier or weak whore?"

Angus said nothing. He stared at the ground, uncomfortable with how much she knew. That was probably her magical skill. Everyone here had magic… but not all dedicated their life to it. Why?

She stood. "Wiley warlock. You will have your hands full with that one, Saka."

She motioned to two of the demons in the room. "Hold him."

Angus looked up. Saka gave a small shake of his head. Then the demons had him. They forced him to his feet. Their hands gripping his arms tight as they held them out horizontal. Angus curled his toes against the rough fabric of the floor.

Miniti sat on her lounge. "I do love some entertainment in the morning." She leaned forward and rested her chin on her hands. Her smile was too wide and her eyes too bright.

Angus clamped his teeth shut. He was not going to give her anything to enjoy.

Saka walked around him and the demons holding him, making a formal circle. The air shimmered then settled. This magic was different. The circle not as strong. He realized why as Miniti made her own, snapping it around the tent with barely a movement of her fingers.

He refused to look down, so he stared at her.

Saka ran a hand down his back, over his butt, over his hip. His hand cupped Angus's groin. He was not going to look down and see if there was a knife missing. There would be.

What was Saka going to do with it?

Like last night the anticipation built. Then just before he was about to ask what Saka was going to do, the cool blade touched his shoulder.

"I could make you like this if we had longer. You would get hard at the sight of these blades."

That would never happen. Saka's hand moved over Angus's dick—his body didn't know if it should be afraid or aroused. Miniti was watching his every reaction. Was she waiting for him to cry or plead for mercy?

The blade at his shoulder moved, and his skin stung. He grunted but didn't move. Saka repeated. Angus kept his eyes open and his chin up, he fought to keep his breathing even and to think only of the next breath. When Saka released him, he was hard.

Miniti nodded. "Put your mark on him, Saka."

Saka moved in front of him. He showed Angus the blade. It was clean of blood. What? Had he made no cuts? Saka placed his hand over Angus's heart. His skin warmed.

"Now you will bleed for me." Saka removed his hand, then cut a symbol into Angus's left pectoral.

Angus hissed and flinched. Every drawn-out cut stung. His eyes prickled. He kept his teeth clamped together. He would not give them the pleasure of hearing him cry out. The demons held him up and still until Saka had finished carving a symbol into his skin. Blood welled and shimmered and ran down his chest. Angus watched one rivulet race toward his jeans.

Blood magic made of fear and pain. A little more magic rebalanced in Demonside.

He sucked in several deep breaths. He much preferred sex magic.

Saka dismissed the circle and gave Miniti a half bow.

Miniti watched the blood. "It is a pity they will come. He would be days of fun."

Saka nodded. "I could train him well and get much magic out of him. But one isn't enough to rebalance what is taken." He indicated to Angus. "Would you like more?"

He was there, and they were talking around him. And he was nothing. Something to be used to rebalance the magic that warlocks were using. He was being treated the way demons were treated on the other side of the void. There had to be a better way to keep the flow between the two worlds.

Miniti handed Saka a cup, and Saka collected some of the blood that was still rolling out of the cuts. He didn't look Angus in the eye. He didn't speak or give any indication that he gave a damn. Angus didn't know him at all. Saka had become a very different demon. Angus tried to free his arms, but the demons gripped harder. Theirs claws pressed into his skin. He wanted to yell at them to stop, that he wasn't a walking store of magic from the other side of the void.

But Saka's warning to be silent remained with him.

That, and he *was* full of magic to be returned to Demonside, and Miniti would quite happily take his soul before he was ready to hand it over. Miniti smiled at Angus. He glared at her.

Saka turned away and handed the cup to her as though it were perfectly normal to have a sip of human blood. Just how many times had Saka done this?

Angus didn't want to know.

He knew his father had been through several demons. Drawing magic from Demonside through them and then using up their innate magic, killing them, without a second thought.

Miniti added some liquid to the cup and drank his blood, her gaze

61

on him. Her fingernails tapped the glass. "Take him to the mat to await collection."

She broke the circle. The demons holding his arm didn't release him, but lowered his arms to his side. He tried to break free again but failed. It wasn't like he had anywhere he could run to, but he didn't need to be held either. The demons turned him and marched him toward the door.

"If no one claims him by dusk, I want a public ritual. We must show off the power of the one we caught." Her voice was level as though they were discussing the weather.

Angus stumbled as panic punched upward. There was no way he was doing anything in public, and he certainly wasn't getting cut again. His back stung, and the symbol Saka had cut into him burned. Saka had freaking marked him.... For all Angus knew, that had magical consequences. How was he going to explain that back home? How was he going to be able to talk about any of it?

He couldn't. He didn't want anyone to know what had happened.

"We must take more like him before the rivers sink deeper and Demonside dries up," Miniti said.

"Or we hope for change on the other side."

"I fear that won't come in time."

Angus glanced back. But the demons didn't stop to let him hear the rest of the conversation. The sun struck his skin, and he squinted. They took him to the mat and made him sit. The guards didn't leave. What would they do if he got up and walked around? There was nowhere for him to go, and he was now painfully aware that things could have been much worse. That had been etched into his skin so he could never forget.

He glanced down at the carved sigil. It had stopped bleeding. The tracks of blood were drying in the sun. He rubbed some dried blood off.

Things could still get worse if no one came for him.

The red sand reflected the heat and light. His mouth dried as he sweated. The sweat stung the cuts. He put his shirt on as a hat and let it fall over his shoulders. He closed his eyes and let the curious stares and conversation around him sink away. In his own mind, time slipped away. He didn't dwell on what had happened or what could happen, instead he let his consciousness connect the world around him. He knew what Earth felt like. Touching the four elements was basic, wizard-level magic. Demonside was different. The four elements were there, but they weren't familiar. Beneath the sand was rock, caverns and tunnels carved out by centuries of water flow. There were things living down there too. Big things. He pulled back to the surface when one sensed him. Gradually he became aware of someone sitting on the mat with him.

Saka.

Angus didn't open his eyes. He didn't want to look at him. While he hated going into Miniti's tent, what Saka had done to him was nothing different than what warlocks did to their demons. Demon blood for a spell, using the demon as a conduit for magic until it collapsed from exhaustion. Or died.

He was far from dead, and Saka had made sure that he was fine after every ritual.

No one killed their demon deliberately, not the way Saka had suggested happened to humans here... did they? But those demons who rampaged through the streets were killed.

His knowledge of the wizard underground and what he'd seen here tumbled together. He'd had reservations about being a warlock before. Now he had more. But if he did nothing, if he walked away, then nothing would change and more would be taken. Demons used for magic. Humans sacrificed to rebalance.

If there was no balance, Demonside would die and there would be no magic.

"They are bridging the void." Saka's voice was soft.

Angus opened his eyes. "How can you tell?"

Saka smiled, but there was no joy in it. "I have been working magic for longer than you have been alive. I can feel the tear starting to form in my world. It was how I was able to make ready when you bridged the void and answer your call." He fisted his hand and placed it against his chest. "You are my warlock. Do not forget. I am your Demonside master."

"I am your earthbound master." He repeated the words by rote, but here there was a shimmer of power in them. Something changed in the air. It sharpened.

Saka put his hands on the edge of the mat Angus was sitting on. A circle sprang up. "I look forward to your summons, warlock." Saka nodded, then stood and stepped back.

Everyone watching stepped back, forming an even bigger circle. They linked hands and started humming. The vibrations rumbled through the ground. The air crackled, and then there was a person standing in the circle with him. Behind her he could just make out a room and figures, but it wouldn't come into focus.

The woman glanced around with a sneer on her lip, then looked down. "Angus Donohue." She said his name clearly as though expecting a demon to challenge her. She paused for a moment. None did. "You walking out of here, or are you injured?"

Angus stood. He glanced at Saka. There was no way he could come to Demonside again. But Saka would come if summoned. He had no choice. Angus had an inkling of how that must feel.

The woman took his arm, much like the demons had. One step and they were across the void. The room was cold and dim after the heat of the desert market. A vampry demon and another warlock also stood in the circle. While he knew there was a circle, Angus couldn't see it. It was like being blinded.

On the other side of the circle were three other warlocks, including his father.

CHAPTER TEN

Saka stood there for several moments after Angus was gone, returned to Humanside. He was glad that someone had come for him. He was. He just didn't feel it within him. He was strangely empty. The same way he had been when he'd realized that Kitu was gone.

He breathed in the hot air and then exhaled.

He had more of a connection to Angus than he'd ever had with Kitu. The bond between warlock and demon could only be broken by death. Usually the demon's. He closed his eyes, aware of the people moving around him and the chatter.

They were impressed with Angus and the way he had handled himself and the amount of magic that had been released. They were happy with him. It was always good when the people had faith in their mage. If the people liked him, it would be harder for Miniti to remove him if she found him too troublesome.

If things went badly with Angus, Saka could become a problem. The one thing in Saka's favor was that he'd handled a warlock before and had succeeded in making him see the flaws in what the humans were doing.

With Angus he was already two steps in. Angus knew something was off, and he had been a willing participant in the magic. A smile formed on Saka's lips. His penis started to thicken at the memory.

The liquid heat cooled just as fast as it had formed. There had been cold metal in Angus's eyes after the knives had been brought out. Saka hung his head. The rules of the college tied Angus as much as the rules of Demonside bound him. If he'd refused, Miniti would've done it. Or worse the other mage would've. Usi's specialty was blood magic, and she was very good at extracting every drop. But where Saka created pleasure—usually—Usi went for fear and pain.

Miniti liked that about her other mage. She also liked that she got the soul. However, as much as she liked inflicting pain, she wasn't stupid, and she knew that sex magic was a nonlethal replenishing source. She also knew that many mages didn't have the skill or patience to do it.

Angus had made him hungry for more.

A smile formed. He'd really like another attempt.

But if Angus came back, he would need to be retrieved again, and Saka knew that while getting taken once was allowable, twice would be seen as a failure. Angus was more valuable alive and on Humanside.

Saka opened his eyes, sensing Usi approach.

Her green skin glimmered, shifting color from light to dark. Her short pink hair stood straight up from her skull ridges. Many considered her to be very beautiful.

She smiled, her teeth small and sharp, as she stood opposite him. "Missing your new toy?"

"Wondering how long it will be before he summons me."

"There will be an audience."

"Of that I have no doubt." He turned away. "The gathering draws closer; we must plot a way."

Usi nodded. "The scouts brought no good news. Our previous wells are dry. The river has sunk again."

Saka swore by the sun and the stars on both sides of the void as he stood. "How much more do we need to do?"

Usi hooked her arm through his. As they left the mats, someone rolled them up and took them away, honored to have been the mat provider for such an important event. "We take stragglers and too few."

"We take too many and they will retaliate and kill more of us." That method had been tried a hundred years ago. The unwritten rules had come out of it. Saka hadn't been born at the time, but like all mages, he knew his history.

"Then we retaliate and take more of them," she snarled.

"And then we chase our tails and become buried deeper in the sand." He shook his head as they made their way through the town. "We must convince them to stop sucking us dry."

She gave a gurgling laugh. "Is that what you said last night?"

Saka stopped walking. "It was productive."

"He'd still be screaming and sobbing if I had him."

"True, but I would rather not alienate someone who could be an ally."

"Humans don't care about us."

"No, but if Demonside collapses, Humanside will not fare well." It was a theory that some mages had floated at the last gathering. It made sense to Saka, and he had supported it. Others did not. They felt that the only effect would be the loss of magic from Humanside. Now he knew they were wrong. Angus had said his world was growing colder.

"They will kill him like your last warlock. They will learn he is a traitor."

That was a risk. But Angus had already been figuring out the truth. Saka had seen the doubts, and lust, in Angus's eyes in those first few seconds. It had been that first impression that had made him want the warlock. He'd rather keep Angus than let him die and try again.

Better the warlock he knew.

"Perhaps. Have you received any fresh traitors?" He knew she hadn't. They had to wait for the warlocks in charge to send traitors across. They controlled how much magic was restored, and they were sending fewer humans.

She purred. "Did you want to help me question one?" She leaned in

67

and licked his ear with her long pointed tongue. "You could fuck while I cut."

"My knife skills are not rusted." He'd taken the time to learn to meld his skills together so one ability emphasized the other. Usually he could separate ritual from his own pleasure. Angus had blurred that line this morning.

"I forget you like them to cry for entirely the wrong reasons." Usi opened the tent flap for him, as was protocol. He was the senior mage, the favorite. Something that Usi would love to take from him even as they worked together.

Saka smiled. "I prefer them to beg me for more."

CHAPTER ELEVEN

THE CHAIR WAS cold and uncomfortable. The heater was noisy. And there were too many sets of eyes on Angus.

He'd been given a shower—to remove the taint of Demonside— and had his cuts treated by a healer. The whole time she'd been working her magic, he'd been thinking about the demon not that far from her and the way the magic was coming across the void to be used to heal him. Saka could've healed him if he'd wanted.

Saka shouldn't have made the cuts in the first place.

The magic that Angus had rebalanced in Demonside had now flowed back to heal him. Part of it, or all of it? Did any warlock ever think about the cost, or were demons and Demonside just a resource to be exploited?

Now the cuts on his back, that had never bled, were nothing but fine scars. The mark on his chest was a knotted scar that looked as though there was red metal trapped in the wound. As though part of Saka was in his skin. He remembered the heat of the demon's hand before he'd done it, seen the look in his dark eyes. There had been no glee, but there hadn't been regret either.

Angus suppressed a shiver. He should've asked more questions instead of withdrawing into his own thoughts, but the shock of what had happened and the anxiety of waiting for rescue had taken over. He hadn't wanted to see any demons. He was regretting that now as he sat before the warlocks who had rescued him. They had observed him in the shower, watched him get healed, and watched him some more as he sat there wearing only a towel.

His father hadn't rushed to his side or asked about his welfare. He was sure his father was thinking only of the humiliation of having his son taken to Demonside.

"There is no hold over him," one of male warlocks said.

"That marking can't be removed. It was made with blood magic." The warlock who had healed the cuts had her head tilted to the side as though perplexed by the problem.

Only the healer's demon was now present. A green skinned man with impressive ridges on his skull and dark orange hair tufting out of them. He stood there silently. Why didn't he fight back? But Angus already knew. If the demon did anything wrong, his warlock would kill him and move on.

The unwritten rules were meant to protect everyone. There were three that he was now clear on.

Demons can't kill humans in Humanside, only in Demonside.

Demons had to wait twenty-four hours before killing a human to rebalance the magic.

Humans can't kill demons for magic.

And yet they were. The occasional rampage was an excuse to take a huge amount of magic. It was no wonder that some demons were unhappy with the way things were.

"Check his memories," his father said.

"Or you could talk to me, since I am sitting here." Angus really wanted a hot meal and some sleep. He was tired of being ignored and treated like some kind of experiment. There had been little concern about how he was coping. No one had asked. They had just ordered him to wash, to stand, to sit. He had expected more from his father. He shouldn't have.

"We may not get the truth. They may have altered your mind." His father looked as though he were serious.

Angus lifted one eyebrow. He really didn't want them in his mind. They would see what he'd done with Saka. That would not go down well. "Ah, no. They used me in some kind of ritual, thus the cuts."

"Did they say what it was for?" The man with the beard leaned forward.

"Rebalancing the magic. We take, we have to give back." That sounded a lot like underground wizard propaganda. Could it be propaganda if it was true? He looked at the five warlocks facing him. Even if they knew this truth, they wouldn't acknowledge that it was a problem.

"And they let you live?" his father said that as if it were a bad thing.

Angus ignored that bite. Had his father been hoping there would be no retrieval? He looked at his father. "Sorry to disappoint you again. I can't even die at the right time… that is what you wanted right? Now all your friends know that I wasn't strong enough to hold my demon."

"Yes, let's talk about your demon." The woman who had stepped across the void to retrieve him crossed her arms. "Was he the one opposite you?"

Angus nodded. "He was. A common black-horn." He had no idea what the students or lecturer had told these people.

"Why was he able to snatch you? Can't you hold a circle?" His father's eyes narrowed.

He'd heard that tone of voice his whole childhood. Only now it had no effect. He'd survived Demonside, had a powerful demon and knowledge that he didn't know what to do with. All of it reinforced his instinct that using demons without thought was wrong.

The five waited for an answer.

They would never give up their demons or make a personal sacrifice to keep the magic. That was why they sent criminals across the void. Why they waited twenty-four hours before even attempting a rescue of a taken warlock. How many people were never retrieved? How many humans and demons had died so that a few warlocks could have power?

"I can, but that day…." It seemed a lifetime ago. "Something felt

71

off." He wasn't going to admit that he was trying to fail. Nor was he going to admit that Saka was a mage. That might mean admitting to the other ritual, and no one would approve of that. His skin heated as the blush crept over his skin. He cursed silently and then lied. "I had a migraine, but I knew I couldn't skip the class. The demon summoning is important. He appeared in the circle, and that was fine and... and then... when I tried to draw some power, he reached through...."

"Why didn't you see someone about the migraine? You know better than to perform magic when not fully alert." What his father said was true, but Angus didn't want to compound the lie.

"I know better than to admit weakness too, Father."

Silence.

The five considered him.

Angus tried not to move. He was aching and tired and hungry. He didn't know what he needed to deal with first.

"I'll check his memories." The woman who had retrieved him stepped closer.

Angus pressed himself against the back of the chair. "I don't want you in my head."

"Have you got something to hide?" She smiled, and it was all malice.

Yes. "No... how do I know you won't mess my head up?"

"We aren't the monsters, Angus. We just want to help you and get you back to college and your studies." She placed her hand on his forehead and tilted his chin so that he was looking into her eyes.

A circle snapped around them. He should've eaten, grounded himself better so that she couldn't use him in this ritual. The warlocks hadn't let him eat for a reason. He tried to pull away but couldn't move. His memories of Demonside started to flicker to life. The heat, the demons, the tents. Saka. Miniti. The knife being brought to his skin. The pain of that first cut.

Then nothing.

ANGUS WOKE up in his room on campus. His stomach was growling and trying to eat itself. He squinted and looked at the alarm clock. It hadn't gone off yet. He winced as he sat up, glanced down, and saw the scar on his chest.

It was almost an S with a line and two dots. He rubbed it. But couldn't quite remember how he'd gotten it. Or how he'd gotten to his room. He lay back down, tracing the shape and trying to remember.

Wiley warlock. You will have your hands full with that one, Saka. The demon's face was close to his, and then she pulled back. Her black eyes had bored into his as she worked some kind of magic. He couldn't blink as she looked into his mind and memories.

He frowned, and his finger stilled. He'd been in Demonside.

How had he got back here? He traced the shape again and tried to remember everything about the demon who had been in his head. Nothing.

What did he remember about being retrieved? He knew he'd been retrieved and hadn't made it across himself. It was unsettling to have so much missing time. He should remember getting such a knotted scar.

Any scar.

Shadowed figures. Voices but not the words. A hand on his forehead as a human woman had looked into his eyes.

Magic stabbed, dug deep, and twisted. He clutched his temples and curled up, but the searing pain was within him and nothing he could fight. The warlock had done something to him. The scar had been made with blood magic and couldn't be removed. It was his link to what had happened. He had to think about the scar.

The demon's white face and her dark eyes flashed in his mind again. She'd done something to his mind too. In his head the two magicks slammed together and tried to tear him apart.

His alarm started going off, but he couldn't move to shut it off.

Fragments of Demonside and being questioned by the warlocks scattered.

The demon hadn't tampered with his memories, warlocks had. What did they not want him to know? He needed to remember. Acting on instinct he dug his nails into his chest near the scar. In his mind he brought up a circle around himself. His nails broke the skin, and he traced the scar with his blood.

By my blood I will remember. Show me what was lost.

The veil that had surrounded his memories of Demonside tore away, and he gasped, unable to move in case his brain somehow melted and leaked out of his ear.

He saw Demonside red under the orange sun. Saka gleaming like metal. The blue crystalline circle that had surrounded them as they had indulged in… he swallowed at the memory of what they had done… sex magic. The demon's kiss. The glowing glass orbs. The release of magic. Give and take. Take and give.

Miniti—he knew the demon's name now—had somehow protected his memories. She'd known that someone would try to take them. Everything that had happened after her working her magic was virtually gone, erased by the warlock who didn't want him to know.

He couldn't remember how he'd got from Miniti's tent back to his room. All he had was a vague impression of being retrieved, of being questioned. And the scar?

Saka had carved it into his flesh. It was Saka's mark that he wore. He was sure of that even though he didn't remember anyone making the cuts. The warlocks had tried to take Angus's memories of his demon.

He drew in deep breaths and gradually released his head. Was it possible for a mind to feel wounded and bruised? As though it had been trampled on?

It wasn't just the pain. It was the knowledge that the warlocks who'd retrieved him had tried to take his memories. That was why no one ever talked about it. They literally couldn't because they didn't know what had happened.

Why had Miniti made sure that he would?

He didn't want the chance to see her in person to ask. That would mean returning to Demonside, and he was sure there would be no second retrieval.

He groaned, rolled over, and slapped the button on his alarm clock. His room fell silent. While his body was tired, he was hungry.

He had no idea how long ago his last meal had been. He had to get up, eat, shower, and get ready for class. Go on as though nothing had happened. He touched the scar on his chest, now smeared with blood. That scar would always remind him of what had happened in Demonside.

He made himself move and find some painkillers. Then he got ready to face the world outside his room.

He made it halfway to the bathroom.

"I thought you were dead." One of the warlocks from his class slapped him on the shoulder. "I saw you get taken."

Angus nodded. "I got lucky."

A small crowd gathered around him. All were excited to see him again and they wanted to know what had happened.

Angus opened his mouth to tell them about Demonside and everything that he'd learned about how magic worked between the two worlds. He was taking a demon's word over a warlock's. No one would believe him, or they'd report him for being an underground sympathizer. Worse still he might get his mind messed with again. His temples throbbed. He just wanted to get to the bathroom.

"I'm not sure what happened. I barely remember getting taken, or retrieved." He shrugged. He didn't know who he could trust. These were his friends and classmates, but how many would be happy to suck their demon dry for more power? How many would draw away in disgust if they knew he'd had sex with a demon and been part of a demonic ritual or three?

That was why the warlocks had taken his memories. So the victim never questioned their place.

Trouble was, he only felt like a victim because warlocks had invaded his mind. If not for Miniti, he'd be the Angus he'd been before. Filled with doubt and a gut instinct that something was wrong.

Now he knew for sure what that something was, and it wasn't the demons.

CHAPTER TWELVE

SAKA WOKE AND LISTENED, trying to work out why he was awake. It was dark; the breeze moved through his tent but didn't ruffle the bed sheets. He'd changed them, but in his mind, he could still smell Angus. He'd been dreaming of him. He ran his hand over his erection. Perhaps that was why he was awake.

Awareness glided over his skin. A faint aura formed around him.

He sat up. Fully alert now. He was about to be summoned. It was just after midnight. This was not good. He lunged for pants but didn't make it in time. Great, now he was going to have to face Angus and a cluster of judgmental warlocks, naked and with a hard dick.

He crossed the void in a rush of cold air and landed on one knee with his hand over his genitals. There was no visible circle, but he could feel it binding him in place, firmer than the first time Angus had summoned him. He blinked and let his eyes get used to the light.

There was no room full of warlocks.

Just Angus. A bed, and a light, and a table.

This was odd. Saka stood, keeping his hand in place. "Aren't you supposed to have supervision when you do this?"

"Yes."

Saka checked the room again: there was definitely no one hidden in the shadows or under the bed.

"They are making me repeat the demon summoning spell tomorrow. They are acting as though I failed." Angus rubbed his temples.

"So you summoned me on your own?" Saka frowned, and his tail whipped in annoyance. He had a life and couldn't jump every time Angus called—except he had to. "I could drag you across the void now, and no one would know where to start looking."

The idea had a limited appeal. Angus would be bound to him and in his bed... until the human's spark went out from spending too long in Demonside. Then Miniti would eat Angus's soul. Saka didn't want that. Angus was more use here as a voice of the truth. The circle tightened as Angus strengthened it. Not enough to stop Saka if he really wanted to break it. Not yet anyway. There would come a time when they were more equally matched.

"They tried to take my memories."

Saka tilted his head. "Which memories, and what did they do with them?"

"Everything from the time you took me. Miniti did something. I got them back." He pressed his hands to his head. "It hurts to remember. And I'm missing bits." Angus pulled aside his shirt. "What is this?"

Saka took a step forward, then stopped. He could break the circle; Angus was losing concentration. But Angus stepped back and pushed more energy and then Saka's own energy into it. The circle strengthened. It was much harder to break a circle he was helping feed. He could close the void, but then the magic would be draining out of him. He left the void open and waited to see what Angus would do.

There was wariness on Angus's face now, a distance in the way he held himself. The warlocks might have forced him to forget Saka's knives, but part of him knew something had happened. Saka wanted to hold Angus as he filled in the gaps. He wanted to kiss him. He wanted to do more than that. His dream lust was still thick and heavy in his blood.

"Strengthen your circle, for it would be a simple matter for me to tear it down." Saka took a half step forward, not that he needed to move to destroy the circle.

Angus lifted his hands and concentrated.

"More." Magic flowed through Saka and into the circle. Should he be teaching the warlock?

The young warlock frowned. The circle became something that Saka could feel. It became almost solid. It would take more effort for him to bring down, but it wasn't impossible. He'd been doing magic for too many years for a simple circle to trap him.

"This would hold a scarlips or other creature. It would even hold your average demon, but not a mage. Not me."

"Why did I connect to you when I cannot hold you?"

"You would not be the first warlock to be outclassed and then taken."

"Were they retrieved?"

Saka shrugged. "I do not know every ritual that occurs. But you did get retrieved...." He stopped covering his penis. They were alone; there was nothing to hide. "Why did they mess with your memories?"

"Why did Miniti?"

"She didn't, all she did was anchor them to the blood magic I then worked. She isn't a mage." But she had invested her trust in him and Angus with that small action.

"All demons have magic."

Saka nodded.

"Why aren't you all mages?"

"Why aren't all humans warlocks or engineers or librarians... being a mage means putting your leader first. It means years of grueling work. How do you think we get good at magic? I spent years getting cut and learning to cut. Longer working out the intricacies of sex magic." He paused. "Being a mage is an honor. Not all who volunteer are chosen. The kick is that all mages feel the void open. Many shun the call of a warlock because if we have one, we must treat the warlock with respect and encourage the same because we are in a position to influence, to teach. Warlocks do not give the same respect."

He still remembered the pride of passing and being accepted, but of only realizing the enormity of the undertaking once he was already in too deep. He wouldn't change it. He liked what he did; he even liked that touch of danger of knowing that he could fall out of favor.

"I could've done something easier with my life."

Angus rubbed his forehead. "I don't remember the blood magic."

"That is probably for the best as it was a crude effort done to convince your fellow warlocks that we had used you in the way they expected. They would probably not appreciate the truth." How much did Angus actually recall of the night they had spent together?

The warlock's cheeks turned pink, then red. Oh, he remembered it all. Saka smiled. *Good.*

"They don't know."

Saka inclined his head. "For the best, then."

"I want to know about the blood magic. I need to know what I've forgotten."

"Let me out of the circle."

Angus considered him for a moment. "If I do, you could take me back to Demonside."

"That is true." While demons couldn't open the void from Demonside, they could from Humanside. Or at least mages could. He could. "But I do not think they would retrieve you again."

Angus nodded.

"Then it is in both our interests to let you live here."

Angus didn't break the circle, and Saka was very tempted to bring it down. His fingers curled, but he waited.

"Is it? What about the rebalancing of magic?"

Saka smiled. "That can be done from this side. Some warlocks do pay for their magic."

Angus sat on the end of the bed with his head in his hands. He let the circle go. "I didn't know who else I could turn to. I don't know who to trust. I don't know what to do tomorrow."

Saka went to him, kneeling before him. "Tomorrow we can worry about in the morning." His fingers trailed along Angus's jaw. Then he lowered his hand and undid the first two buttons on Angus's shirt.

"This is my mark. I do not regret putting it on you, only the manner in which it was done."

"Did it hurt?"

"Yes. I do not like to inflict that kind of pain."

"Miniti does, yet she protected my mind."

Saka nodded. "And she will expect to be repaid at some point."

Angus looked down. "Have I made friends or enemies?"

"One can never tell. However, I will always choose those who serve others over those who serve themselves."

Angus had doubted the power of the warlocks even before he'd stepped across the void. He could work for human and demon if he trusted himself to bridge the void.

"And who do you serve, Saka?"

"Miniti, the mages, Demonside. You." Saka tilted his chin, his lips now close to Angus's.

"It felt more like I was serving you."

"And in doing that, you served Demonside. They all knew that. Miniti knew that. She saw the value of having you alive, and in protecting your memories." That warlocks were actively erasing or burying the memories of those who were retrieved was concerning.

"I have to act like I don't have those memories. Tomorrow I will have to summon you and prove that I have control. If I don't, I will fail and be kicked out."

"What do you want?"

Angus looked at him. His blue eyes filled with worry, and Saka could feel the tension and uncertainty radiating off him. It would be best if Angus stayed in the college, honed his skills, and looked for clues. It would also be more dangerous.

"I don't know."

Saka knew he should leave, but Angus had summoned him because he didn't know who else he could talk to. Saka couldn't leave his warlock when he needed help. "You can't be caught summoning me on your own."

"I'm not stupid. I went to a cheap motel far enough away from campus. One that doesn't have magic suppression."

"You have that? I remember it being talked about as a possible measure." That had been years ago with his last warlock.

"It's been around for nearly five years. They say it is to stop rogue demons and wizards. The underground says it's to make sure only certain warlocks have power. There are overrides that qualified warlocks get."

The idea of blocking magic was distasteful. Like blocking air or water. It was part of the world and should flow freely. "Would it be safe for you to make contact with the underground?"

Angus shrugged. "I could look up my ex, Jim. He's a wizard. He used to have connections."

Saka flinched. He shouldn't be jealous, but he was. He smoothed his thumbs over Angus's temples. "Let me take away the headache and settle your mind."

"I don't want someone else messing around in there."

"The two different spells are still operating against each other, thus the headache. There may be permanent damage if I don't do something. I don't want that, and I don't want to hurt you."

"But you did." Angus touched the scar.

"Yes, but we both have rules to obey, and not all of them make us happy. I will play the subservient demon tomorrow as expected, if you want to stay in college." That would be the safest for him too. "If I make a move to take you or break free, I suspect that the watching warlocks will either capture or kill me."

"Then there is no choice, is there?"

"There is always a choice, even if you don't like the options."

"If you can stop the headache, I will happily pay for the use of magic." Angus glanced down, then reached out to run his fingers up Saka's arm.

"I do this freely... but I could stay a while." How much of what they had done did Angus want to repeat? Tonight he would tread gently, and he would let himself enjoy. He rarely did that these days. It would be nice to have a partner he could work magic with as well as enjoy their time together.

Angus moved closer; his lips brushed Saka's. Saka kept his hands on Angus's temples as they kissed. He felt the warring spells. The anchor Miniti had made and the warlocks' shield that was supposed to stop Angus from ever finding the memories of Demonside. Those that Miniti hadn't protected were sealed—including the blood magic. Right now Saka didn't want to try to unravel that so he left them wrapped and tucked away. The rest of the spell was trying to wrap the anchored memories, an impossible task. Saka bundled that up on itself. Destroying it would leave a trail, and if a warlock looked inside, they'd expect to see the memory bubble. They wouldn't be able to see that it was empty, only the spell's creator would be able to look inside —it was a risk but not a big one.

Angus sighed, and the tension in his muscles eased. "Thank you."

Saka undid Angus's shirt the rest of the way. He couldn't lie; he did like seeing his mark on Angus. His fingers brushed over it. He wished Miniti had warned him what she was doing with the warlock's mind.

"Did I interrupt your evening?" Angus murmured as his hands skimmed over Saka's shoulders and chest.

"No. I was asleep and dreaming of you."

"Maybe because I was thinking of you. It took me hours to work up the nerve to try this on my own." Another kiss. Here Angus wasn't so hesitant about revealing his hunger.

This desire had nothing to do with magic. It was a dangerous lust that would serve neither of them well. Calling it ritual made it safe, yet it was clear that neither of them wanted that tonight.

Tomorrow he would worry about what was happening. A lot could change in daylight. So he wouldn't waste the dark.

He undid Angus's belt, and then his jeans. The warlock's erection jutted forward, constrained by black underwear. Saka pushed him back so Angus lay on the bed, then pulled down the jeans and underwear, freeing Angus's cock. It rested thick and heavy and dark against the human's pale skin. The change in color fascinated him, as had the shape. Where demon cocks were smooth, human ones had texture and only the dome was silken.

He wrapped his fingers around Angus and caressed, enjoying the feel without having to worry about either of them coming too fast.

There was no pressure. It had been a while since he'd had sex without it being part of something more. Tonight there was no circle binding them.

He lapped at Angus's sac, then tongued the shaft, finally tracing the head. Angus groaned as Saka took him into his mouth. The warlock's fingers brushed the demon's horns, then propped himself up to watch.

His lips parted, and his chest lifted with each breath. "Please, don't stop."

Saka stroked with his hand. "I have no plans to unless you keep making me talk." He licked the smooth crown, flicking his tongue over the slit. When Angus didn't say anything, Saka went back to sucking. He planned on enjoying the taste of him this time.

Knowing that there would be no delay to his release, Angus relaxed a little. His hips started to rock, thrusting into Saka's mouth. When salty precome coated his tongue, he was tempted to make Angus wait just once tonight, but decided against it. He wanted to have fun and show Angus that, even though he was a mage, he could have sex without controlling everything and making it part of something more.

The human's back arched, and he groaned as he came.

Saka swallowed, surprised that there was so little, then moved over Angus. He kissed him.

Angus's eyelids fluttered closed. "There is lube in my jacket pocket."

Saka smiled. Angus had obviously thought about this before summoning him. That was interesting. It was also interesting what he was offering. Had Saka left him unsatisfied? That had never been a problem before, but then he'd never had a human lover before.

Angus wasn't his lover. He was a warlock. And he'd brought lube.

Saka drew away and picked up the jacket lying over the chair, located the lube, and walked back over. "Planned ahead?"

Angus's skin turned a pretty shade of pink. "I thought you might want something since I called you."

Saka stroked himself with the slick lube. It was different from the

TJ NICHOLS

oil on Demonside... cold too. "I wanted something, but not because you called me."

He couldn't deny that thoughts of Angus had made him hard. That he had thought about this very thing but had held back because he didn't want to push the warlock too hard. "Are you sure about this?"

"Yes. Unless you don't want—"

"Oh I want." He just didn't let himself have.

He pressed his cock against the tight ring of Angus's ass, then pushed in slowly. This time he didn't have to hold back, and he didn't have to keep part of his mind focused on the magic. He could sink in and let go. He watched Angus's face as he thrust in. The way Angus gasped or bit his lip. Saka gripped Angus's hips, seeking his own release. He pumped hard, enjoying the simple building of tension and the craving for release without the need to do anything but enjoy.

He threw his head back and snarled as he came. Energy traced through him. He hadn't performed any ritual, but magic had gathered anyway. He reveled in it, absorbed it. After a few breaths, he withdrew.

Angus lay there, limp, watching through half-closed eyes. Was he too young for what was going to happen? He would be caught in the middle of a fight between warlocks and demons. But he had magic, and had been accepted into Warlock College. Angus was old enough to make his own decisions. He was already choosing to break the rules of the Warlock College. That they were in the same bed would bring trouble.

And not just for Angus.

Saka shouldn't feel anything for his Humanside master, and yet he did.

CHAPTER THIRTEEN

ANGUS AND three senior warlocks walked to the sparse forest where they did the demon summonings. Students always summoned outside in case the demon broke free. He flexed his fingers and tried to ignore the flutter in his stomach. He really didn't want to be doing this. The three warlocks had all lied to him and told him that he'd failed to bind a demon and that was why the demon had taken him. Maybe he had failed by their standards... but he and Saka were connected. He bit the inside of his cheek to keep from smiling at the memory of last night.

He felt better than he had in several months. Not only had he summoned a demon, but Saka had fixed the mess the warlocks had made of his mind and then they'd screwed—no one was taking that memory away. His demon had been gone when he'd woken up this morning. Angus had made his way back to college in time for the first class. Everyone seemed to know that a demon had taken him across the void. All he could say was that he didn't remember. It seemed like every word out of his mouth was a lie.

He glanced at the warlocks with him. He'd fit right in.

Except he knew more about Demonside than these three put together and he'd been there. At least he hoped that was the case and they weren't deliberately harming demons for personal gain. How deep did the conspiracy run? Was it something that everyone knew once they became qualified warlocks?

Surely not. That would make the secret too big.

It had to be just the top level, people like his father and above.

His world seemed colder and drearier after being across the void. The heat, the color... it had all been weird and interesting, and he wanted to know more. He wished he was summoning Saka in private so they could talk.

The warlocks stopped in the clearing the class had used only a few short days ago.

"When you are ready, Mr. Donohue," the lecturer said, obviously unhappy that one of his students had been taken right in front of him. Statistically the first time a wizard bridged the void—to get a demon and become a warlock—was when they got taken. After that it was fairly safe.

When Angus heard "Mr. Donohue," he still looked for his father. Mercifully he wasn't here today. Today nothing could go wrong with this summoning. He'd done it last night. Everything would be fine.

Unless the warlocks watching planned on betraying Saka and him. Would they send him back to Demonside, or would they punish Saka for taking him? Now he was dwelling on what might happen instead of focusing on what he needed to do.

He had to focus. He wouldn't make that mistake again.

Couldn't.

He drew in a breath and found his center, created the circle in front of himself—a little farther away this time. He pushed energy into its invisible walls. In Demonside it would be glowing blue. He could see it in his mind, and it formed more easily.

Then as if cautious, he started the walk that had begun this drama. Three times around the circle, widdershins. With each step he felt the fabric between the worlds weaken. He pulled it apart a little farther. By the time he stopped, the void was open, and Demonside was on the other side, a smudge of shimmering red was all he could make out. If anything rushed through, it would be contained by the circle.

Someone had let those rampaging demons through.

Someone had then justified killing them. Angus doubted they were killed straight out.

Someone had caught them and used them for ritual magic.

He exhaled and in his mind called to Saka. He had a name this time. He wasn't calling for a demon the way he had the first time. Saka stepped across the void, wearing black pants and his machete. The mark on his chest heated as it had last night when Saka was close.

Saka held his gaze, defiant.

What had happened to being subservient?

Behind Angus the warlocks murmured, deciding that yes this was the same demon. Angus needed to prove that he had Saka under control—or at least look as though he did.

"I am your earthbound master," Angus said, his voice more confident this time. He almost expected Saka to come straight back and claim that he was Angus's Demonside master.

But he didn't.

There was a small pause, and then Saka bowed his head—although not so much that he couldn't make eye contact. "I accept your command."

Angus released the breath he had been holding. He wanted to turn around and see if the warlocks approved, but he didn't dare take his eyes off Saka.

"This seems like a dangerous demon for such a young warlock," one of the warlocks behind Angus said.

"He is a common black-horn demon… I thought they were considered safe." Angus still didn't turn. They would never admit that Saka had already dragged him across the void. What lies would they tell to make him appear dangerous?

Certainly nothing close to the truth. Saka was dangerous because he was a mage. A stronger warlock might have been able to control him. A stronger warlock might have been killed in Demonside and not given a chance. There were two reasons the demons were letting him live. He already doubted the Warlock College, and he was young and untrained. At what point would he become dangerous to Demonside? Were they weighing him the way the warlocks were assessing Saka?

It was an unsettling thought.

Saka stood waiting, his fingers loosely curled. Angus had no doubt that Saka could use magic as effectively as his machete. Behind him was the void and Demonside. For a moment Angus thought that he could smell the heat and the spices, hear the noise of singing. If it were easy to come and go, he would visit again.

A place where you could see magic was fascinating. How did the warlocks assessing him and Saka not see the opportunities... the expansion of the use of magic if it were constantly being replenished and if the demons worked willingly instead of grudgingly? The opportunities to learn and share knowledge.

"He is armed," a warlock finally replied.

"A soldier?" Angus continued to play dumb.

"They have no armies in Demonside. He is not a good selection. We should start over."

"No. He is my demon. The connection was made for a reason." As he spoke Angus realized the weight of those words. The connection had been made for a reason. Not because of strength or ability but because of knowledge and desire. He met Saka's gaze, the endless black of his eyes.

Saka straightened a fraction. This time when he dipped his horns, it was in acknowledgment. He understood.

So did the warlocks. They went back to muttering amongst themselves.

Angus couldn't shrug because the warlocks were watching him, but he rolled his eyes and smiled, glad no one could see his face. Saka couldn't do much in case a warlock noticed, but the mark carved into Angus's chest became hotter. He thought Saka might have winked.

A warlock coughed. "Very well. Let's hope you have him under control. Your father would be most upset if you were taken to Demonside."

Angus pressed his lips together to keep from either laughing or arguing—he wasn't sure which. Saka's eyes narrowed, and his tail flicked. He looked as though he'd like to smite that warlock and drag him off to Demonside.

"Shall I draw up some power and then let him go?"

"Yes, yes finish this off."

He didn't have to draw energy as Saka gave it. The scar heated further as the magic sank into him. Whatever the rest of the day held, he had more magic than he could handle, or need. It would of course dissipate overnight. Magical energy couldn't be stored in bodies, but it could be shared.

In Demonside it could be stored. He'd seen Saka's glass orbs.

Could it be stored on this side of the void too?

Now wasn't the time to ask either Saka or the warlocks. He probably wasn't even supposed to be thinking of those questions. He was supposed to be listening and obeying. Learning by rote to become a good warlock.

In his heart he knew he was already becoming a rogue warlock.

ANGUS SAT in his room and stared at the website. Saka had said to seek out the underground. The idea had occurred to him after the warlocks tried to hide his memories. That Saka wanted him to make contact was intriguing. Were the demons in charge already working with humans? If so that meant that things were changing.

He had no proof, though. All he knew about the wizard underground was what Jim had told him—which wasn't that much as at the time Jim had been on the fringe, trying to decide if he was being edgy and cool or if he actually cared and wanted to make the world a better place. Right now all Angus could think about was surviving college. If the underground could help with that, then that was where he'd look for answers, or at least look for someone who could help him.

Hopefully Jim wouldn't be a prat. Over the last four months, they hadn't kept in touch, except through the occasional post on Wheel, a social network for warlocks and wizards. When Angus had entered college, most of his nonmagical friends had fallen away.

Angus pulled up Jim's profile... he was dating someone else already. A woman. Well, that was unexpected.

What should Angus say to him after all this time?

You were right? No, they both knew that Warlock College wasn't where Angus had wanted to be. They had both believed that there was something going on behind the magic of the most powerful warlocks. They had bought into the conspiracy theories of the underground.

Asking for help wouldn't get him anywhere, and he wasn't sure what help he needed. He wasn't sure what help Jim could give. Angus tapped the desk. Why would any wizard help a warlock? Especially those in the underground who were fighting for demonic rights and the end to drawing magic across the void.

Why would Saka point him in this direction? He had the feeling that Saka knew more than he'd let on. Yeah, but if he were Saka, he wouldn't trust a warlock easily either. While it wasn't expressly forbidden for students to make contact with the underground, it was one of those things that if discovered could go against a young warlock when trying to get a job. It was a smear and mark of untrust-worthiness.

His name was already marked because he'd been taken. There wasn't much else the college could do to him... getting kicked out was what he'd wanted in the first place. The underground might be interested in all the things he wasn't supposed to remember.

That would get Jim's interest.

He was, of course, assuming that Jim was still in the underground and hadn't dropped out. Maybe that was the place to start.

Hey... are you still connected?

Angus watched the screen. Nothing. Jim obviously wasn't answering even though he was online. He couldn't sit here and wait. He had homework to do. He had theory to study as well as the various rituals for protection. Until the students had mastered protection, there would be no progression. They would spend the last year of college on a specialization. Like healing, or retrieval, or policing, or advertising.

After another few minutes, he got out his books and started working.

A message came back.

Yes.

We should catch up. It's been a while.

Haha... too late to get me back.

Dickhead. What had he liked about Jim again? But Angus smiled. Jim had always done things his way, and he wasn't afraid of making the wrong move. His parents actually cared about what he wanted.

He'd wanted to be brave like Jim... fearless.

Jim came back with another message. *Let's go to the Drake and Ribbon. Tonight at 8?*

OK

He gave up on homework, had a shower, and got changed. At eight o'clock he walked into the Drake and Ribbon, a small bar on the good side of town. There was a darts competition going, sports on the TV, and it was the kind of place that Jim had hated.

Angus spotted Jim at a table with four others. He had his arm around a dark-haired woman. How fast *had* Jim moved on? Actually Angus didn't want to know as he hadn't dated anyone since Jim. Sleeping with a demon didn't count.

He forced himself to walk over. Had he told them that Angus was a warlock? Did they know that Jim was a wizard? Some people didn't tell. If you couldn't afford Warlock College, it was easier to keep quiet about the magic in your blood. The Warlock College had done a good job of convincing the general population that wizards were dangerous because they were untrained. The government had tried to bring in mandatory training, but the cost was too much and not everyone wanted to get their very own demon. So it had all been swept under the nearest mat.

Wizards still offered their services, nice and cheap, and the Warlock College still reminded people that warlocks were better trained and more powerful and that magic was worth paying for. Most people couldn't afford the college's high rates for magic.

Jim lifted his hand in greeting. "This is Angus."

Jim rattled off a bunch of names, but all Angus remembered was Lizzie the girlfriend.

"Hey." He'd wanted a private chat with Jim not a social one.

Everyone looked at him. There was a distinct frost in their smiles as conversation all but dried up. Oh, they knew exactly what he was, and it carried zero status.

Not everyone loved warlocks.

Some people hated all magic users equally. Had Jim fallen in with a group of them and decided to suppress his magic? If he did it for long enough, it would wither away. It was alleged that when some kids first showed magical tendencies, some parents would force them to stop. They called it therapy.

That was worse than being forced to be a warlock. Not being able to use magic and to feel it dying inside would be horrid. Once dead it couldn't be rekindled.

"I told them a bit about you. Hope you don't mind." Jim smiled.

Exactly what bits? Did Lizzie know that he and Jim had dated for nearly two years? He hesitated, not sure what to say. "I guess that depends on what you said."

That smile again. Once it had made his chest tighten in lust. Now his chest was just tight with anxiety. He took the last seat at the table —they had been expecting him.

"Just the truth… your father made you go to college." It was clear from Jim's tone which college that was.

The temperature dropped a few more degrees. They really didn't like warlocks. Angus had decided over the last couple of days that he didn't like most warlocks. Even the other people in his class only seemed to care about who had what demon and how much power they could control. Since getting taken, and the initial rush of curiosity at his return, they had taken to avoiding him. He was seen as weak.

Maybe he was. The scar on his chest was a warm reminder of the things he had agreed to. But he didn't feel weak. He had the support of Demonside—or at least part of it—and a mage for a demon.

He looked Jim in the eye. "Yeah, he did." He glanced at the other people. "You're all wizards?"

There were a couple of nods. A few were still hesitant about admitting to anything.

Jim leaned forward. "Some of my connections. They didn't want me meeting a warlock on my own."

Right, so all underground.

Did Angus trust them? He didn't trust anyone at the moment. But alone, he couldn't figure out what was going on. At least Jim had people who cared. All Angus's father had done was lock up the memories.

Were the warlocks really afraid of what he'd do or learn?

"I never wanted to be a warlock, but I can't change that now. I have a demon." He glanced at Jim. Jim had probably guessed. "But that doesn't mean I agree with what is happening."

"Oh yeah and which bits don't you agree with?" Lizzie asked with one eyebrow raised as though she didn't believe a word out of his mouth.

He couldn't say all of it. "The killing of demons for power."

"Would you prefer that they let them rampage through the streets killing humans?" The other woman scoffed, but there was an edge. This was a test.

Angus took a few breaths. Either he parroted what he was supposed to, what everyone had been led to believe, or he admitted to believing in the underground's argument. He didn't just believe; he knew it was true. He couldn't open a tear in the void from Demon-side. There was no way those demons were doing it. "Demons can only cross the void if someone on this side opens it for them. They can't just pop across for a quick holiday killing spree."

They looked at him. What he'd said was not what the papers were saying.

"And what would a first-year warlock know about demons that a master doesn't?" The man with short spiked hair narrowed his eyes.

Angus swallowed. He knew that he shouldn't be talking about it and that he shouldn't even be able to remember it. But he needed to share what he knew. He needed help to be able to find out what was going on. He wasn't going to get that in college.

"I have been across the void."

"Nah. Not possible. People don't come back from there." Jim shook his head.

Lizzie stood. "This is a trap. Warlocks will snatch us."

Did the college still try to catch underground wizards to silence dissent? Hadn't that all ended years ago? What happened to the wizards they caught... oh... magic had to be rebalanced. Angus was willing to bet that they were sent across the void. Nobody would miss a few missing troublemaking wizards. The college barely tolerated those that kept their mouths closed and worked alone. If the college had their way, there would be no practicing wizards at all. "If anyone is watching me, they are seeing me catch up with an old friend."

Jim tugged on Lizzie's hand, and she sat. "Let's assume that you did go. Your father actually sent a retrieval squad after you? That implies that he has a heart—I don't believe that for a nanosecond."

"He sent a squad because me getting taken was embarrassing, not because he cared. He hasn't changed." Angus shook his head. "I know what goes on there and what happens to those who don't return."

"We all know what happens." Lizzie leaned against Jim. Her gaze was calculating. Was she trying to work out what Angus had done while he was there?

"The balance is out. We can feel it," the other woman said.

"Feel it how?" He couldn't feel magic in the air, not like he'd been able to in Demonside.

The other woman smiled. "We don't need demons to work magic. It comes from us, from the earth and nature. Magic can't be created or destroyed. It obeys the laws of physics."

Saka had said much the same. Angus nodded. "The people responsible for the upset need to be stopped."

"You and what army?" Lizzie crossed her arms.

"Angus needs to talk to Ellis." Spikey slapped the table.

"Don't drag Ellis into it."

"How can we even trust Angus? He could be lying, trying to draw out contacts for the college."

"He's not lying. I'd have sensed it," the other woman said, although it was clear that she still didn't trust him. "That said, he could still be bait from the college. They'd love to smash us as we are the only voice united against them."

Angus's gaze darted around the table as they argued about if he should be invited into the underground without actually using that word.

"Who is Ellis?" Angus said, not sure how deep he wanted to get. The college would hunt him down if he left. A rogue warlock was highly dangerous—more so than a wizard, as a warlock had the demon's power to draw on. Right now he wasn't feeling dangerous. But the scar on his chest was still warm. He still had enough magic to get himself out of danger if he needed to.

Jim looked at him. "Ellis knows more about demons than any human. Word is she also survived Demonside."

CHAPTER FOURTEEN

SAKA PLACE his hand over the cool black stone. He calmed his breathing and thought of Guda. He hadn't seen the winged mage in almost a year—since the last gathering—but they talked regularly via the telestones. She had been his instructor in all things blood and cutting. It had taken decades for the scars to fade from his skin.

Her image formed in his mind. He held it, giving her time to sense his call and answer. If she was too busy, she would contact him later, but he needed to speak with her. Miniti wanted to make travel plans, and the hunting hadn't been very good here. The watering hole was little more than a patch of mud. He and Usi were contacting their counterparts to build a fresh map of the rivers and active wells and watering holes. They were also supposed to head to the gathering, which meant they couldn't wander wherever the water was, the way they normally did. They had to head toward Lifeblood Mountain.

It was requiring more and more magic to bring the river up so they could tap it. He didn't like to think about what would happen if one day he couldn't draw it up. If he couldn't, Usi wouldn't be able to either, and then everyone would die. He hoped that water still flowed at Lifeblood.

Guda's mind touched his, and her image solidified. In his mind it was as though they were standing in the same tent.

Saka inclined his head. "Thank you for attending to my call."

"It is always a pleasure to talk." Her mouth opened a fraction in what passed for a smile on her snout. She was what humans fancifully called a dragon. She hadn't needed knives to mark his skin, as her talons were lethal. He shivered at the memory of the pleasure and pain he'd learned by being at the pointed end of a claw first before graduating to turning the blade on her and then finally a human.

"I look forward to seeing you at the gathering. How goes your journey?"

"We have to leave sooner than planned because the Golden Lake is almost dry." That had never happened before. This camp was supposed to be one of the regular stops because it was reliable. They were running out of safe sites. It would take more than one young warlock to put things right. The task before him, before all of the mages was too huge. "And Lifeblood spring?"

"Still bubbles." She made the sign of protection. "It will be a bad day when it no longer flows."

"Agreed. We are taking action, though I am sure that you have heard." He smiled. He had caught a warlock and not just any warlock, but one who didn't follow blindly.

"I have. Quite the success. I hope he doesn't slip free or betray you."

Saka was well aware of the risk. He'd thought for a moment when Angus had summoned him in front of those other warlocks that his time was going to come to an abrupt and unpleasant end. Instead he seemed to have reached a new understanding with Angus.

"So do I. We need him." That left a bad taste in his mouth. Humans were the ones destroying Demonside, and yet, it was humans that they needed to stop the power drain.

Guda grunted. "We need more than one at the rate the rivers are sinking."

Saka could only agree with that. "And how deep are the rivers? Below the spikes?"

There were spikes sunk all across the desert, ready for whatever tribe needed to draw up water. Once it had been possible not to require a mage—that had been before he'd been born. Now no tribe would be without one, and a strong one.

"Some. I feel you will have to raise the water as you travel. It is becoming harder to stabilize the rivers. It used to be that a blood and soul sacrifice would lift them for a season... now?" Her leathery wings flicked.

Saka nodded. "I know."

The magic he had released with Angus was already fading away and the river sinking with it. The hunters were returning with tales of dried-up springs surrounded by the bodies of animals.

More blood was required. More souls. More sex.

"A point you might find interesting, Saka. Do not wait for the warlocks to send through their criminals. Take their animals the way they take ours. Their blood achieves the same."

It would be a simple painless kill. No demon would use an animal, a creature incapable of giving consent, in a prolonged ritual. Humans didn't have that many scruples. While there would be rebalancing from the death of the animal, it wouldn't be as much as from a human.

"The flesh was also edible." Guda gave a silent laugh.

Saka smiled. "I am glad the whole creature was used."

It would be a horrible waste to kill an animal and then leave bits to rot.

"We can't be fussy." She shared some other stories of dry springs and wells and the death of the herd animals. It wasn't local. It was wide spread. Things were getting worse fast. Faster than they had predicted at the last gathering.

"Thank you for sharing your knowledge, Guda."

"Always. We'll meet at Lifeblood." She inclined her head and was gone.

Saka's mind cleared, and he took his hand off the stone.

He let himself come fully back into his body and stretched his legs. It was times like this he wished that he could open up the void and drag someone or something across. Instead they had to wait while the rivers sank. Wait while their world died. Wait until a warlock bridged the void.

He snarled and stood.

While he knew releasing Angus to the retrieval squad had been the right thing to do, part of him had wanted to keep him right here. For the magic....

He couldn't fool himself.

Angus had been something special. He understood what was going on, and he cared. Even now that he was home, he still cared.

That didn't help Saka now.

What he needed was a sacrifice from the human world. He knew which demons in the town had warlocks. He was going to have to get them all together with Usi and wait until one got a call up. Then they would have to grab whatever they could.

He would have to sharpen his knives.

CHAPTER FIFTEEN

THERE WERE whispers around the college that another warlock was missing. The silence that had surrounded Angus thawed, and the other warlocks started looking at him with questions in their eyes.

He had been retrieved. Would the other warlock?

The twenty-four hours was almost up. There was a hint of fear in the air as if the other students realized for the first time that it could happen to any of them. Apparently a third-year warlock had been completing an assignment when it had happened. There had never been a problem between warlock and demon before.

This time it was hard to stop the gossip. The questions about why it was happening more frequently, and the demands from other students who wanted to know what had happened there.

Angus knew exactly what was happening. While he didn't know which mage would be responsible, Angus had the horrible feeling that there would be nothing for the squad to retrieve. He knew how badly Demonside needed the magic rebalanced. It would take more than the blood or soul from one warlock, or even one night of bone-melting sex, to put back what was being drained across the void.

The missing warlock didn't make the news.

A demon on the loose tearing up the streets of New London did.

Angus watched the footage with a few other students in the common room. A large gleaming, golden demon raced down the road, picking up and tossing screaming humans aside with tusks as thick as a thigh and twice as long as a tall man's leg—they were the lucky ones, the unlucky ones got eaten in a couple of quick bites.

"Look at it go."

"The power it must contain."

Others exclaimed in awe as they watched. Angus wanted to correct them. This was an animal, not a powerful demon. A big, terrifying animal with multiple rows of teeth and what looked like armor plates on its shoulders and spikes on its tail, but still an animal.

"How do these things keep breaking through?"

"The bigger they are, the easier it is apparently."

Angus bit his tongue. That was what they were told. That was what everyone believed. But it wasn't the truth. It was propaganda put out by the college so that people didn't blame the warlocks. Much better to blame the demons.

The footage replayed.

Where had the demon materialized? Where was it going?

A third-year student who tutored history remained grimly silent. As Angus watched the TV and ignored the comments of the other warlocks, he realized that the creature was wounded and it seemed to be running away, not running to something. It kept glancing behind as though it was being herded.

"Is it being chased?" Angus leaned forward and wished the footage were sharper and wider.

Everyone looked at Angus.

"Chased by what? Look at that thing."

The third-year student laughed, but he fixed his gaze on Angus. There was no smile in his eyes. "That thing isn't scared of anyone."

The school rugby shirt said his name was Erikson. Angus had seen him play. Angus didn't watch the rugby games because he loved the sport. He liked watching the men in shorts. He suspected that many of the female spectators felt the same way.

Angus frowned at Erikson—he couldn't remember his first name since he wasn't one of Angus's tutors, which was a pity. Although right now Erikson was giving out a weird vibe. What that vibe meant, Angus had no idea—perhaps he secretly agreed with Angus, or perhaps he was trying to remember Angus's name so he could report him.

He returned his attention to the TV and the animal. The demon was in a strange place and wounded. It was probably running from the warlock who had opened the void and summoned it. Was it someone's demon, or had a warlock demanded that their demon supply a sacrifice. How much control did a warlock really have over their demon? In Angus's case it didn't appear to be much. But then Saka was a mage.

Most of the warlocks in his class had ended up with animals, not people. After being told all of his life that a demon was just a demon, separating them out into different groups should've been hard. However, his twenty-four-hour stay in Demonside had given him a glimpse into what it was really like. They were not that different than humans. They had families and they ate and drank and sang and bathed and followed the will of their leader.

They also had heat and sinking rivers. Magic was part of their world naturally. Magic had to be brought here. Who was the wizard who had first stumbled onto demon magic?

As he watched the reporter and the warlock talk, he realized that no one wanted the truth revealed here. The warlock was lying, and everyone in the room believed him. Angus glanced over his shoulder at Erikson. He wasn't joining in the talk. Erikson looked at Angus, and in that moment Angus was sure that there was an understanding. Neither of them was buying what the college was selling.

In Angus's case he wasn't supposed to remember. He shouldn't question what was being broadcast unless he wanted people to start poking around in his head again. Which he didn't. He looked away, determined not to make eye contact with Erikson again. Angus had to fit in, not stand out.

Was there something wrong with him that he couldn't accept what he was told as the truth? Did believing the words of a demon make him gullible and weak-minded? And worse he listened to the wizard underground? The warlocks painted the underground as a dangerous organization full of rogue warlocks and untrained wizards. If not for Jim, Angus would've never opened his eyes. If not for Saka, the truth would have remained hidden.

The more he watched the news, the more he wanted to believe that the warlocks were right—there was clearly magic behind the warlock's words or the broadcast. He fidgeted, not wanting to be even in the common room anymore. Logic twisted and turned like a leaf in the breeze. Who did he trust?

Surely the body governing the use of demons and magic wouldn't fabricate such lies? What would they gain? What would they lose?

He rubbed the scar on his chest.

The news topic changed to the thickening of the arctic sheets and the heavier than usual snowfall in northern Vinland.

Around him the other warlocks were talking about the increase in the numbers of demons breaking through. He wanted to tell them that it wasn't possible. That the void could only be opened from this side, but that would mean admitting to remembering his time in Demonside.

Better to stay silent.

He stared at the TV without seeing. Had he already said too much? He wanted to turn and glance at Erikson again, but resisted. He didn't want to give the senior student any reason to remember him. He had to pretend to be an obedient warlock. But he also had to do something about what was happening. The student that had been taken and the rampaging demon were all connected. Trouble was he was a first-year student with a powerful demon he had no control over. No one would listen to him and take him seriously. Not even his fellow students.

"Angus." Someone snapped their finger in front of his face. "We're going to get a drink unless you're too scared to go outside."

There was laughter.

"I'm not scared of demons." He knew exactly what would happen to him in Demonside. It was the warlocks that he was worried about.

He stood up. He needed to fit in and be one of them on the surface, even though his blood was churning and his mind was a dangerous storm full of bits of information, but not enough to make sense. As he left he stole one last look at Erikson. Erikson was watching him. There was no way he was going to forget Angus.

ELLIS HAD AGREED to meet him, but meeting her wasn't a simple process. Getting there had involved a car ride and a blindfold. He had no idea where he was, but he was acutely aware that if the Warlock College discovered he was fraternizing with the underground, they would throw him out before he could take the blindfold off.

Someone pressed him into a chair, a soft armchair with cold leather that wanted to suck the heat out of him. The room smelled faintly of sandalwood and something else. There was talking, three maybe four people, but he couldn't quite hear what they were saying.

If they were talking about him, he hoped they were saying nice things.

Someone cleared their throat. They were much closer now.

There was a tug as they removed the blindfold.

In front of him sat an older woman with stark white hair, wound loosely into a bun. She crossed her legs up on the chair and rested her hands on her knees. It was clear that she was a magic user of some power from the way she held herself and the aura around her.

"I am Ellis. I'm not going to apologize for your treatment in getting here as it is necessary."

Angus nodded. Ellis had been to Demonside. The thought consumed him. This was someone who would understand what he knew... maybe knew more and be able to answer questions.

Then he became aware of the demon in the room. A tall elegant demon with wings, a tail, and a snout, and yet it was obviously not an animal. It would be a dragon according to the official warlock books. They were supposed to be powerful, even though they were only a little taller than a man, scraping in at seven feet.

"He looks young. Is he a child?" The dragon-demon drew closer.

Why was there a demon here? Was the underground planning on sending him across the void again? If the underground didn't like what he said, that was probably a reasonable expectation. He hadn't realized how closely the underground was working with Demonside.

Despite his curiosity he was starting to regret making contact with the underground. This was becoming dangerous. He didn't like danger. He didn't want to be mixed up in any of this. But that moment had passed when he'd summoned Saka.

His dreams of a nice, normal life had been stolen when he'd started at Warlock College. Maybe even earlier, when his father had realized Angus had magic.

He was in too deep to walk away. He wasn't even sure that he'd be allowed to if he tried. The college wouldn't let him go, and there was only one way he was getting free of Saka. Angus shivered and blamed the cool room, not the fear that was lodged in his stomach and twisting with every breath.

There was no one else in the room now except Ellis and her demon. Angus tried to look relaxed, but he was worried. No one knew where he was, and he was putting his trust in people he didn't know and who received a whole lot of bad press on a regular basis. He fidgeted while the demon and Ellis assessed him.

"Angus, this is Guda. My demon," Ellis said as though it were obvious.

He blinked. Ellis had a demon. "You're a warlock?"

"I am. I work in the medical industry."

Angus was still processing that information. She was in the underground and a practicing warlock. And a doctor. For a moment he glimpsed a possible future for himself.

"They told you that you would not be able to speak of this meeting to anyone outside of this room?"

"Yes." He nodded too. He was getting very good at keeping secrets and lying. He didn't want to be that person either, but he had little other choice.

"It will be a magical binding. I have to protect my position." She smiled. "I can do more work for the underground by continuing to be a warlock respected by the college. It is something you should consider—there are risks of course."

"I am aware." It seemed, no matter what he did since his trip across the void, there were risks. Getting out of bed to go to school was a hazard. One wrong comment and people were looking at him funny. He hadn't forgotten Terrance Erikson—he'd looked him up. But no one had come to speak to him so maybe the rugby player had said nothing. Which made the thing that had happened between them extra weird.

"Good. Then tell me about Demonside as I'm sure it has changed since I was last there."

Guda snorted. "I can tell you that."

"I want to know what he remembers, and I want to know who his demon is." She smiled again. It wasn't any friendlier. It felt a lot like the retrieval squad was once again grilling him about his visit to Demonside.

This time he was more cautious. "You aren't going to make me forget?"

"No... although I am curious about how you remembered."

Angus told her about Miniti and what she had done.

He'd barely finished speaking when Guda spoke. "I know Miniti's tribe well. Who is your demon?"

"My demon is a mage, Saka."

Guda clapped her hands and purred as though thrilled. "Saka is a good man. A strong mage and very level. He will work with us. I vouch for him, and if he let Angus live, then we can trust Angus."

He relaxed a fraction. Getting the demon's approval was obviously important—that and there was more to demon society than what he'd learned. Were there demons who would refuse to work with the underground? Who weren't level? He was assuming that level meant something like cooperative, but he wasn't going to ask for a definition.

Ellis nodded her head. "No one gets out of Demonside untouched. You still have your soul... so tell me, Angus, was it blood or sex?"

Angus swallowed as his face burned. His heart beat a little faster.

He'd kept that a secret from the warlocks, and he didn't want to be sharing it now. He went with the simple lie and opened his shirt to reveal the mark.

Ellis and Guda studied it for a few seconds.

"He signed his name," Ellis said. "That isn't the magic you participated in. Like I said every human in Demonside is used in a ritual. It's why they leave us there for twenty-four hours."

Guda opened her mouth and laughed. "I know Saka, and I know why the young warlock is changing color."

Ellis gave a small chuckle. "Is it so hard to say you joined in sex magic…, or is your embarrassment because you enjoyed it?"

"He should enjoy it; that's the point." Guda crossed her arms, her wings moving as though she was still silently laughing.

"When I was in Demonside forty years ago, small rivers cut the red sand. Oasis weren't rare, and small forests grew around them. It was very beautiful," Ellis said. There was a touch of wistfulness in her voice.

"Were you in a different part of Demonside?" The whole continent couldn't be desert. He didn't even know how many continents there were.

"The sand now stretches from coast to coast. I talk to the mages in all the tribes, Angus. There are no surface rivers anymore." Guda's voice was soft.

"Their world grows hotter while ours grows colder… coincidence? Where do you stand on the use of magic and the balancing of magic between the worlds?" Ellis leaned forward, her gaze piercing as though daring him to try to lie.

He wasn't that brave. "If Demonside dies, then there will be no more magic."

"That isn't true. Wizards draw on nature and themselves. They can do sex magic." Ellis dismissed his reasoning.

Angus had to do better. "There will be no warlocks without demons, but if Demonside dies, will our world freeze over? The worlds need to be in balance. There is no need for the rivers to be sinking."

Ellis gave a harsh laugh. "No need. Just the desire of a few to want more power."

"They must know what is happening." The warlocks at the top couldn't be blind to the reality. Their demons must say something.

"You would think, but if they know and they choose to ignore, then they are guilty of a greater crime—genocide of all demons," Ellis said.

"It's not just the damage done to our world, Angus. There is anger among my people. They talk of going back to the old ways—of grabbing a herd of humans and using them in a ritual to balance. They blame the unwritten rules for this disaster. Your warlocks take too much. And for what? Why do they need so much magic? They suck their demons dry. Demons fear getting a warlock where once it was something to be proud of." Guda spoke calmly, but there was a bite to her words. "When the level mages lose control, there will be trouble on both sides of the void."

Angus didn't think the mages would be messing around with anything less than soul magic—and they would be going for quantity.

"I'm only a student." And not a very good one. "I didn't even want to be a warlock, now I'm part of this mess. I don't know what I can do."

Ellis smiled; her lips were narrow as she considered him. "There are others who walk this fine line, but we must move softly. We relay information to the underground but often do not act ourselves or draw attention."

"My friends knew who you were." Her identity wasn't that secret.

She nodded. "They know a name. It is not my real one. You will remember my name, but little else."

"Who do I trust at the college?"

"No one in power. They want to keep the lies watertight and educate young warlocks that demons are disposable."

"Do you know who is bringing the demons across to rampage?"

"No... not yet. But we have suspicions. But there will only be one chance to act. The underground must get it right."

Angus glanced at Guda. "Would their demon not give the warlock up?"

"Some of the most powerful warlocks have animals. They select them because they don't argue and their large size contains a lot of energy. I would get no more sense from a scarlips than you would a cat." She shrugged, her wings lifting in a shrug.

"I didn't choose Saka."

Ellis and Guda laughed.

"Of course you didn't. You wouldn't know how. Saka chose you," Guda said as if that should've been obvious. "The mages knew we needed a warlock. Saka's previous one died, so he knew how to secure another."

"His warlock was killed by humans." He hadn't just died. Prickles ran down Angus's spine. Would he be next?

"His warlock wasn't careful. Don't make the same mistake, Angus. You cannot be seen with the underground." Ellis's voice was firm.

"Then who can I talk to?" He couldn't connect with the other warlocks in his class because they had swallowed the lies and were happy to be blind. He needed someone who understood. A tiny part of him wished he hadn't remembered what had happened to him in Demonside. Then he could go back to quietly failing until the college kicked him out and his father left him alone. That was never going to happen now. He couldn't walk away and live with the knowledge that Demonside was dying and would take the world as he knew it with it.

"I will put someone in contact with you. A mentor, perhaps? You are struggling with some subjects, aren't you?"

Was there anything Ellis didn't know about him? He nodded.

"Good, then. Our meeting is done. I shall erase it." Ellis stood up and walked over to him. "Don't worry. I'm not a hack like the retrieval squad. There will be no echoes or headaches."

He shrank back into the chair. "I'm just getting really wary of people messing with my mind—it can't be safe."

"It's not. If it is done too many times, people develop holes in their memories. I have seen it too many times." Ellis didn't seem particularly worried.

"Punch too many holes in a cloth and it falls apart," Guda added unhelpfully.

"Can you not touch my mind?"

Ellis considered him for a moment. "It would be easier for you if I do. You already have to keep your knowledge of Demonside a secret. You know how the warlocks deal with traitors?"

Angus nodded. "They send them to Demonside to balance the magic."

"They know it needs balancing, but I don't think that they realize the scale. After all they have never been there." Guda bared her teeth.

"We do the same, Angus. People who betray us are sent across the void. The criminals on death row... sent across the void."

That was common knowledge, but the media made it seem as though the demons demanded humans. As though human sacrifice was what kept the demons from crossing the void and killing them all.

"Even if they appear in the desert alone, their death still helps Demonside?"

Guda nodded. "Much less effective than a ritual."

The interaction between the two worlds was more complex than Angus had thought. Those in power were either willfully ignorant or gleefully corrupt.

How many were involved?

"I will remove only my image from your mind." She didn't give him a chance to disagree. She placed her hands on either side of his temple. "Close your eyes."

He couldn't resist as his eyelids became heavy.

Then he couldn't remember what the person he'd been talking to looked like. And while he thought that there had been a demon in the room, he couldn't be sure. He tried to recall exactly what had been said, but couldn't. With his eyes still unable to open, a hood was placed over his head. It was only once he was escorted from the room that he was able to force his eyes open. Not that it mattered since all he could see was black.

Pinpricks of light made their way through the weave of the cloth.

He had to remember that nothing was ever totally black, not even the night sky. There was always hope.

Destroying the Warlock College and bringing down those in power was the only way to rebalance both worlds. It was an impossible quest.

CHAPTER SIXTEEN

AS THEY TREKKED TOWARD LIFEBLOOD, there was no denying the changes in the landscape. The red sand shimmered in the afternoon sun, and the demons cast long slanting shadows.

Few trees were left to do the same.

Where there had been plenty of the deep-rooted fingerfruits, now there were a few gnarled trunks and nothing more. Their roots couldn't stretch deep enough to reach the ever-sinking rivers.

No fingerfruits meant no smaller animals, and no smaller animals meant no big animals. The hunters had returned with very little after straying far. Soon they would be forced to eat their pack animals and leave their belongings in the desert.

Saka sighed and walked on, searching for water and a place to camp.

He could feel the tribe's fear. They all knew the cause. Most campfire talk was now about how it had been. There had always been desert, but there had been oases and rivers cutting through it. It had once been filled with life, now there was only a harsh landscape where little thrived.

If the whisperings he was hearing were right, he might not survive the next gathering. Some were now calling for drastic action.

Action. Did they think that the void could be ripped open from this side? That he could do anything other than wait for a summons?

Demonside had always been at the mercy of the humans. Being aggressive and stealing life wouldn't help in the long-term, and the level approach was working. They just needed more time.

He lifted his gaze to the sky and sighed.

They might not have more time. He could feel the world dying every time he reached out. Behind him the tribe stretched out. He had to find water soon as they needed to stop. The water they carried with them would last through tomorrow, but making a camp without water was a bad sign.

Footsteps behind him drew closer. He knew who it would be before he turned. He slowed out of respect and to allow Miniti to fall into step. She expected him to have the rivers in hand. If he faltered she would replace him. Usi was all about the short-term solution and wetting the sand with blood from Humanside.

"Where is the water, Mage?" Miniti's voice was sharp.

"Deep." They both knew that. "But beneath us. We have been following the river's path since moving." They had rested through the hottest part of the day.

"No spring?"

"There should be a rock formation that marks it. We are two days from Lifeblood." The sand now contained rock fragments. There were signs of old riverbeds that they had crossed.

Miniti narrowed her eyes. "There should be water and trees this close."

"I know." Did she think that he didn't realize how dire the situation was?

"We should have kept that warlock. He could have bled our whole trek."

She had a point. But Saka was trying to think past a solution that would last only days. "He is more use returned."

Miniti growled. "I am running out of time and patience. We are running out of water."

He could tell. He didn't need reminding. "I hear the talk. I share the same concern."

If he lost the support of his leader, he would lose status on the council of mages. The council contained many like him who had been working behind the scenes, but it also had plenty who wanted to drag every warlock through and bleed them out the way they were being bled out.

He also shared their anger. "My warlock is now in the underground. Do not forget that there are humans working to discover who is taking and killing demons. They side with us."

"As if humans can be trusted."

"Their world is icing over. Not all seek power. The same as not every demon seeks to be leader." He smiled, and she inclined her head in acknowledgment of the point scored.

"Would you be averse to keeping a human for ritual? I think we may need to revert to the old ways to survive—to buy us the time you need."

"It has been discussed. But a formal vote will be cast during session." Much of his time would be spent in meetings or rituals at Lifeblood. Some would see family; some would find a partner. Children would be reunited with parents. Those who were old enough to travel would join their tribe for the first time.

Mages didn't have families. Their family was the tribe—the smaller and the greater whole. That didn't stop them from taking lovers. Despite being surrounded by people, he did get lonely. He had enjoyed Angus's company.

He almost looked forward to being summoned. It had been several days. He would need time with Angus to offer a rebalance soon and keep Miniti appeased.

Miniti grunted. "Bet you would've liked to keep the warlock for ritual."

Saka smiled. It wouldn't be blood getting spilled. Would Angus be happy here, his energy feeding Demonside? He might be for a while, but a human on this side of the void only had so much to give. Angus would wither and die. Much like a demon drained of magic on the other side.

"I did enjoy using sex magic again. It is powerful."

"It is why you are stronger than Usi. You can draw more out. But without a human to lie with—" She gave an elegant flick of her bone-white fingers. "Your magic isn't saving us, and neither is your warlock."

Saka stopped as a ripple went through him. He knelt and placed his hand on the warm sand. "The river is rising."

Miniti lifted her hand to shield her eyes. "There."

She pointed to a spot about two hundred paces away. He'd been looking for trees growing by the spring. All he saw were rocks.

He swore under his breath.

"Your warlock would come in handy now." She turned and started walking away.

"Next time I shall bring his blood."

Miniti glanced over her shoulder. "Just his blood?"

Saka grinned. "Blood alone isn't powerful. It's all in the collection."

"Then collect away, Saka. Prove why I should back you when I meet with the other leaders. I will not appear weak before them because you have chosen the level approach."

She strode away, announcing to the tribe that water had been found.

It hadn't... but the river was rising, and if the spring still trickled, he'd be able to draw up more. He stood and walked on ahead to assess the spring, one hand resting on his machete, and singing to himself to dissuade a riverwyrm from rising with the water and dragging him under. Although getting eaten by a riverwyrm at this point in time would be the least of his worries.

ENERGY SHIMMERED over Saka's skin like the call of a lover. A need. He had been resting under the communal canopy that had been erected. Most people were napping. The trek was hard... harder now. Even in their sleep, they looked anxious.

Quietly he got up. At the edge of the shade, he studied his tribe. The people he had to protect. Angus's reasons for helping were different, and while the result would be the same, they were not on the same side.

Saka had to remember that.

A few noticed him leaving, they watched. He ignored them. Angus would be working the ritual to open the void. It was in Saka's best interest to be ready and to obey. At this point anyway because he had no idea if Angus would be alone or in class. It would be nice to know in advance if it was a class or a private meeting.

A private meeting would be better, as then he'd be able to get what he needed.

He took another step, and the void opened before him. It shimmered black like obsidian. He stepped into the cold before it could drag him through.

He blinked. It was a class, but they weren't in the forest anymore; they were in a field.

Angus stood in front of him, something held in his hand. His lips twitched as though he wanted to smile. Saka gave a flick of his tail in greeting. Something lower down also twitched. While not as bone white as a Vampry, Angus was pale, his red hair a contrast, and freckles covered his skin. Saka knew exactly how covered.

Unlike a demon, his skin was buttery soft, making him seem fragile. Saka wanted to play with him again—in his tent, watching the glass orbs light up as the lust built.

He could think about that later... alone.

The teacher was talking about drawing magic and using it for something constructive. Creation must be learned before destruction.

"Let us use our demons to grow this seed into a tree of your own height."

No one moved. A couple of demons yawned. They had their own lives to get on with. Were they already at Lifeblood or on their way? He wanted to ask, to talk to the few sentient ones here. Most were animals.

However, he knew that wouldn't be appreciated, and at the first sign of trouble, the teacher would make a report that would get Angus in trouble and put a target on Saka's heart. He really didn't need that.

So he waited.

At the students' obvious hesitation, the teacher clapped his hands. "Come on. You all know how to draw up power, and I'm sure you all know how to plant a seed. This is about control. Those of you who want to go into healing will need to master your craft on plants before you move on to animals."

Angus squatted and made a small hole in the ground. He put the seed in and buried it; then he paused and glanced up at Saka as if wondering what to do next. There was only so much magic that could be taught. Ethics, the theory, even a step-by-step explanation of what to do, but the most important part was what the practitioner did. They had to find a way to connect with and feel the magic in order to be able to direct it, and no two people ever did that the same.

The mages had spent plenty of time discussing their processes for drawing up water and comparing notes to try to be more effective, but what worked for one failed for another. Magic was as personal as a heart or mind. It could be educated or guided, but in the end, it did what it wanted. Maybe it was more like a penis, with a mind of its own.

Angus placed one hand over the now-buried seed and then held out his other hand to the circle.

Saka squatted too. Hesitated a moment, and then placed his palm near Angus's.

Magic began to trickle though Saka's body from across the void. He lowered his head. While these kids practiced and planted trees, they were draining his world and trees were dying. He wanted to stop the flow, but that would mean making trouble, but he kept it to a trickle, barely all that was needed.

Those warlocks with a demon animal had a harder time control-ling what was going on.

Someone yelped. Angus didn't flinch. He lifted his hand as the seedling broke through the ground. Then he lifted his hand as though pulling the seedling up. It grew so easily in the cold ground. Saka shivered, not used to the chill. He'd need a cloak next time. He hadn't needed one in Demonside for years.

Together demon and warlock stood, and the seedling became a sapling, waist high, shoulder high. It was killing him to watch. This was why his world was dying and their world was freezing. Why were they so blind?

Angus lifted his hand head height, then stopped. A small tree now stood as though it had been growing for years. Saka let his hand fall to his side. Angus had done a perfect, measured job. Saka had to admire that. He took a moment to glance around at how the others had fared. Some were still going. Someone had grown a tree that was over twice the required height. Others were struggling to get the tree to grow up and straight.

"Nice work, Angus... a little risky to be so close to a demon. Maybe next time you could attempt to keep your hands to yourself." The teacher lifted his eyebrows.

"Yes, sir." Angus's cheeks turned pink.

Saka kept his lips in a thin disgruntled line, as though he didn't appreciate being here. It was a good thing that the teacher didn't know exactly what Angus's hands did out of class.

"You may dismiss your demon." The teacher made a couple of notes and moved on.

Angus touched his chest. The place where Saka had carved his mark. He knew then that Angus would summon him later and pay for the magic he had used. Saka was looking forward to it. More than he should.

His affection for Angus could be seen as a weakness when the council met. With tensions rising in the lead-up to the gathering, he couldn't be seen as weak.

CHAPTER SEVENTEEN

ANGUS HAD PICKED another cheap motel, and he knew that he wouldn't be staying the night. Not this time. He suspected that the college and the underground were watching him, but what else could he do? Knowing what he did, he couldn't take magic from Demonside and not rebalance.

He summoned Saka as soon as he arrived, and the demon appeared. He had three glass orbs on strings in one hand and a vial in the other. Angus swallowed as he noticed the knives strapped to the demon's forearm.

For a moment his need to do the right thing faltered. But if he didn't, he was only furthering the destruction of his world too. He pushed down his fear. He didn't want to live in a world covered in ice —Saka probably felt the same way about living in a desert.

"I can't stay… I have to find a safer way of summoning you in private for this." He tried really hard not to look at the knives.

"But you took the risk anyway."

Angus nodded.

"That took courage."

"Or stupidity. If the college catches me doing this without supervision, I'll be in trouble."

"And how do your studies go?"

"Fine." He watched as Saka placed his things on the bed. "I met with the underground. There are other warlocks there. Working from the inside." They really didn't need him. No, but Saka did. They had been brought together for a reason. Maybe Angus's doubts about the way demons were used had been enough. "You knew that already, though."

"Yes, I knew. But there are mages who want to drag humans through en mass every time the warlocks open the void. They want oceans of blood to bring our rivers back. They want humans too afraid to ever open the void."

"But it would still happen by accident." Everyone knew the stories of a wizard who accidentally summoned a demon and was taken or killed. They were often blamed for the rampaging demons, reinforcing the notion that wizards were untrained and dangerous.

Not half as dangerous as warlocks with a thirst for power.

"And magic would still leak across and need to be rebalanced. I think they might gain enough support at the gathering." He met Angus's gaze, and for the first time Angus saw absolute fear in Saka's eyes. "Things are dire, worse than I let you know. Your fellow warlocks, planting trees and playing, have no idea that every drop of magic they wasted was another drop of water gone. My trees are nothing but dried, twisted trunks."

"I'd gladly give a forest if I could. If the whole class could cross the void and learn and work magic over there. How fast would healers learn if they could see what they were doing? They could return and know and feel magic even if they couldn't see it." Angus sighed. "It's because I saw it in Demonside that I was able to grow my tree. I could see it in my mind."

"No. It is because it is in you." Saka tapped Angus's chest over his heart. "You have it in your blood. You know in here. The others, they think they know. They want to play with power, but they don't understand how to use it. But a knife in an unskilled hand is still a weapon."

"Maybe I should learn. I could leave you something."

Saka laughed. "It is more than making a cut and drawing blood.

There is magic in the liquid, but it is the emotion that gives it true power."

Angus closed his eyes for a second and thought of the blood Saka had taken the first time.

"But I do need blood. I need to take something back to show that I have you under control and that sending you home wasn't a mistake," Saka said.

"I need to make regular donations to stay alive?"

"Something like that. Miniti could force me to bring you across."

Angus stepped back, his blood cold. "If I go back, they won't retrieve me a second time."

"There would be no chance of rescue. You would be sacrificed. There is a push to go back to taking human slaves. I am going to have to vote in favor. If I don't, I will have no voice on the council, and that would be worse."

"You'd keep people to use. Like farm...." Angus stopped midway through his horrified objection. That is pretty much what warlocks were doing. Keeping a demon on call for when they needed magic.

"We need more return of magic. The humans would be treated well. They would be free to move around, fed, and given what they wanted."

"Everything except returning home."

"Would it have been so bad, Angus?" Saka touched Angus's cheek. His fingers were warm and smooth.

Angus turned his head into the touch. No, it wouldn't have been bad. He could see himself learning about magic and enjoying Saka's company. "Humans don't survive there. The same way demons can't live here."

"That is true. They would weaken. But they would have a good few weeks, maybe even months."

"They wouldn't all consent to sex magic, or blood magic." Most humans wouldn't consent to even going.

"Then find some who would is my suggestion. Otherwise when it gets passed, and I'm sure that it will because we have no choice, people will be taken."

Angus saw the reluctance, but also the acceptance that Demonside had to be saved through any means. One person wouldn't be enough, not when there were warlocks out there using magic all the time.

For everything, for the highest bidder.

Businesses needing additional security, the police needing to find a criminal, healing for the rich and dying, the college training warlocks. Magic was no longer a special thing to be revered, the way it had been two hundred years ago. It was a business, a commodity, and the mine they were digging was running dry. How many people would the mages need to raise the rivers?

"I'll let the underground know."

"They already know. All mages with a warlock are saying the same thing—not all warlocks are listening. We would rather have volunteers." There was the pointed reminder that humans tended to treat demons as slaves without freewill.

If the underground succeeded, that would change. But as Saka had said, they were running out of time to make that change. Angus glanced at the clock; he was running out of time if he wanted to get back to college. He didn't want to spend the night out since someone would be paying attention to his absences. Too many and there would be questions.

He pulled his shirt off. "I'm volunteering now. Don't make me regret it."

"Never. I want you to summon me on a regular basis." Saka kissed him. His mouth was hot and demanding. His tongue pushed in to Angus's mouth, and his hand roamed over Angus's skin as though it had been months since they had seen each other.

Saka's hunger fed Angus. Lust heated his blood, and he ground his hips against Saka's, pleased to feel the hardness and length of the demon's erection.

Clothes came off, and Saka pulled the covers on the bed back. In the soft light, Saka's skin was dark. It didn't shimmer the way it did across the void. Angus lay down and brought Saka with him. He was sure that the demon could've resisted, but he didn't. Angus stroked

Saka's length. He was hot and hard as he rocked his hips, thrusting into Angus's hand.

Angus needed to feel his touch. When it was clear that Saka wasn't going to give it, Angus moved a little and then wrapped his hand around both of their cocks.

Saka gave a low laugh. "Desperate, are you?"

Not desperate, but he wanted Saka in a way that he couldn't quite voice. It was more than magic and rebalancing.

"Just fuck me or whatever you have planned." Whatever it was, Angus knew he'd enjoy it. That was what Saka wanted. It was the magic he liked to use.

"I don't plan. I go with what is happening. But if you're bored." Saka pulled away and turned around, so his cock was close to Angus's face.

Angus didn't need a further invitation. He licked along the length of the demon's shaft before taking him in his mouth. Each time he took a little more. He almost preferred it when Saka was over him, thrusting into his mouth so that his whole world became nothing but breathing and sucking. He moaned as Saka's tongue swept over the head of his cock, then as the demon took him into his mouth.

It felt incredible to be sucked deep. Then Saka's hand was cupping his balls, caressing and squeezing. A moment later a finger circled his ass. Angus didn't know if he should thrust up or push back.

In the end it didn't matter as Saka penetrated him as he took him deep, the head of Angus's cock brushing the demon's throat. For a moment Angus was sure he was about to come. He couldn't move. His balls were tight, and then the unexpected climax receded a little. Saka wasn't unaffected. The burnt honey taste of his precome was on Angus's tongue.

Saka released him. "Make me come. Then you will get your release." His finger pushed a little deeper.

It sounded easy, but Angus knew how good Saka's control was.

Saka rolled onto his back and stretched out, giving Angus the appearance of free rein.

Angus moved too, straddling Saka's head, then he went back to licking and sucking the demon's thick, ridged cock. He fisted the length and tongued the head, and was rewarded with a bead of precome that he hungrily lapped up. Saka's hands caressed Angus's thighs, his lips brushed his dick, but only to tease… or was that taste? Angus glanced down his body to watch as Saka lapped away another single drop of white precome. Angus shuddered and had to fight the urge to lower his hips and thrust into the demon's mouth.

He drew in a couple of deep breaths, then refocused on the cock in front of him. Sucking him as deep as he could and then drawing back slowly, his tongue lashing the hot skin of Saka's shaft. Then repeating as Saka lifted his hips, thrusting up.

Saka was close now. Angus prayed that he wouldn't hold back. Saka's tail brushed the back of his neck, his tongue teased the throbbing head of Angus's cock. He would come before Saka if he kept going. But Saka pressed his fingers behind the head, and Angus found himself left wanting to climax but not being able to.

He shuddered and moaned but kept giving head, wanting more than just a taste of come. He wanted it all.

Saka growled, his hands gripping Angus's thighs hard. Angus pumped his hand and worked the head of the demon's cock, sucking and licking, his mouth starting to ache. Then the come was flooding his mouth. He moaned as he swallowed and sucked, knowing that there would be more. When he was sure that Saka was done, he released the demon.

Angus's body was quivering with need. He expected Saka to drag his hips down and return the favor, but he didn't, the demon rolled Angus onto his back. Angus drew in several deep breaths, trying to steady himself.

"Take yourself in hand." Saka drew a knife and placed the flat of the blade against Angus's outer thigh.

Angus's heart stopped, and his breath caught. Saka planned on actually using them. He wasn't ready for that.

Saka caressed Angus's balls. "You will like it."

Angus wasn't so sure. He held Saka's gaze. He had known this wouldn't be just sex when he'd summoned him, but he'd hoped that it would be. But Saka needed more to take home. The more was his blood, made all magical by lust. This wouldn't be a gift for Miniti, though. This was a gift for the whole of Demonside.

He was paying for his magic and for other people too, and it still wouldn't be enough. This was the price, and he had to pay... he didn't need to like it. Without blinking he took himself in hand and stared into Saka's black eyes. It was like falling into the void.

Saka didn't look away either. "For every drop of come you spill; I will spill blood. But you will keep stroking yourself because I want to watch. You will come when I tell you."

Angus managed a half-choked laugh. "Yeah... I don't like my chances of holding out." Even as he spoke, a bead of precome formed and rolled over the head. Angus was acutely aware of the tiny sensation as it slid down his shaft.

The blade bit into the skin of his thigh.

He gasped, and his hand stilled. The sting spread through him, and the lust dampened.

Saka smiled. His tail reached out and grabbed the vial. This one was bigger. The length of a hand, wider too. Angus watched as Saka's tail moved the vial into place.

"Don't stop, now." Saka's hand traced up Angus's inner thigh, teasing, caressing, but not giving him what he wanted.

Slowly Angus gave himself another stroke, now torn between wanting to come and fearing being cut. But even the uncertain movement of his hand was enough to wind the lust higher. Saka's touch on his balls only added to the need.

He tried to tamp it down and think about something else, but he couldn't fight his body. Another drop formed. Angus's stomach tightened in anticipation, and he flinched at the cut.

"Each drop brings you closer to release." Saka's voice had lowered.

A little part of Angus's brain—the five brain cells that weren't thinking about coming, the knife, the demon between his legs, or even how the hell he'd ended up a demon's sex toy and why was he enjoying it so much—realized this was true. Instead of fighting out of fear of getting cut, he could give in. It didn't hurt that much. He already knew that. It wasn't going to get any worse.

His stroke became firmer. The bite of the blade more regular, but now he welcomed it. His eyes closed as he sought release. Every so often Saka would place his finger near the head of Angus's cock and squeeze, pulling Angus back from the edge. He knew he had to wait, but it was torture.

He couldn't keep going. His hips lifted with each stroke, and then Saka's hand wrapped around his. For a moment Angus thought it was to stop him from coming, and he growled in protest, but Saka increased the pace.

"Yes. I want to see you come."

Angus groaned. It was raw and didn't sound like him. But the release was worth every moment of the wait. He shuddered as he came. His body bucking. No come hit his skin as expected, though. He opened his eyes. Their linked hands were still stroking, and every drop of come had been caught in the vial. The vial that also contained glistening ruby blood. His blood.

His heart was still pounding, and a sheen of sweat covered him. Saka put the stopper in and inclined his head.

"It is a pity we can't see the magic here. I'm sure it would be beautiful."

He stared at the vial. As the euphoria left, he became aware of the throbbing of his thigh. His leg would be a mess. He wanted to know how much damage had been done. He went to sit up.

Saka put his hand on Angus's chest and made him lie still. "Rest a moment. I will tend the wounds."

Angus remained lying down, but he didn't relax. Saka went into the bathroom and came back with a wet face cloth. He wiped Angus's thigh. Without the sexual distraction, his skin was starting to burn, but with each wipe, it lessened.

"You may look now." Saka drew back. "And judge me accordingly. But I have enjoyed what I did to you and much more during my training."

Angus waited a moment. He didn't feel lightheaded. His heartbeat had slowed. He felt okay. Tired. Drained. But he propped himself up and glanced down at his leg. There were only six cuts. Each one the length of a finger and exactly a finger width apart. None looked deep. Certainly not deep enough to bleed.

"You partially healed them."

"It isn't good form to leave a lover with open wounds that could get infected."

"You didn't heal them completely." Why leave them at all?

Saka pulled a knife out of his collection. It didn't match the others. "So you can claim to have been practicing should the college ask."

"Blood magic isn't allowed." Or at least using blood magic on others... on himself, though, surely that wouldn't count, and it would get him in less trouble than summoning his demon.

"I wonder why that is?" Saka tilted his head. His horns gleamed black in the light. "Those in power don't like making sacrifices for magic? However, the greater the sacrifice, the greater the magic."

Angus frowned. "So they could be more powerful if they gave blood?"

"I'll let you ponder that on your way back home." Saka leaned over and kissed him. "I look forward to our next meeting."

CHAPTER EIGHTEEN

THEY WOULD ARRIVE at Lifeblood tomorrow. But before they left the temporary camp, Saka went to what had been an oasis. It was once again a small puddle. He had lifted it last night, but it had sunk while they slept. There were a couple of trees grimly hanging on to life.

The orbs hanging from his hand burned like stars. They were hot to touch. Every time he held one, it was like he was holding Angus again and feeling the desire run through him. Saka should have slept well last night, but he hadn't.

There was no joy for him in returning to Lifeblood like there should be. He wanted to see old friends, but he no longer knew which side of the argument they had picked. He didn't like the side he had to pick. Taking human slaves was wrong.

But without them Demonside was doomed.

So was the human world.

They might not be acting so rashly if the warlocks knew how bad things were getting.

He sat down on the edge of the oasis and reached his mind out to feel the water below. There was plenty there; it was just out of reach.

What he was about to do would bring the oasis back for several days. He'd carve his mark and let every other tribe who followed know that he had done this. Miniti would appreciate the show of power since it would reflect well on her. Her mage had a warlock on tap.

Saka shivered, remembering the few hours he'd spent with Angus.

He drew up a circle and released the magic held in the orbs. The air smelled like rain for a moment. He missed rain. The rains should come soon, but for the last ten years, the rainy season had been too light and too short to do little more than dampen the sand. They needed a heavy rain this year. Perhaps having human slaves would bring it. He wished it didn't take death to bring life.

Saka felt the bubbles before he heard them. The magic drawing the water up. He didn't know why it had sunk. Perhaps the water was attracted to magic on the surface. He opened his eyes and smiled at the sight of the oasis shimmering in the dawn light. He wanted to be able to show Angus the changes that such a small act could bring about. He got up and walked around to the trees. In his pocket he had a few seeds that he'd scavenged from the dead trees while on the trek. The seeds would be fine once planted.

So that's what he did. Six small holes. Each one got a seed, and a piece of Angus. Much like Angus had done, Saka placed his hand over each one and got it going. The delicate blue leaves breaking through the sand, taller until they reached his knees. He gave the rest of the blood and magic mix to the existing trees feeding them. For a moment he bathed in the energy of new growth. Of life. He wanted his world to be like this again, to be vibrant. Alive.

There would be hard choices ahead to get there without all-out war across the void.

Saka opened his eyes and carved his sign in a tree, healing it so the tree wouldn't be vulnerable to insects that would burrow in and eat its center. Then he dropped the circle. Magic rippled away. The work he had done would spread a little. He hoped that the tribe would appreciate what he'd done and realize that power wasn't always big actions.

As he stood there, he watched the leaves growing. He smiled and sighed, then turned around to head back to the camp. Usi stood there, watching him. He couldn't avoid her, but he didn't want to talk to her either.

She would vote for the short-term solution.

He knew that. Miniti had picked her mages so they wouldn't hold the same beliefs, so they wouldn't only give her one viewpoint back from the mage council. She was smart, and she knew how quickly sentiments could change. If the level approach fell from favor, then he would be gone.

"You must have had a productive trip across the void."

Saka gave her a single nod. The now-empty orbs and vial in his hands. It was obvious what he'd been doing. Usi considered him weak for even having a warlock, but he was doing more than she was to rebalance the magic.

"I don't think even you can have enough sex to heal the damage the warlocks have done."

Saka glanced back at the oasis. No, he couldn't on his own... what had Angus said about the class coming here and seeing the magic, learning how it really worked? It was something he would need to think about, before he spoke to Angus again. The Warlock College would never send a class, but what about the underground? Most of them were wizards who had no demon.

But if they got demons... mages... then the underground would grow in power. How far should demons trust warlocks, even those who came from the underground?

"Maybe not, but you would need the blood of a lot of humans. A lot of death. Sex never runs out. And if you do it well, they always want more." Saka smiled. "But you wouldn't know, would you, as you don't have a warlock."

"You love humans too much," she sneered.

"I understand the different factions at play on both sides. I volunteered to get a warlock despite the danger. I am working for the good of the tribe and Demonside. What are you doing, aside from stirring up dissent and worry?"

"One pretty oasis does nothing. Proves nothing."

"You would be surprised what one oasis can do. Not every battle needs a winner, and not all battles are fought with weapons." Saka walked past her.

Angus had better summon him again soon because Usi was right. One oasis wasn't enough.

THE CLOSER THEY got to Lifeblood, the more signs of life Saka saw. There was a river that flowed between the rocks before disappearing into sand. Trees and other shrubs were growing wild, not magically cultivated. Some of the tension he'd been feeling melted away.

He'd been worried that Lifeblood would be dry or little more than a trickle.

This year it wasn't... but would it be next year if they did nothing?

He might not like the course of action, but it was better than letting his world dry up. While his heart was pained, Saka would not vote in a way that harmed Demonside. He would, however, do everything he could to ensure that there was no rush to bloodshed either. He was the embodiment of the level approach to finding a solution.

Tribes were still arriving and finding places to camp near the mountain. No one was allowed to camp on its slopes because the mountain and the springs that flowed from it were sacred. The mages would meet at the top and make offerings. New mages who had been training would be tested and either accepted or sent with a different tribe for more training with a different mage—having an apprentice fail was a strike against that master, not the student.

Tribe leaders would meet, and children who were old enough would be given a place in their mother's tribe, where they would become youths of the whole tribe. Loved by all. Pregnant women would remain here, safe and protected. Leaving Lifeblood after the month of celebration and trading and talk was always sad. Some people moved tribes because of new partners. Some would spend the month trying to get pregnant and return next year in preparation for birth.

There had been fewer pregnancies and babies in recent years.

Everyone had noticed.

Miniti directed her tribe to set up near the river, but not so close that they would block other tribes' use of the water. A surface river was something his tribe hadn't seen since the last gathering. Saka left following those rivers, if indeed they still existed, for the tribes without strong mages.

With no need to help until his tent had been unpacked and erected, Saka went to see who was nearby and make greetings. While he spoke to many with the telestones, he wasn't friends with all.

Still, greeting was part of the job. Miniti's standing would increase with his welcome. She would be seen as open and inclusive, but it would also give Saka a better idea for what other tribes were saying and how they were feeling. Were they all as fearful as his? Was everyone hoping to spill human blood and draw up the rivers immediately? Or were some thinking of the future. Going to war with the humans when demons couldn't open the void was a dangerous strategy as it gave the humans all the advantages. Of course if they sacrificed enough humans, then perhaps they would stop summoning demons.

Saka took it as a good sign that he was welcomed and not turned away as he made his greetings. Eventually he sat down in the shade of a tree with Lox and Becha. Mages he counted as close friends, even though they only saw each other at Lifeblood.

They wanted to know more about his warlock as well as the humans and their plans. Saka took the opportunity to give information—truth and not speculation. The other mages needed to know that they had allies on the other side.

"Why would they risk their world? What good is power if it only destroys?" Lox sat cross-legged opposite Saka. She looked much like him, but her skin had more of a purple sheen and her horns were perfectly straight; she was quite a beauty.

Since Angus was his second warlock, he forgot that he knew more about the human world than most. And even though he had tried to share the details, many were not interested. Or they hadn't been, until recently.

"Their society is different. To them power means wealth."

"They are like children who don't know any better." Becha shook his head.

"They haven't been taught any better. Their masters have failed their students, and now those students teach others the flawed learning. The underground is trying to fix it, but they do not have demons. Many have shunned demons, believing it unhealthy." According to Guda, even the underground was split. Some believed, like Angus, that demon and human could work together, and others believed that it was best to avoid getting a demon.

"We cannot wait for their faults to be corrected." Lox sighed. These were both level demons, and even they were starting to lose hope.

Saka shrugged. "I think we have reached a tipping point." On both sides of the void.

The three of them nodded.

"Do you find working with a human odd?" Lox tilted her head.

"He is willing and interested, so it makes the rituals more effective."

Becha laughed. "You have a human apprentice. He who has avoided teaching while entangled with warlocks has finally succumbed to the need to share knowledge."

Saka lowered his head in acknowledgment. That was true. He did want to teach Angus. Most mages reached a point where they wanted an apprentice and to pass on what they knew—not all received permission to teach. He had always been more worried about Demonside as a whole than teaching. He had volunteered twice to have a warlock, despite the danger. Yet the need to teach had caught up with him.

"Let us hope I am a good teacher, for all of our sakes."

The demons nodded. A large green demon dropped out of the sky and landed near them. Saka had thought she'd been a hunter, circling, but it was Guda. He bowed to his old teacher while Lox immediately told of Saka's new apprentice.

She looked down her snout at him and nodded. "I have met your warlock. I think you teach him well."

It wasn't only Angus who needed teaching. "I think we need more mages willing to get a warlock."

Becha wrinkled his nose. "Many would disagree. The idea of being summoned is abhorrent. Living at the whim of a warlock... do you not struggle with the bonds?"

He did. But there was always a tradeoff. "The magic I bring back is needed. Imagine what more mages could accomplish."

Becha lowered his head, conceding the point. Then he signaled to a passing demon and asked for refreshments for the mages. No one would be rude enough to say no.

Saka wasn't hungry, but he wouldn't turn down the hospitality. He was trying to gather allies and assess numbers. He was sure that was what other mages would be doing too. As much as he loved coming to Lifeblood, this year there was less joy, and it wasn't only affecting him.

"Your head is heavy with thought, Saka," Guda said.

"I don't know if my thoughts are tidy enough to be told." He wasn't going to embarrass himself with half-formed ideas like a child. A mage was supposed to be able to order and present ideas.

"I am interested if it involves warlocks and bringing back magic... we need it, and as you have said, a willing human sits better within." Guda tapped her chest.

"An unwilling human bleeds fear, which is just as powerful," Becha countered.

"But once trapped here, they lose their potency," Guda said. She was the most senior mage in their small group.

They all knew that she was right. A willing human on the other side of the void could rebalance the magic for the rest of his or her life.

"Very well. Angus, my warlock, made a comment that has stuck like a thorn. He said it would be better if all warlocks spent time here to learn about magic so they could see it."

"What? They do not see magic?" Lox's tail flicked in surprise. "How do they know what they are doing?"

"They do not, or they would see the damage," Becha replied.

Most mages had never been across the void. In the same way Saka could sense the void opening and had felt the call of the warlocks summoning a demon and accepted it, most mages turned it away from them so they wouldn't suffer at the hands of a warlock. It also meant that they didn't know their enemy the way Saka and the few like him did.

"It is not visible on that side of the void. So if they could see magic, they would learn faster, but also learn the truth." Guda saw immediately where Saka was going. "The flaw is that once here, they could not leave."

"Not on their own, but at the end of the time, the void could be opened by someone on the other side and they could return," Saka said.

"And while here they rebalance." It was obvious that Becha could see the advantage. "I don't know a lot about warlocks, but I suspect they will not agree. They do not retrieve all who come here accidentally."

Some humans were sent here to die, an offering that was no longer enough to rebalance what the warlocks were taking.

"You would be correct." It was always polite to acknowledge a truth preceded by the admission that it was a guess. That showed both humility and a sharp mind. Becha and Lox were both younger than him. Maybe it was the younger mages who would be more willing to try something dangerous instead of going back to the old ways of grabbing humans every time the void was opened. "I was thinking of the underground."

There was silence for a while. Saka knew his idea wasn't well enough formed to be shared.

Becha poured watered-down wine and offered the plate of dried fruit and cheese. Instead of talking and rushing to respond, each mage took their time to think. If his own thoughts had been clearer and his mind more certain, perhaps they would've formed their response faster.

The shade of the tree moved, sliding around as the afternoon edged closer to dusk. While the mages were silent, the camp they were near wasn't. Children raced around, chasing pets and livestock. Those children had never seen a real rainy season. They didn't know that their world had once been more blue than red. That there had been swathes of vegetation that followed the rivers. For most of those children, a surface river was a novelty.

People sang more out of habit than out of need. There were too many people for a riverwyrm to attack—they hated noise and always attacked the isolated heartbeat. No one ever wandered from their tribe alone, not even the airborne hunters. The scents of cooking started to reach them. A hint of something spicy, the deeper taste of boiled ynns. Even the staples of their diet were becoming hard to grow because there was no river to plant them by. Usually a tribe would plant when they left so there would be more for the next people. That was becoming harder to do.

Would they even be able to leave Lifeblood?

While everyone loved coming here, this many people in one location would cause friction.

Last year some tribes had decided to head for the coast. Last he had heard, several months ago, they had reached it. Had they prospered? They wouldn't be coming back to Lifeblood this year. Saka returned his attention to the very serious-looking mages sitting with him. While it was nice to wait for perfectly formed ideas and ideal times, perhaps those times were over. Now was a period of quick action, where daring and bravery were rewarded like the heroes of old who had fought with the humans hundreds of years ago.

Finally Guda spoke. "It is an interesting concept, one that should be debated with other mages. One that I should perhaps take to the underground?"

Saka nodded. He was hoping that Angus would end up in the underground. Was he pushing too much, instead of letting Angus find his way? Possibly, but time was something he no longer had.

"That would be appreciated. For it to work, they would need willing students and we would need willing teachers." He glanced at Lox and Becha.

Both were thinking.

Taking on a wizard—even if they were part of the underground and had a mutual interest in the equitable use of magic so two worlds weren't destroyed—was entirely different than getting mixed up with college-educated warlocks.

Becha spread his hands. "In theory it is a fine idea."

Many things appeared to be good ideas until put into practice. The warlocks must have realized their error at some point but had too much hubris to admit it and make corrections. Here if a mage had done that, he'd have been tied to a stake and left for scarlips or riverwyrms.

Pride was dangerous. It led to mistakes that could wipe out a whole tribe.

"Student of mine, I would like a word." Guda remained sitting, so Lox and Becha made their excuses and left.

Saka sipped his wine, expecting her to tell him off for speaking. She didn't, though. She was still looking thoughtful.

"Your idea comes late."

"I have only been working with Angus a short while. He has an untrained mind full of unusual ideas." Truthfully he didn't know if the underground would be willing even to consider such a proposal. There was too much trust required. Just because the underground didn't want Demonside destroyed, didn't mean that they were on the demons' side. The increase in magic on that side of the void was also affecting their world.

"That is the joy of youth. It is why taking an apprentice is a good thing, Saka." Guda had been trying to convince him for over a decade to take an apprentice.

"My hands are full with warlocks."

"Is that all?"

"There is an affection. I have perhaps spent too much time around warlocks." Saka knew that there were mages who thought less of him for that, while at the same time being glad that he had volunteered so they didn't have to.

"Perhaps. It makes your opinion unusual, and that scares some. How many mages have warlocks now?"

"A dozen, I believe." There had been a few mages to step forward to get a warlock. The rest had been accidental because the mage hadn't been quick enough to turn away from the opening in the void. "I do not know if they are underground or college, though."

"I suspect that many wouldn't say because it is dangerous to be a warlock and underground supporter. Most warlocks were college trained before finding a better way. Still a dozen is an increase."

"Not enough." Change would only come when more mages took the chance to get a warlock.

"No. But mages do not need a warlock if they take a human apprentice." Guda tilted her head. "It may be more palatable to those who would like to keep their freedom."

"We all make sacrifices. Some choose what they will be." Saka shrugged.

"I will take your idea to my warlock. She has influence in the underground. If we can get agreement from them, it will make our argument more persuasive." Guda sighed and paused to gather her thoughts. Saka didn't interrupt. She lifted her head and spoke firmly. "I request your presence tonight for a ritual."

That was part invitation and part order.

"Gladly. It would be an honor." Saka lowered his head. Being asked to assist in opening the proceeding on Lifeblood was an honor. Why had Guda thought he would need the order to agree?

"You would not say that if you let me finish. I have been gifted two humans for wetting the sand."

Despite the heat from the sun reflecting off the sand and the warmth of the rock he was sitting on, Saka shivered.

"They are ill and dying, so they have donated their lives. They are willing."

Saka nodded. He trusted Guda's word on that. She didn't like the idea of taking human slaves any more than he did. He needed to be there tonight as it would be seen as a sign of strength even though he was arguing for change and refusing to go back to the old ways.

"I will be voting for the sacrifices."

"So will I. There is no other choice. I hope to buy time."

Saka laughed. "That is never for purchase."

CHAPTER NINETEEN

ANGUS STARED at his magical theory homework. He knew what he was supposed to be learning, but it didn't fit with what he already knew. He'd struggled with the theory the whole time he'd been at college because it hadn't made sense to him. The lecturer said that innate ability wouldn't be enough for him to pass.

Because of his trip to Demonside, he was being watched more closely. Because he'd been trying to fail before that unexpected visit, he had months of bad marks to try to fix. If he did get kicked out, at least he'd be able to join the underground properly instead of pretending that he was a real warlock and biting his tongue every time another student said something about demons that wasn't right, or worse one of the teachers. He didn't know if they believed the lies or were just ignorant. Either option was bad.

The library was quiet. Around him second-year students were studying for their upcoming midyear exams. At least in second year, he'd be able to summon Saka without supervision. While he understood the need for care, especially if the demon was a wild animal, the restriction made his life extra dangerous.

He'd spoken to Jim a couple of times, but they hadn't met since that night at the bar. His father would no doubt be angry that he'd even done that. Jim had been considered a very bad influence, which had made dating him all the more fun. It was a good thing that his father had no idea just how bad Jim was. It was one thing to associate with a lowly wizard, but another entirely if that wizard was in the underground. While it wasn't called a criminal organization, they were considered to be antagonistic and full of lies according to the college.

Occasionally there would be news reports of a raid on the underground and the arrest of rogue warlocks—who no doubt ended up in Demonside with a minimal trial. More frequently there were reports of things blamed on the underground. Now Angus wasn't so sure that the underground was doing half the things they were accused of doing. If the college lied about demons running amok, it wouldn't be hard to lie about the underground.

Ellis's warning about not contacting anyone in the underground directly had stayed with him, even though he couldn't remember who Ellis was. He knew it had been another mind-tampering spell. This time it was probably for his own good.

He refocused on the page in front of him. He was supposed to be looking up references for an essay. It was exceedingly hard to do when he didn't agree with the topic and even some of the books didn't support it. But then he had selected older books because he'd been hoping to find something outside what the lecturer was teaching. There must have been a point where magic was more freely examined and contemplated, before the rigid structure and training were enforced.

"You will never pass theory if you are reading Henkins et al. He was controversial two decades ago," said a dark-haired guy as he sat opposite Angus.

Erikson. Angus swallowed. Why was he here? Was he watching and reporting?

"Terrance Erikson, third year and your new tutor." He offered his hand.

Angus shook it because refusing would be rude at best and suspicious at worst. They had never officially met, but Angus was well aware of who he was—and not just because of the common room incident. There were some men who were always going to be out of reach, but that had never stopped Angus from looking. Terrance was handsome. He looked as though he should be working on a farm, not studying the finer points of magic. Big strong hands and broad shoulders. He could probably fight off most demons without breaking a sweat.

Angus swallowed again before finding his voice. "My father that concerned about me failing?"

If that was all his father was worried about, that would be a good thing. Better for him to worry about Angus's grades than his views on magic and his closer-than-safe dealings with his demon. But the last thing he needed was an official watchdog trailing him.

"Your father and others. We have mutual friends." Terrance's smile widened.

On another day, and if his life wasn't already so complicated, Angus would've welcomed the attention. Terrance had a very nice smile. Now all he wanted to do was run.

Was this the liaison that the underground had promised, or was this a test from a suspicious warlock?

"Let's leave the books. Walk with me." Terrance closed the textbooks Angus had been reading and stood. He was right; he wouldn't pass if he quoted from those books since their theories had fallen out of favor.

Angus packed up his things, shoved them into his bag, and followed—still unsure if it was a setup or an offer of help. They went outside. It was dusk, and the air was cold and damp. It would be snowing soon, and they were predicting another long winter, the same as last year. It felt like there had hardly been any summer.

There were warlocks supposedly working on the weather, but using magic to fix a problem caused by too much magic didn't seem like the right approach. Unless there was something he was missing. Which he probably was, even though he was reading more news from official and unofficial sources.

Terrance walked through the formal garden, out the front of the library. On the other side of the garden were the accommodation blocks. With the fancy hedges and winding pathways, there were plenty of hidden corners. Should he be worried about someone jumping him? Terrance seemed calm.

They passed a couple making out. A woman with earphones in typed away on her computer as she sat cross-legged on a bench. Angus sat out here on weekends, reading or pretending to study. In daylight it was a nice garden. Right now as the shadows deepened and darkened, he wasn't so sure.

Terrance eventually stopped in a very secluded nook. "This will do."

Angus went still. If Terrance opened up a tear in the void and tossed him through, no one would know what had happened to him. Just another missing person.

When he'd been dating Jim, there'd been a spike, and the media had been all over it, asking questions. Wondering if criminal gangs were taking each other out. Jim had said that the warlocks were rounding up petty criminals or people on the street and tossing them over. At the time Angus had assured Jim that couldn't be the case. The college was investigating the disappearances with the police.

The media didn't report on it anymore. Angus was willing to bet that people were still going missing and being sent over the void.

Terrance lifted his shirt with one hand and conjured light with his other. His whole hand glowed and soft blue light illuminated the scars on his ribs. "To put your mind at ease. I pay."

Angus nodded. He was underground. But he still didn't want to say too much, anyone could be listening.

Terrance let his shirt drop back. "I'll get you passing your classes, but you'll struggle with the theory for obvious reasons. But there are ways. I also have other things for you to learn." He smiled. The light from his hand illuminated the nook they had taken over. "Sometimes we'll meet here; other times I think it would be more convenient for you to come to my room. As a third-year student, I have certain privileges."

Angus knew exactly what those privileges were, but that didn't mean that Terrance was allowed to share them with another student. There was a reason why first-year students weren't allowed to summon their demon on their own.

He kept his voice low. "You could get in trouble."

"I could get in trouble for many things... what's one more?" He smiled again, and Angus hated the way it made Terrance more attractive. "But before we go any further, I have a request."

Right, Angus had known that the underground would want something. He wasn't about to rush in this time. He'd already given up blood. What more did people, and demons, want from him.

"What?"

"Fix your relationship with your father."

"Huh?" How was that any of the underground's concern?

"He is powerful and in the upper echelons of the college. If you showed the error of your ways and an interest in becoming a warlock instead of fighting it, you could move closer."

They wanted him to spy on his father. While they didn't see eye to eye, this was asking too much. "I don't know... can I say no?"

"You could, but you require our help too." Terrance raised one eyebrow.

"Why do they want to know what my father is doing?" He knew his father was important... but was he that important?

Terrance shrugged. "I don't know. I do what I'm asked. I'm not privy to the big picture. Best that we aren't, as then it could be leaked."

The college came down hard on traitors. The media loved to remind people of the trouble rogue warlocks caused. It was more likely college members seeking to keep the reporters looking somewhere else instead of at the real threat. He stopped his mind from racing in circles. He couldn't believe the conspiracy theories any more than he could believe the college or the demons. He had to listen and work out what was real for himself. At the moment all he knew for sure was that his world was getting colder and Demonside was getting drier, and someone was summoning demons through the void to kill them for their magic.

Was his father involved in setting demons free or killing them for gain? Angus didn't want to believe it, but if he wasn't involved, he probably knew the people who were. Angus deliberated. Laughter and talking were filtering through the garden on the cold air. This was where all warlocks trained and received the stamp of approval for employment as warlocks. Without that, the only people who would employ him as a warlock were criminals.

Angus remembered why he'd never wanted to come here. The politics were too messy. There was a joke often told that was a twist on the college's approval: College warlocks, the only ones who can be trusted.

When should you trust a warlock?

When their heart has stopped beating.

Most people thought the only warlock who could be trusted was a dead one, even if they were paying handsomely for use of their services. Wizards weren't trusted either, but they had no demon stain, and they were cheaper so they generally received less scorn.

While he didn't agree with his father, he had trusted him. And that trust had been betrayed when his father had let the retrieval squad seal his memories of Demonside.

"I need to take your answer back," Terrance said.

"We aren't exactly talking. I have no relationship with my father to fix." When he called home, he spoke to his mother. His father was probably on campus sometimes or at the business headquarters across the road. He probably didn't lower himself to mixing with students, and he certainly didn't teach.

"So call him up and thank him for paying for the tutor."

Angus lifted his eyebrows, then gave a small laugh.

Terrance joined in. "Good fun, eh?"

"Now as well as helping with your theory, I have a few other things to teach you." He moved his glowing hand then, let the light go out. He leaned in close, close enough that his breath was on Angus's ear. "I don't need demon magic for the small stuff."

"You use wizard tricks?" Jim had been dabbling, they had both been dabbling in the small magics that wizards could do. Finding things, lighting candles, making things float…. It had taken a lot of effort to do anything, and most of it had been fairly useless.

"Not tricks. I can gather the magic that has already bled across."

He and Jim had tried sex magic once. It hadn't been anything like what he and Saka had done. Was Terrance going to be teaching that too? That didn't seem quite right… but then ritual sex was just sex, supposedly. Maybe he wasn't doing it right as he felt something when he was with the demon. He liked Saka. The demon was smart, as well as being just a little more dangerous than Angus was comfortable with.

Intoxicated. That's how he felt with Saka. Like he wasn't fully in control, but he was having fun anyway, consequences could wait. Consequences always had a way of catching up.

He glanced at Terrance. "Why you?"

"Because they thought I stood a better chance of teaching some of the more delicate points of magic than a woman." His hand was on Angus's shoulder, but it just rested there and it didn't demand any response.

Angus wasn't about to admit that he had noticed that Terrance was rather attractive. Terrance had probably taken one look at him and thought "what a weed." A freckly weed. Although Terrance had spent too long looking at him in the common room. Had he been watching him even then? "Did you pull the short straw?"

He wasn't sure that he wanted to be doing that kind of magic with Terrance.

"When you're in a circle and doing it right, it's about the other person's magic and their willingness to be open. I think we could have some fun studying."

Right, another person who liked him for his magic.

He didn't have time for a relationship anyway. And he was keeping far too many secrets to make it work. He should take what was on offer and enjoy it. He had with Saka. The one time there had been no magic between them had been enough to make him want more just like it… but it hadn't happened. He touched his thigh in memory of the knife marks. He still didn't want to admit that he had liked that, the way Saka said he would.

"How many other people do you tutor?"

"A few, not all need the same help."

He needed someone to talk to, an ally. Saka was a demon with his own agenda. Terrance worked for the underground, and they had their own reasons. There was no one he could really trust except himself. No one else needed to know that. He'd play along for the moment.

"I'll call my dad."

"Good." Terrance took his hand away. "We'll start tomorrow afternoon."

"That quick?"

"With the easy stuff. You've got to know how to gather the magic within yourself and from the earth before you can go deeper. But if you want to catch up for recreation, let me know." He grinned. "See you tomorrow straight after dinner."

"Where?"

"I'll find you." Then he was gone into the darkness. Angus headed back to the library. He still had to do this theory assignment. Terrance was right; Angus needed to pull recent textbooks that supported the current beliefs and not go looking for reasons to doubt.

And not give people reason to doubt him.

ANGUS STOPPED when he turned the corner after dinner. He'd been waiting for Terrance to find him since classes had finished. Terrance had, but it was not the friendly kind of finding and more of the stalky kind of finding.

Terrance came around the corner and took a step back when he saw Angus casually waiting.

"How long have you been following me?"

"I saw you leave dinner and I thought…." He trailed away.

Angus shook his head. "Don't lie."

He was sick of getting lied to or only getting partial pieces of information.

As Terrance drew in a breath and stared back, Angus realized it probably wasn't in his best interest to argue with the rugby-playing warlock.

Terrance sighed. "Since you came back. It's one of the things I do. I watch those who are retrieved."

Did he watch for the underground or for the college or both? And if the underground watched, then Angus was damn sure that the college did too.

"We can talk about this later." Terrance gave a pointed glance at the other students walking by.

"Fine." Neither of them needed people listening in. "Did you have plans?"

"Yes. And they involve you." Terrance grinned.

From anyone else that might have been a pickup line, but Terrance was talking about magic, and that was all Angus was interested in. Mostly.

"Put your coat on. We're going outside." Terrance pulled on his coat and started walking.

Angus followed even though he'd have rather stayed in. It had been raining on and off all day. They went outside, where it was already cold and almost dark. Again Terrance led him through the hedges of the library garden. The light rain was keeping most people away. He pulled up the hood of his coat, but rain had already trickled down the back of his neck.

Terrance stopped at a bench mostly protected by a tree. "This should be fine."

"For what?"

"For a little practical work."

"We couldn't do that inside?"

Terrance sat on the bench. "It's easier to learn outdoors because there is more flowing around. Inside it gets trapped in corners and there is less flow."

Kids with magical ability usually had favorite places, and those favorite places had a buildup of magic. What was here was very weak compared to what was across the void. He'd been able to gather it easily over there.

Angus knew he was looking unconvinced.

"You need to be able to use what is around you. And you need to be able to do it fast. Yes, you have a demon, but this is faster. In the time it would take you to work through a summoning, I could've already attacked you."

"But I will get faster at summoning."

"True. I don't need to walk widdershins. I do it all in my mind, but this is still faster. Think of it as self-defense."

"If that were true, then it wouldn't be banned." They were both keeping their voices soft. Angus was standing with his hands shoved in his pocket.

"If you have to use your demon for everything, then you are weak. They knew that. They don't want warlocks running around who can draw up magic on a whim. It makes magic look easy and safe. It's why they always take great pains to reiterate that wizards are pathetic."

By the college's definition, Saka was a wizard. There was nothing pathetic about his magic.

"You still didn't answer my first question. How long have you been following me?"

"I did. You just weren't happy with the answer. If you'd said another dangerous thing in the common room, I'd have shut you down."

That explained the looks from Terrance. He'd known it couldn't be anything else. "And who would've reported me?"

"I don't know. But someone in your class would've been told to keep an eye on you—the college would have said it was in case you suffered any side effects from being taken. They would've made it sound innocent."

Which was even more disturbing. Someone in his classes was making sure that he was okay and thinking they were concerned about his welfare when that was the furthest thing from the truth.

"So draw up energy and then what?"

"You haven't done much yet, have you?"

"Tree growing?"

Terrance shook his head. "That's just shifting the energy from the demon to you to the tree. You aren't actually doing anything with the energy. The seed already knows what to do. You're just feeding it. They'll probably have you making light and then heat. They're very simple."

"Like fire?" Standing in front of a fire would be nice. He couldn't feel his toes.

"No fire today. Draw it up, try and hold it in your hand, then change it from magical energy to light." Terrance did all of that while he was talking, and he made it look as natural as breathing.

It wasn't.

Angus could feel the magic, but it was slippery and so hard to gather. There wasn't enough of it. There was a reason wizards used blood or sex to draw more magic.

He didn't know how long he'd been trying when Terrance got up and put his hand over Angus's. Immediately Angus felt the magic in his palm. He managed to hold it for a few seconds before it slid away.

"I suck at this."

"Everyone does at first. It's the hardest thing to learn. But once you can...." He smiled. Rain slicked down his dark hair, and his face was mostly hidden in shadows, but it was enough that lust took hold and Angus had to remind himself to breathe.

The magic reformed between their palms.

Maybe he was only good at one kind of magic.

THAT SATURDAY NIGHT Angus had been invited home for dinner. One groveling phone call was all it had taken to smooth his father's ruffled feathers and to show that he was really trying to please.

It had left a bad taste in Angus's mouth. He didn't want to please. And he didn't want to go to dinner. Yet here he was, ringing the doorbell and waiting to be let in. He shouldn't have needed an invitation to have dinner at home. He wouldn't have needed the invitation if his father hadn't banned him from coming home until he'd turned himself into a warlock, and a good one.

That ultimatum had been what made Angus decide to fail the demon summoning. That hadn't worked out as he'd expected. What would he be doing now if the college had kicked him out? Would he have turned to the underground anyway? Or tried to get into a medical college? He would've needed to find a job because he would've had all of his funds cuts if he'd been tossed out of college.

Or would his father have pulled strings to make sure Angus stayed in Warlock College?

He crossed his arms and pulled his coat tighter around him. What was taking so long? Was his father giving his mother a list of topics not to talk about?

Just as he was about to ring the doorbell again, his mother opened the door and hugged him. She was shorter than he remembered, more like he'd grown. "I am so happy you and your father are speaking again. Are you enjoying college?"

"I am." That wasn't a lie. He liked history. But he liked the other things that he was learning on the side more. With Terrance he was learning to gather the magic that was around him and in him. He couldn't do much with it, yet, but he was learning how powerful wizard magic could be.

He was also discovering the magic that was really in his blood. His dad had known that he'd never be able to ignore it, so had wanted him to be able to use it in what he considered a proper manner. In his father's mind, sending his son to college had been the right thing to do. Most warlocks didn't question what they had been told. Why would they when it was working for them?

His life would've been easier if he'd never questioned the use of demons for magic. For that he blamed Jim. Jim had been the one to interest him in the underground, and at the time, Angus had thought him exciting and dangerous.

"Good. You'll be a fine warlock. Have you picked a specialty yet?" she asked.

"That's at the end of second year, after they have sampled the different areas," his father answered for him.

Angus's heart clenched, and he forced himself to keep breathing, slow and even. He wasn't supposed to remember seeing his father at the interrogation after being retrieved. He wasn't supposed to remember anything about the incident, just that it had been horrible and that the demons had hurt him.

Every time he blinked, he saw the retrieval squad and his father sitting there as the woman dug into his brain.

"I have always been interested in medicine. I doubt that will change," Angus added. He had always wanted to be a doctor. Now he'd end up treating those with an overinflated self-worth and bank account instead of those who needed genuine care. Maybe he could also volunteer at a clinic.

"Softhearted," his father countered.

"Big money." That was why warlocks went into healing.

It placated his father, and he nodded as though he could respect a love of money more than he could the desire to help. How involved with the college was his father? Was he one of the warlocks releasing demons into the streets to create havoc and reinforce the lies spun to the media?

His mother served up dinner while Angus and his father sat at the table in awkward silence. Was his father looking for flaws or signs that Angus knew too much? What would Angus have to report to the underground? All well, no news. How long until that was no longer enough... how long until his father trusted him?

They could be waiting until the glaciers receded and Demonside had surface rivers.

"The tutor is really helping. He makes things really clear."

"Good. Sometimes you have to hear things a new way to understand. I want you to pass. We have a family reputation to maintain."

Three generations of warlocks before Angus. Had any of them ever questioned what was going on? The clock on the wall ticked, counting out the silence. That was a question he was never going to be able to ask his father.

His father cleared his throat. "I heard you saw Jim."

Angus glanced up sharply. "Yeah." There was no point in denying it, but he could certainly deflect. "He wanted to show off his new girlfriend. I don't know why I bothered. It would've been better if I'd had someone on my arm."

"You don't have time to date. You need to get your grades up."

"Thus the not dating, Dad." *Thanks for your concern.*

Angus shouldn't be surprised. It wasn't as though he'd been worried about what might happen to his son's mind when they were trying to play seek-and-destroy in there.

His mother placed chicken pie in front of him. She'd made his favorite. He smiled up at her. He'd missed her while living on campus. He hadn't missed living with his father. In that respect living on campus was better than living at home. Before it had been clear he had magic, she'd encouraged him to chase his dreams. One of his favorite toys had been a medical set... He remembered his father scoffing ten years ago and saying something like in the future they wouldn't need doctors for anything. It would all be done with magic.

Then when he'd been ten, he'd felt it. He'd be drawn to certain places because he felt better there. He'd said nothing. Everyone knew the signs to look out for, and he'd spent almost a year trying to hide them because even back then, he hadn't wanted to be like his father.

A need to be outside. Restlessness. Intense focus. Anger that resulted in objects levitating. He'd shattered a mirror when his father had started hassling him. In hindsight his father had probably been testing him.

"Thanks, Mom. I didn't think you'd remember." Or care.

"Of course I remember. I haven't made it since you moved out. How is life at college? I'm so relieved that nastiness is over. You are fully recovered?" His mother spoke fast, as though she could stop the silence from coming back.

That he was only here to spy on his father—no, fix things so that he could spy later—wasn't fair to her. He needed to be here for her. He didn't give a damn about his father. Angus didn't get the chance to answer the questions because his father butted in.

"Of course he's all right. Why wouldn't he be? The best doctors checked him over." His father picked up his fork.

Angus looked at the man he barely knew. That bullshit wasn't going by unchallenged. If he was here, having to sit through dinner, he would get something out of it. "I don't remember anything." *Certainly no doctors.* "Can't have been that bad."

"Demons like to drug warlocks so they are less trouble. That's why you don't remember."

Angus started eating, forcing down each mouthful without tasting it. He should be enjoying it. His mother was a great cook, and he loved the way she put cheese in her chicken pie.

His father had just lied to his face. And in front of his mother. His mother, like the rest of the general nonmagical population, was buying into those lies. Why wouldn't she believe her husband? She loved him and trusted him. His father was part of the college and all that stood between demons breaking through and killing humans for their own corrupt desires. People feared the demons. They *should* be worried about the warlocks.

And people like his father who perpetuated the lies.

The lies were so thick and pervasive. There was no room to question until, like a blanket, they were torn away. For Angus it had happened slowly over his time with Jim. Saka had removed the last bits.

Now Angus could barely breathe for all the misinformation that was everywhere.

"What about you, Dad? How is it going at the top?"

His father paused, eyes narrowed, as if concerned about this sudden interest, but Angus had made sure that there was snark in his tone. Too much? Was his father about to tell him off for being rude?

His father rearranged his face into something close to a smile and acted as though nothing was wrong. "I seem to be spending half my time trying to stop the demons who break through."

"That must be tough." *Given they couldn't break through on their own.* "Are they killed or returned?"

"Killed. Be a waste of magic to return them." His father looked up from his plate. "You getting interested in law enforcement?"

"A friend at college is." That was a lie. He didn't have any friends. Being taken had lowered his standing, being good at the practical side of magic had dropped it further as now he was too smart.

"There are many branches. From working with the cops on crime to policing our own." His father stared at him. If he'd stared any harder, he'd have been scanning Angus's brain for illegal thoughts.

Angus held his gaze and nodded, but wondered if that was meant as a warning to him.

"So tell me about your demon," his father said as though the conversation was going smoothly. "I hear you have him under control now."

"Just your average black-horn demon. I don't remember what went wrong the first time."

"Inattention most likely. Demons are tricky and dangerous." His father pointed the fork at him. "Glad you learned your lesson."

"What about you? Do you still have that black, scary-looking thing... what is it? Nightshade?"

"No. Now that was a dangerous demon. Not too many of them around fortunately. Got a dragon now."

A dragon. Was it also a mage? He wanted to ask what had happened to the Nightshade, but didn't because he could guess. His father had either drained it of magic and it had died, or he'd killed it in a ritual for its magic. Either way it was bad. The unwritten rules were there for a reason. If humans were breaking them, then the demons would. Then the accord that had existed across the void would be gone.

As fat snowflakes hit the window two months earlier than when Angus had been a kid, he realized that the unwritten rules should probably be written, or etched in stone next time, as they were already being ignored on both sides of the void.

CHAPTER TWENTY

FROM THE TOP OF LIFEBLOOD, Saka could see for several days of travel. Not as far as to the ocean, though; that was much farther. He remembered standing up there the very first time. He'd finished his training and passed the test. Dawn had risen after his initiation and promises to serve his tribe—meaning the greater tribe of all demons.

Back then he hadn't imagined ever having a warlock.

He hadn't imagined being the head mage of a tribe.

He hadn't imagined that he'd ever stand here and not be able to see rivers or oases shimmering on the sand. He turned so he could see the one Angus's blood had created. There was another tribe there at the moment. He smiled. They would see his mark and be impressed with the new trees and the way the oasis hadn't dried up fast. It would need to be maintained.

All water needed to be maintained carefully. Not a drop taken for granted.

There were tribes still trickling in. Some would be late, and some would leave early. There would be much talk about where the water was, and where they were heading. It would not do for too many tribes to cluster together, that would put pressure on an already fragile world. Even before the drought, they had always moved, taking advantage of the herd migration.

There were fewer herds of animals now because there was less water. The mages would need to look at that issue, as well as trying to stop the warlocks from making the problem worse. Beneath the red sands were the riverwyrms. They could hear their prey as they moved through the sunken rivers. By the time a riverwyrm broke the surface, it was too late for the creature being hunted. Were there still riverwyrms? No one had mentioned a sighting in quite a while. No one would risk being complacent either.

Yet that was exactly what had happened. Somehow all the mages had failed the tribe. They had let magic be siphoned across for too long. They should all be doing some searching and asking what went wrong.

His lips twisted as he realized that there were some similarities between warlocks and demons—change was hard.

He lifted his gaze to the sky as a couple of winged mages landed on Lifeblood. This was the first official meeting. He had gone up early to think. There had been a couple of others, but they had simply nodded and continued with their silent contemplation. Those mages who couldn't fly made their way up the mountain on foot. The climb had also given him thinking time.

More thinking time about things he didn't want to think about.

The keeping of human slaves still sat wrong in his heart. But going against the council of mages on this issue would not help him. He needed them willing to listen to his wilder ideas. A murmur swept through the gathering mages.

The humans had arrived.

They had been carried up the mountain, given cushions and meals and treated as honored guests for their time here. He had avoided speaking to them at the foot of the mountain out of guilt, but he needed to offer his thanks since he would be holding one of the knives.

He turned away from the expansive view that made him feel like a grain of sand and returned to the reality of the first sitting of mages at the gathering. The two humans were there to shed blood and souls. They were positioned in the middle of the plateau in preparation. Mages walked around them, starting to form a loose circle. All nodded or bowed, few stopped to talk. There was an awkwardness about this. Even the mages known for their blood and soul magic didn't seem entirely comfortable with having humans up there.

Humans hadn't been sacrificed on Lifeblood in Saka's lifetime.

Guda had said these two were volunteers sent by the underground, not offerings sent across by guilty warlocks, hoping that someone else would pay for their magic. Had there ever been human volunteers before?

Saka went down on one knee in front of the humans. Up close it was clear they were not well. What had his old warlock called it? Cancer. It rotted a person from the inside. It could be cured with magic. They could be healed here. The humans probably didn't know that, and they hadn't been told. So they were going to die instead.

"Thank you for your sacrifice." There was nothing else he could say.

"I'm glad to stop fighting," the man said. "I have enjoyed several pain-free days, seeing a world that I could never have imagined."

"Yes. My death will have meaning," the woman said, and then her face crumpled. "That doesn't mean I am not afraid."

Saka looked at her. "Fear of the unknown is normal. We believe that the spirit goes back to the land to give life to the next generation." Her soul and blood would lift rivers and give his world a reprieve.

"That is a nice thought." She didn't sound convinced.

Was she having second thoughts? No doubt it had been explained, but being in a strange land surrounded by demons had to be unsettling, along with knowing the manner of her death. He glanced at his hands.

"I will be one of the mages performing the ritual." He was trying to lighten his own burden and reassure them both. He had never been involved in a sacrifice on Lifeblood with all the other mages watching, not even the more common killing of animals. He didn't like death, unlike some, but Guda had asked and he couldn't refuse the honor or the political maneuver. "You will bring life back."

The woman nodded. "It won't be enough, though."

"I wish it was, but I won't lie." He was aware of other mages watching. He needed to get ready. He bowed his head and then stood. Even if the humans changed their minds, it was too late.

Guda was already at the bloodstone. A sacrifice of an animal from across the void marked the start of the first meeting. Was Guda old enough to remember human sacrifice? The stone was stained dark, and the hole in the middle went deep into the mountain. The blood from the sacrifice feeding the Lifeblood spring.

He looked at his old teacher. It had been she who suggested that he volunteer to get a warlock the first time. "Change would be needed on both sides" had been her words. She had been one of the first to choose a warlock, putting her life on the line for what she believed.

Now they were about to bloody their hands and prove the tales that humans told about demons being blood-hungry savages.

He lowered his head in acknowledgment of her presence. He was no longer her official apprentice, but she would always be his teacher. She had guided his whole journey. But he had chosen to walk those paths, enjoying the danger and the chance to cross the void.

"I will support your idea when you speak," she said as though their conversation from yesterday had never paused.

"Thank you. I hope others will listen."

"Blood will calm the anger."

"I hope you are right. It could wet more than the sand." They might desire the easy way of more blood. The humans would retaliate, and demons with a warlock were vulnerable. Warlocks could take whole tribes and slaughter them for their magic.

Demons had to be smarter. That wasn't usually hard. Humans were easily distracted by shiny metal or power.

"I think most people are here. Those who are late will have to wait beyond the circle."

Saka glanced at the setting sun. The timing had to be perfect. "Will you lead the walk?"

"No. You do it."

"These are your sacrifices." While other tribes had brought animals from across the void, Guda's humans were far more prized, thus the privilege of opening the first meeting.

"But you need the honor. I would not take that from you." Her mouth opened. "I am old. You are my legacy. I want to make sure you don't make a mess of it."

"You will be coming to many more gatherings."

"No, the magic no longer flows through me the way it once did. My river is sinking."

There was no time to process that thought as the mages were already assembling to make the walk and create the circle. They would follow the lead mage until the circle was closed. With their collective wills feeding the circle, the sacrifice would be made. Then the circle would be dropped and the meeting would start. Here every mage was supposed to be equal, but they all knew who was more powerful, and who was in favor.

Saka started walking, each step leading him away until he reached the halfway mark, then he was drawing closer to the end of the line and closing the circle. The humans sat on the stone in the center watching; they gasped as the circle came in to being. A brilliant blue that crackled with the energy of over fifty mages.

It was awe inducing. People at the bottom of Lifeblood Mountain would be able to see it shooting up into the sky. He'd wanted to be a mage from the first time he saw it. He wanted to know what went on up there.

Tonight he didn't feel the awe, or the swell of accomplishment. He felt the failure of every mage that had brought them to this moment when they had to sacrifice two humans to rebalance what was being stolen.

His failure at treading too gently for too long. No more.

He closed his eyes and drew in a deep breath. The thrum of magic swelled within him. This wasn't his first sacrifice. His very first one, at his initiation, had been full of self-importance, that it was somehow his right to take another life. He hadn't even known what the humans had called that type of animal back then. He'd learned later it had been a sheep.

Saka stopped in front of the bloodstone.

His blood was like the ice taking over the other side of the veil. For a moment he couldn't breathe. He was sure that if he lifted his hand, it would shake. He reached to the power around him and the ebb of the water in the mountain.

This was about the humans' lives making a difference. This was about them.

He breathed deeply, then turned to face the gathered mages.

"The first meeting of this gathering has been honored by the presence of these two humans. They have offered their blood, their souls to Lifeblood. To Demonside. To us." Saka turned and bowed to the humans. His words had been specific because he wanted the mages to know that these people had chosen to die for Demonside.

They were starting to look happy, as though they were enjoying the experience. Guda was lulling them. Had she made them forget what was going to happen? The humans were relaxed, expressions dazed as though on the edge of bliss. It was better to die with a smile than a scream—not all mages agreed with him—but having someone enjoy their death was a little odd.

There was a murmur behind him from the other mages. No one would dare say anything, except to express gratitude. Privately they would wonder why Saka had been given the honor, and they would ask why, and how, Guda had found willing humans. All of which would leave an opening to deepen relations across the void—look what can be achieved if we work with the humans.

Gently he laid the woman down. Guda did the same for the man, and then Guda unsheathed her claws. Saka drew a knife. The opening sacrifice was always fast and always about the blood. The elaborate rituals and orgies would come later.

Any prisoner or traitor sent across the void and captured by a tribe was given a choice. They would also be offered the same mental relief that these two were getting. Some chose not to, as though they thought screaming would make it stop. They were wrong.

The sun was almost ready to kiss the sand. Saka watched, waiting for the moment.

As one Saka and Guda sliced the soft skin on the neck of the sacrifices. The small cut was all it took. The blood was black in the flickering blue light of the circle; it spurted out onto the stone, then drained down the hole and into the mountain.

The flow slowed to a trickle.

The woman stared up at the sky, her eyes losing focus and her breathing shallow.

Guda licked her claw, and Saka wiped his blade and sheathed it. Already the magic was swelling.

"Demonside thanks you." He had no idea if the humans heard, but it needed to be said.

While he'd been distracted, a few more had arrived and were waiting for the circle to be dropped. When the sun had fully gone, Saka would let it fall. Then the talking would start.

He already knew that tonight they would talk about water, which would turn to the talk of human slaves who could be kept for more regular rituals. He suspected that some tribes were already keeping the criminals sent across alive for longer than they were strictly supposed to. He didn't blame them. Raising rivers, even just enough so the pumps could reach them was hard work. Tiring.

The vote on slaves would be overwhelmingly yes.

Tomorrow or the next day, he would raise his idea. He was hoping for a discussion, not an outright no.

CHAPTER TWENTY-ONE

MORE TREE PLANTING. Now Angus understood why there were such nice forests around the college. Saka stood in front of him, waiting to act as the conduit for magic from across the void, but Angus had something else in mind.

Terrance had been teaching him how to gather up magic. It was all around him, but in much smaller quantities than in Demonside. This was the magic that wizards used. It was small, which meant they could never take on a warlock in a magical fight. However, it was fine for finding lost pets or jewelry or any of the other little things that wizards did when offering their services.

It was why Angus had never had a problem finding things as a kid... he'd been using magic without realizing. Because his father was a very active warlock, there was more magic than usual around the house. He'd never realized. Consciously gathering, though, was much harder than having it eddy around him and accidentally using the available magic.

But he'd been working hard with Terrance and now he could draw it to him. He was more aware of it. He wasn't sure that he could do it in class, though. What if people noticed that he wasn't using his demon? If they could see magic, then they definitely would be able to tell what he was doing.

As before, he planted the seed and held his hand over it. Because he'd been warned about touching Saka, he held his hand out but not enough that he could touch the demon. Saka seemed to understand and kept his distance.

Angus smiled.

Instead of drawing from Saka, he drew from the land and himself. He had prepared for the class, and it wasn't hard to run his thumbnail over the cut he'd made on his finger and reopen it. Blood magic, the kind that involved blood from the magic user, was seen as weak by warlocks.

Terrance would be disappointed that he was cheating. Especially when there was so much around because of all the tears in the void, but Angus wanted to make a point. He didn't need a demon to do magic. However, it was a whole lot easier.

If he was caught spilling blood, he'd be in trouble. Angus glanced over, but the lecturer was helping a student whose tree was rather twisted. A drop of blood hit the ground and was absorbed by the freshly turned earth. Saka's tail flicked in question, but otherwise he didn't move.

Angus noticed, but he had to concentrate on what he was doing. There might be less magic for him to draw on, but it was also less contained. He could feel the difference between drawing from a demon and drawing from the world around.

As before, Angus got the seedling going, carefully drawing it up. It was much harder this time. The concentration and the energy needed were making him frown and sweat. It trickled down his back, despite the cold air. He was never going to be able to get the tree to his height by his own magic. And because he'd done it before, he couldn't screw it up this time. He glanced up at Saka and then lowered his gaze, admitting defeat... this time.

Angus was going to have to draw on his demon. He was playing with magic while Demonside dried up.

Saka tilted his head slightly as though acknowledging the effort

Angus had made. Angus opened himself up to the push of power from Saka, accepting the magical boost. The increase in magic was heady. He could understand why warlocks got addicted to the feeling. For those few minutes, Angus was invincible.

He grew the tree rapidly, yet carefully.

Before they had finished filling this field with trees, he would be able to grow one all on his own, without his demon. That would make him a better magic user than all of his classmates who couldn't do a spell without a demon.

"Very nice, Angus." The lecturer walked by. "And without touching your demon. You can move on to drawing the power, dismissing your demon, and then see if you can continue growing the tree using one of the methods described in yesterday's class."

Angus swallowed. It was one thing to draw magic and let it dissipate, the way they had been doing, and another to hold on to the magic for later use. Saka used the glass orbs. Warlocks had nothing like that. They had to find a visualization that worked for them, which was made harder by the fact that magic wasn't visible here. Too much of learning how to use magic was trial and error. He studied Saka and wished he could ask him. His lecturer wouldn't appreciate his student taking tips from a demon.

With Terrance he'd been holding it in the palm of his hand, but that wasn't going to be practical in the long run. The scar over his heart tingled. Saka gave a very small grin that revealed his pointed teeth. Of course. That was how Saka had given him magic before. The scar could act as a focus... Would it glow in Demonside? He'd never know.

THAT ANGUS and Terrance were spending time together had been noticed, but if other students assumed they were dating, it was a good thing. Much better than if they found out what was really going on.

Angus knocked on Terrance's door.

"Come in if you're horny" came the reply.

Angus hesitated. He'd never been in Terrance's room, and he

wasn't turning up for sex. The door swung open. Terrance was wearing track pants and a dressing gown, but bare feet. Warm air wafted out into the cold corridor.

"That was a joke," Terrance said without a smile.

"I knew that." Would he be this confident by the time he was a third-year student? Was Terrance not worried about people noticing him and wondering what he was up to? Right now it was hard for Angus to imagine making it through the rest of first year.

Terrance laughed. "No, you didn't. Come in; you're letting in the cold air." Terrance grabbed his arm and pulled him in, then locked the door. "Better to let them all think you're here for one reason."

"Which I am."

Terrance winked at him. "I know that... I'm having fun. You should try it."

Walking along the edge of the knife between two opposing sides wasn't fun. He was going to slip and get cut in half.

There was a circle marked in the middle of the floor, a couple of socks lay over the line, but Terrance kicked them clear.

"You really are allowed to do summoning and spells in here?" Angus bent down to touch the circle. It was metal inlaid in the wood flooring, and it resonated with old magic.

"Yep. You want to go first, or shall I?"

Angus looked up. "Now?"

"I'll show you mine if you show me yours."

Angus's face started burning even though Terrance was referring to demons. Half the time when Terrance opened his mouth, his words were flirty. It had to be his personality. He was unsettling with his confidence and manner, as though he didn't care what everyone else thought, or even if they discovered he was working with the underground. Maybe it was an act and he was bluffing his way through college while praying that he wouldn't get caught.

He did want to know what kind of demon Terrance had, though. Not a big one if it fit in this room. "What is your demon?"

"Scarlips."

"You have that in here?" That was a large catish-scorpionish thing that, according to Saka, hunted in packs and had occasionally been known to kill demons wandering too far from their tribe. However, they much preferred the smaller animals that lived in the desert. He was more likely to be seen as a threat than a meal. That didn't make the idea of having one in a confined space any more comforting.

"Don't freak out, she's fine. She knows if she is good she gets some blood."

"You don't expect her to kill you?"

"We chased around that tree over a year ago. I'm still here, and Aqua behaves."

"Aqua?"

Terrance shrugged. "She needed a name."

Right…. This room was not big enough for a scarlips and two humans who no doubt looked like large juicy steaks. "You summon her in here regularly?"

Terrance nodded. "And I let her out of the circle."

"Maybe I should go first." That way if the scarlips tried something, Saka could help.

Both men stepped back from the circle, and a couple of minutes later, Saka was there and looking very unimpressed. His lips pressed into a thin line, and his head was tilted so his horns became more of a weapon and less of a decoration.

"You have just pulled me out of a meeting. I don't have long." Hanging from his belt was the damn vial—Saka had obviously expected to be summoned. There would be no fun in the collecting of blood today.

"Would you prefer to come back later?" He wasn't used to Saka being so abrupt.

"I cannot go back empty-handed." Saka glanced at Terrance, and his hand slid to his machete. "Who is that?"

"My tutor… in *all* things magic." Angus tried to imply the underground.

"My lessons are no longer enough?" Saka gave a lazy smile.

Angus vowed to find a magical way to stop himself from blushing. "I enjoy your lessons, but I needed someone on this side."

Angus dropped the circle, and Saka stepped out. He ran his hand up Angus's arm and kissed him as though making it clear that Angus was his. Angus didn't resist, he was hard before Saka's tongue slipped past his lips.

"No fun tonight," Saka whispered. "It is unfortunate."

"Yes." Angus wanted to have sex with Saka, and he looked forward to being fucked by the demon. If the other warlocks knew, they would be horrified. Terrance would be horrified. Angus drew back a little. Even though there would be no pleasure, he wouldn't shirk his responsibility. Saka could take the blood he needed to rebalance. He would go back to his meeting with something more than the shame of being summoned.

Terrance was strangely silent. He didn't look revolted, more fascinated. That eased some of the tension that had formed. While they did use sex magic in the underground, Angus wasn't sure if they involved their people-demons. Maybe he had crossed a line that should never have been crossed.

Angus glanced at the other warlock. "This is Saka, he's a mage. I have been learning about magic from him."

"Yeah, I got that. I... wow. I feel a little lame." But he cast his circle and the scarlips appeared. She was a very vivid shade of aqua. In Demonside she must shimmer. Her black tongue flicked over her lips when she saw Terrance. Then she realized that there was company, and that poison tipped tail arched forward ready to strike. "Peace, Aqua. They are friends."

"Comparing demons?" Saka asked. "I will have to make a rule that whenever you call me there will be blood."

It would still be worth it. "I owe you for today, and Terrance owed his... plus I can't summon you in my room."

Terrance dropped the circle and started petting his poisonous cat as though she was a kitten. "Hey, I can't leave, but don't let that stop you two."

"Angus isn't ready for an audience." Saka smiled. "And I don't have the time. Sorry." His smile vanished.

167

"I understand. You have your gathering thing." From what Angus knew, it was an important gathering of all the tribes.

"We are debating important issues among the mages. It is in *everyone's* interest that I am there, not here."

"Would first thing in the morning be better for you?" Terrance found the spot that made Aqua give something close to a purr. The frequency set Angus's teeth on edge.

"Yes, it would." Saka inclined his head to Terrance.

Angus should've asked that. "I'll summon you in the morning in future." Summoning Saka under the watchful gaze of Terrance took all the fun out of it. Maybe he could go to the motel again. Although if he got caught, he suspected the warlocks would do a better job of wiping his mind. This was safer. "You'd best take what you want."

"What I have time for." Saka corrected as he pulled a knife free.

"Wait, let me get Aqua sorted, otherwise she might try and taste Angus." Terrance got off his bed and picked a ritual knife off his desk. Aqua's ears flicked forward, and the dangerous tail curled around her back leg.

Without even blinking Terrance sat on the chair and rolled up the leg of his track pants, then sliced open his skin with several shallow cuts.

The way it was done was so calm and cold, Angus didn't quite know what to make of it.

Terrance glanced up. "You get used to it."

Saka shook his head. "You could do a better job."

"You offering?" Terrance raised an eyebrow. In jest or seriousness?

Jealousy spiked in Angus. He didn't want to share Saka, but if Terrance was teaching him, wasn't it also fair that Saka teach Terrance? It would be better if more warlocks knew how to rebalance.

Saka's touch on Angus's arm tightened a touch. "Not tonight."

Gently Saka pushed Angus to the bed. Angus sat on the edge, really not looking forward to what was about to happen at all.

Saka smoothed his hand up Angus's arm, pushing his sleeve as he went. His touch was hot, and Angus craved more. He leaned forward to kiss Saka. Maybe he could distract himself. Sink into the moment and enjoy what he could. Saka's other hand slid up Angus's thigh as he knelt in front of him. The tips of his fingers grazed Angus's erection.

The demon made a small growl of frustration and drew back a fraction. "I have no time."

"Then do it and go." *Stop teasing and making me want what I can't have.*

The warlock and mage glared at each other.

Saka drew his blade and traced the tip down Angus's forearm without breaking the skin. Angus shivered.

"Remember, the higher the emotion, the more value, the more magic is rebalanced." Saka didn't take his eyes from Angus, but he was speaking for Terrance. "Fear, lust." Saka caressed Angus's length. It was obvious which emotion Saka caused. "It makes no difference—I prefer lust. It is more fun for everyone."

A kiss and the sure stroke of the demon's hand. Angus groaned and then realized that Saka had cut him. The vial held by his tail.

When Saka drew back, the vial was full. Saka pressed his hand to the wound, and then it was healing. "It should be gone by morning."

His hard-on wouldn't be.

Angus glanced down and saw that Saka was at least suffering from the same problem. The demon's breathing had even quickened. He stole another kiss, then stood and stepped back... gone. He didn't need Angus to dismiss him or open the void.

Angus looked at his arm to be sure that Saka had actually been here. There was the proof in the mostly healed cut.

Terrance sent Aqua back and looked at Angus. "It's not just blood, is it?"

"No." He closed his eyes. Admitting that he liked sex with a demon would be too much. Years of being told that demons were bad and immoral was hard to shake. But he remembered their tents, the colors, and the way they had looked at him after the night with Saka. They saw nothing to be ashamed of.

"I could feel the magic rolling between the two of you."

"You should see it." Angus bit his lip; he wasn't supposed to remember that.

"So it's true… it can be seen over there."

"Yeah. But Saka really knows what he's doing."

"I could tell." Terrance put some antiseptic on the cuts he'd made. "I should be cutting myself now after watching that. I know what I will be doing in the future."

Angus frowned.

"Not with Aqua… on my own. Ew." Terrance threw a shirt at him. "You are lucky to have a mage."

"Yeah." If he'd had a regular animal demon, he'd have never been taken across the void. Luck had nothing to do with it, though; Saka had wanted a warlock and had chosen him.

Terrance looked at him, his eyes dark. Was he still feeling the lust? Angus pulled down his sleeve to hide the cut. The moment stretched between them. Angus's dick twitched. If he went back to his room, he'd be entertaining himself.

Terrance got up, walked over, and sat on the bed next to Angus. "Stay awhile."

Angus wanted sex that had nothing to do with magic. Did Terrance want him, or was he just seeking release? Did it matter when that was all he wanted? "No magic."

"No magic." Terrance took off his dressing gown. There were old scars all over his ribs. They were evidence that he paid for his magic, and dangerous if seen by the wrong people. They needed to be fully healed so no scars remained. Saka could do that for him.

Angus stripped off his shirt and undid his belt. Terrance's hands were there, tugging the jeans down as Angus toed out of his shoes.

Naked, they were soon on the bed, stealing first kisses. Touching, caressing. Their legs tangled. Angus was hungry for release without games, and he didn't care how he got it. He wrapped his hand around Terrance's long shaft and stroked.

The older warlock groaned and thrust into Angus's hand, before grasping Angus. His touch was firm and sure. "Do you want more?"

"Just keep going." The words were mumbled against lips, but the need burned within him. He wanted simple, easy. He realized that as much as he liked Saka, what they had was all about the magic. They worked together because they had no other choice.

He closed his eyes as his breathing quickened. His fingers slicked with Terrance's precome. The kisses deepened as lust pushed harder. Then the climax rolled through him.

Terrance groaned. His cock hardened further, and then he was adding his come to the mess between them.

For a moment they lay there, catching their breath.

He'd needed that. He needed the human connection and to feel like he was something other than a warlock only good for magic. He sighed. Without either of those things, Terrance would never have looked twice at him.

Magic had invaded every part of his life. As much as he had never wanted it, maybe magic was his life.

Terrance kissed him again, slower this time. "I'd ask you to stay, but I know you won't."

"I might have." He knew he wouldn't have. He wanted to go back to his room and untangle what had happened. Maybe he'd have quite happily fucked anyone who'd wanted a bit tonight.

"I like you. But I'm going to run out of things to teach you fast. Your other teacher is better."

Angus looked at the man in bed with him. Saka couldn't help him pass the theory because what Saka taught him wasn't what was being taught. "It might be nice to do stuff that doesn't involve magic."

It might be nice to have a friend. Unless this was just a job for Terrance and he was more interested in Saka than Angus.

"We could do that. Movie?"

Angus nodded and smiled. "Yeah. That would be good."

Terrance was someone who understood what it was like to be caught between the underground and the college. For once Angus wasn't alone.

CHAPTER TWENTY-TWO

SAKA REAPPEARED on the top of Lifeblood Mountain. Mages turned to look.

"Apologies for the interruption. My warlock was rebalancing." Saka held up the vial of shimmering blood, then walked to the blood-stone and tipped Angus's offering down. It would've been nice to stay for longer. He wanted to know who Angus's friend was. There was a tension between the two of them, and while Saka wasn't jealous, he knew not everyone could separate love and sex from sex magic. Humans especially had issues. He faced the gathered mages. "He won't interrupt another meeting."

"How do you know that?" someone said.

"Warlocks can be taught." Saka firmly believed that.

"If you lower yourself to being summoned like an animal."

Saka recognized the speaker as a vampry who wanted blood on the sand.

"There is no shame in teaching the humans or rebalancing the magic that is taken. Perhaps if more of us took that risk, they would have a better understanding." Saka took his seat in the circle. They had been debating what to do next, arguing about drastic action now versus the level slow approach.

An older mage stood. "I have a warlock. I have for many years. He is what they call at college a lecturer, and while he holds firm to their ways, he listens. He refuses to do anything, though, because he has a family to protect."

"Mages shouldn't have family, as it weakens their commitment to the greater tribe."

"We know that. Humans are different." The old mage sat.

Guda stood. "My warlock works at the college and is in the underground. She is trying to make changes from the inside. But where we are equal after our initiation, they have other power structures. It is the people above her who don't want change because they seek to protect their position."

"Can we not remove those warlocks who seek to worsen the damage? Can the humans not do something? Surely they must see what is happening to their own world? Why are they so blind?" The mage spread her hands as though she couldn't understand why anyone would put themselves above an entire world.

Saka stood again. "How can we complain about them when so few of us are willing to take a warlock and teach? We all feel when a warlock is searching for a new demon. Each one of us has the power to answer that call. If we did we could control the flow of magic."

"We could be killed." A mage jumped up. "My warlock has threatened me many times. She wants information. She will ask about this meeting. I would be better dead than betraying those of you who have warlocks. All I can do is make believable mistruths."

"We have said no names," Saka said. He was sure that only Guda and Miniti knew Angus's name. He would have to warn him. "You have not betrayed us yet."

"I will die first, but they keep records of who has what type of demon. They know that there are mages. It is the lower warlocks they keep this information from." The mage who had outed herself as an unwilling traitor sat.

Saka was still standing. He knew there were a few others with warlocks, but none of them would speak now. No one would want a warlock connected to the college as the risk was too high. It was a danger that the warlock a mage took might not be as open as Angus and would use the mage as a spy. Now was the time to offer his idea. There was an alternative.

He glanced at Lox and then Becha. "College warlocks are a danger because they are being misinformed and are afraid of those in power. However, there are plenty of wizards—magic users without demons—in the underground. They would be willing to learn. To come here and learn."

The vampry stood. "And how would they go home... or do they offer their souls?"

This was the two sides, then. Somehow Saka was now speaking for all level demons.

"There is no point in teaching if they do not return to share their knowledge and spread it... but while they are here, I'm sure they would be willing to participate in nonlethal rituals. As for going home, the underground would arrange their retrieval."

"You want to deepen ties with the humans who want to destroy us."

"No, I want to mend the bridge across the void so both worlds survive, and I do not think that the mass slaughter of humans is the way to do it. Human slaves offer a bandage. Taking wizards and training them, here, offers a long-term solution." He hoped it would anyway. If the mages voted against this idea, then the rivers would flow with human blood.

"And the underground would send their wizards? They trust us not to kill them?"

Guda stood. "The underground will send ten wizards on a trial for five days. That means we need ten mages willing to take a human apprentice—not the same as taking a warlock. Many wizards find the idea of needing a demon for magic as weakness."

His old teacher had cleverly phrased it in a way that some would find hard to avoid. Teaching was a duty. He had avoided taking a demon apprentice, but he had taken a human one. As a teacher he was very happy with Angus.

There were a few mutters of disapproval.

Usi stood. Saka swallowed the groan. She would argue against him, he was sure.

"I am the second mage to Saka. I saw his human. I saw the result of the day and night that the human was left here by the unwritten rules. And I saw the oasis that Saka created after spending an evening with his warlock. I told him one oasis wouldn't be enough." There were mutters of agreement. "I am glad that we are getting human slaves, we need them." She paused. "But if Saka can create one oasis after one night with one warlock, perhaps his idea has merit." She shook her head. "Saka and I agree on little, but we both know things have to change." She sat.

That could have been worse. It had been clear that she didn't like agreeing, and that he had a good idea.

"If we give this idea a chance, how long do we wait?" A purple-skinned mage stood and sat just as fast.

It could take years to have full effect. To heal Demonside and remove the taint from the college. But they didn't need years. All he needed was time to prove that the idea worked. The human slaves had bought him that time. "I propose we teach the wizards until the next gathering. It would not be a bad thing to have humans committed to learning and coming to this world on a regular basis."

Conversation swelled.

The vampry mage crossed his arms, not happy with the way this was going. No doubt he'd wanted souls to sacrifice, not teach. Saka stood calmly. On the inside he was tight with anticipation. Now he had to wait while people talked, debated, and tried to find as many flaws as they could in his idea. There were plenty, but he hoped they would see that there were also many benefits.

Eventually the conversation hushed as decisions were reached.

"Before we vote I want to know if we have ten mages willing to risk their life teaching humans." The vampry seemed pretty sure that there wouldn't be.

If anyone stood, they would be identified very quickly as not supporting the vampry's desire for bloodshed.

"Ten would be the start," Saka said. There was no point in hiding the truth. "Unless the ten mages would be willing to take on more than one human apprentice. After all it's not like humans can stay here for the full year while they study. They need to return to their side." Those humans would be trusting that the demons wouldn't kill them. He wasn't sure that Angus trusted him.

"So the mages would be responsible for teaching others too? How many humans will be coming to visit?" The vampry liked this idea less and less. The mages with him were also looking more hostile.

Saka was beginning to feel like he was out on a very fragile branch over a very deep gorge. He'd gone too far to crawl back to safety.

Lox stood. She paused for a moment before speaking. "There is no harm in trying something before resorting to blood. If the humans we train are happy to be used to rebalance while they learn, then I am happy to offer myself as a teacher."

Becha stood. "Only if they agree to rebalance."

"That is what the underground believes." Guda stood again, this time Saka noticed that she didn't spring up as easily as she used to. "The wizards in the underground have refused to take a demon because they disagree with the college. They know magic has a price. Many would love the opportunity to learn here. Are there ten who will teach?"

Lox and Becha remained standing, and another couple of mages followed quickly. Some would be interested in learning more about humans, and that was fine as being a teacher was also a chance to learn.

After a few more heartbeats, there were fifteen mages volunteering. More than enough. If it went well, then others would join in.

The vampry looked unimpressed. "You would waste a year on this? A year while our world dies?"

"You are calling the idea a failure before it has started. Your mind is closed." Saka looked away as though there was no one to argue with. A few of the other mages did the same.

In his push to discredit Saka's idea, the other mage had embarrassed himself by admitting he wasn't even considering the idea. A good mage always looked at both sides before deciding. Sometimes that meant voting in a way that was in the best interest of the greater tribe even though it personally grated. Saka wasn't the only one who didn't like the idea of human slaves but couldn't find another option that provided such a quick fix to a very pressing problem. If his idea went well, then they wouldn't need human slaves for long.

The vampry sat.

A vote was called, and every mage turned around, fists closed or open behind their backs. Saka and another mage counted open hands, open meaning accepted.

Two thirds in favor of a yearlong trial. Next year they would assess both the use of slaves and the training of wizards. Saka sighed and relaxed for the first time that evening.

CHAPTER TWENTY-THREE

Angus didn't expect his father to be so suddenly friendly. They met for tea on campus, and his father asked how it was going with the tutor. It was going very well… although Angus didn't go into details about how well. He was looking forward to going to the movies and pretending that magic didn't exist for a couple of hours. His father wouldn't want to know that. It was unnerving that his father wanted to know anything at all.

"I should get going, or I'll be late for history." Angus picked up his bag.

"You can get the notes. Walk with me." His father stood and headed toward the exit.

It was then Angus noticed the two men who had also been enjoying morning tea had stood. His father hadn't come alone.

The old fear of his father returned like a punch in the gut.

Softly he started drawing magic to him. He didn't know what he was going to do with it, but it seemed like a good idea. If they all summoned demons, he was going to have to run.

"I do need to go to class. I don't want to get behind when I'm just catching up."

"We need to talk about your demon." This time there was no question in his father's voice. That was an order.

Angus crossed calling Saka off his short list of people who would help if things went bad... no they were already bad and getting worse. The warlocks had wanted to kill Saka after he'd snatched Angus the first time, thinking that Angus couldn't control him. They obviously preferred animals to mages. In that moment he knew why.

A mage could spread information that the college didn't want known.

"I have him under control. Everything has been going great." Angus smiled and hoped his father would drop it and move on, even though in his heart Angus knew that his father would never let the issue go.

"Your demon is a dangerous mage. He is a threat to our world."

Your way of using magic.

Angus shrugged. "I don't know what you mean."

"He takes your blood. That is wrong. You know it is." His father turned to face him while the other two men stood nearby. Bodyguards for his father or guards to arrest Angus for not cooperating?

Angus looked his father in the eye. "He has taken no blood."

That was the truth. Angus had freely given his blood to pay for the magic he'd used.

For a moment his father said nothing. "Come to my office, where we can discuss this in private."

"No. I have to go to class." Angus took a step back.

"That was an order, Angus, not an invitation."

The two men drew closer, leaving Angus no choice but to follow or make a scene. If he made a scene, people would ask why, and given that his father was well respected and he was the idiot snatched by a demon, nothing was going to land in his favor.

So Angus followed his father across the road and into the headquarter office. Thick carpet and lots of polished redwood gave it a very opulent feel. Very different to the cheap laminates found in the student areas of the college. Angus had been in here as a kid. Back then he'd been impressed by the high ceilings and the hush as though any noise might distract very busy warlocks from their very important jobs.

The building was still impressive, but the silence was oppressive.

His footsteps were silent on the carpet as he followed. His stomach knotted, and his skin was doing that sweaty, clammy thing. As a kid he'd revered his father. By his early teens, it had become something closer to fear. After being retrieved from Demonside, it was most definitely fear. This man cared more about protecting the college than his son.

His steps faltered, but there was nowhere to run and running would make him look guilty. At the moment there was no proof he'd done anything wrong.

His father opened up the door to a large office. There was a small family photo on the wall, almost lost among the framed certificates and awards.

"Have a seat." His father sat on the other side of the table. He looked at the two men and nodded.

The men who'd followed stepped out of the office and closed the door. Angus guessed they were right outside in the corridor. At least he could talk to his father in private.

"Tell me about your demon."

"He's a red-skinned, common black-horn demon." Angus shrugged. "I'm sure my demonology teacher has told you that. I'm pretty good at using the magic." Angus smiled. "The theory was my weak spot, but that new tutor is starting to make sense. I think." He didn't want to sound as though he knew what he was doing or that he was close to Terrance. He doubted his father would like the idea that the tutor he was paying for had slept with his son in a moment of demon-induced lust. Angus wasn't sure if they were friends and occasional lovers, or if last night had been an aberration brought on by magic. He wasn't sure what he wanted or what would be fair.

If he was tangling with Saka, Terrance deserved better. But then what he had with Saka was just magic. Wasn't it? Didn't he deserve more?

It was all too complicated.

"Show me your arms."

Angus pulled up his sleeves. There wasn't a mark on him. Anywhere, not that he wanted to strip and prove that. "What is this about?"

"I have intel that suggests your demon is far more dangerous than we first thought."

You have no idea. But Saka was only dangerous to the college, not Angus.

Angus frowned. "Really?"

His father sighed. "He took you to Demonside. We were lucky to get you back from them. I don't want it to happen again."

"I don't remember." Would his father tell the truth? He doubted it. If his father was lying, so was he.

"He did something to your mind. It would be best if you summoned him so I can take care of him and you can get a new demon. Something safer."

"You want to kill my demon? What about all that talk about connections made across the void happen for a reason? That the demon revealed a lot about the warlock?" Terrance had tamed a scar-lips with his blood. What did that say about him?

"Your demon is a mage. He probably manipulated it somehow to get a vulnerable warlock. You never even wanted a demon."

Angus managed to contain his shock. His father had listened to Angus for long enough to hear that? "Well, now I have one, and I want to see what magic can do." *And learn how it is abused and how to fix it.* "I want my demon."

"You will get a new one."

"I want to keep the one I have." Angus stood.

"Sit. This meeting isn't over."

Angus remained standing.

His father stood. "This isn't a discussion. You will summon him, and he will be dispatched."

"Why? Are you afraid I'll learn something you don't like? Maybe you just want to kill my demon for the magic."

His father's face blanched, then hardened. It was clear he thought Angus already knew too much. "He has poisoned your mind."

"He has told me the truth that you have tried to hide. You are destroying two worlds for personal power. What do you hope to gain?"

"You have no idea what you are meddling in. Surrender your demon, submit to a mind clean."

"Is that the real reason I don't remember Demonside?"

His father's cheek twitched.

"Give me something... I don't understand why you risk so many lives for magic." *A name, anything.*

"There is more at stake than what you see in the media. Wars aren't fought with guns anymore, Angus."

Angus blinked. He'd heard something a couple of years ago about New Holland experimenting with a unit of battle warlocks. That island in the Southern Ocean was very isolated and secretive. Was his father trying to weaponize magic?

"If the world is iced over and there are no more demons, then it won't matter who can fight the best with magic. There will be no magic."

His father laughed. "You think this is about weapons and wars? There will always be magic. It will be a question of who controls it." He walked around his desk. "Summon your demon."

Angus stepped back. "No."

"His magic won't be wasted."

"His life and his knowledge will."

"Ah... so you have spoken with him. Outside of class? You aren't supposed to be summoning a demon without supervision."

"History has always been one of my better subjects. Until about fifty years ago, there was strict policy of not taking too much magic and of giving a gift to the demon. A rabbit or such. What changed?"

"You are walking on dangerous ground." His father stepped closer.

Angus took a few more steps toward the door. He had no idea what he was going to do when he got there or where he was going to go. Only that the college wasn't safe.

"Are you worried that I'll start talking or that I'll learn too much? This is what you wanted for me. You were the one who insisted that I come to college and study magic when I just wanted to study medicine."

"You can still do that. You can forget all of this. Study medicine if you want. I should never have forced you to become a warlock, despite your obvious talent." His voice was soft, as though he could get Angus to agree by offering what he'd wanted six months ago.

If he'd been allowed to do what he wanted in the first place, he'd have never met Saka or learned about Demonside. He'd lived more in the last month than he had in the last year. He liked magic, and he wanted to find a way to rebalance the magic. That was more important than a magical arms race.

"I don't want to forget."

"You aren't walking out of here until you surrender your demon," his father snapped.

"Then I guess we will be waiting until the world freezes over." That wouldn't be too far in the future. Angus crossed his arms.

"Be sensible. Make this easy on yourself. You are my son... I don't want to hurt you."

Angus looked at his father. "But you would."

Neither man spoke for a moment.

"It would be unfortunate if you were to be snatched again." His father didn't even make the effort to sound like he cared.

"Convenient. Mom would be devastated."

"So don't break her heart. Surrender your demon. Get on with your life and leave being a warlock to those who have the courage to do what needs to be done."

Angus looked at his father. He wasn't sure if his father even liked him or if he was an inconvenience. "It takes no courage to destroy a world, just lies and secrets."

"You value Demonside over Vinland? Demons are tools to be used."

His father had never seen the red sands or the painted tents, heard the singing, or seen the magic created in a ritual. The beauty of

Demonside and demons. "I value both worlds." Not just his country. "No warlock has the power to uncouple the worlds."

"Magic will always flow between the worlds even without demons. The ice will melt, and then only a few will have magic. Think carefully about which side you are choosing. Summon your demon, or you will join him across the void."

"That is a death sentence." There would be no retrieval squad, and if he ended up miles from Saka, another demon would probably kill him. Even if a demon didn't kill him, living in Demonside eventually would. He'd weaken and die.

"Those are your choices. Make the right one."

Angus looked at the man he'd called father and saw no love or concern. If this was how little he cared for his own flesh and blood, then there was no doubt how little he cared for anything or anyone else.

When Angus opened the void, it was to Saka, which meant that when his father opened the void, it would be near his demon. His father had a dragon type, which meant that Angus should arrive somewhere near the gathering.

All he had to do was hope that the demon who found him didn't kill him. How long until Terrance would report him missing to the underground? Perhaps they would attempt a retrieval?

He had no idea, there were so many maybes and ifs that it couldn't really be called a plan, but there was no way he was going to hand over Saka and be part of the damage. Nor did he want his father taking his memories and packing him off to medical school as though Warlock College had never happened.

Angus drew in a breath. "You want me gone. Fine. You will have to push me through the void."

"See reason."

"Like you? A man willing to kill his son for power?"

"This is your last chance." His father's voice rose. Why were the guards not coming in to see what was going on? Or were they there to stop others from coming in and they had known all along what was going to happen?

"You're stalling. How badly do you want my demon?" Angus laughed. "My demon outranks yours. A smart, educated demon will always make for a stronger warlock."

"So you kill him and take his power."

"No. There is no need to kill. Warlocks of old combined self-magic with demonology. They understood the concept of balance. And so do I. So do others. We will bring back the old ways and heal both worlds."

"You are ignorant."

"And you are selfish."

"You are dead to me." His father tore open the void with a swipe of his hand.

Cold swept over Angus's skin. His heart clenched. If he stepped back, death was waiting. He didn't know if he'd be able to survive Demonside a second time.

He glared at his father. "I hope that every time you look at mother, you die a little inside. I hope that the guilt grows like a cancer no magic can cure. I hope your demon eats your tiny heart." There was power behind his words. Not enough for it to be called a hex, but almost. Casting a hex made him responsible for seeing that it happened. He hoped that he lived long enough to have that chance.

His father flinched as if the words had struck him. "Unravel those words."

Angus stepped back, his gaze never leaving his father. His lips didn't open. Another step and his world shimmered as though underwater. His father was saying something, but he couldn't hear him. One more step and there were only murky shadows; hot sun hit his back. He could still run back to the human side of the void. It wasn't too late.

He took a final step, and the void was shimmering blackness in front of him. The tear began shrinking. Angus stepped away just in case someone came charging through.

No one came, and the tear closed.

Angus gasped. He was once again on the wrong side of the void.

There were no tents, just miles and miles of glittering red sand. He turned, looking for a landmark... a sign of life... anything. He lifted his hand to shield his eyes. In the distance was a mountain. In front of that was what he hoped were trees and tents.

He was by himself. But his father's demon must be close by. He wasn't sure he wanted to meet that demon. It probably hated his father. Well, they now had that in common.

What had Saka said about riverwyrms? They hunted individuals, and they didn't like noise?

Angus started singing the first thing that came to mind and clapping, and feeling like an idiot as he walked toward the tents.

The desert made estimating distance hard, and the mountain didn't seem to get any closer. The singing was making his throat dry.

He knew what he'd forgotten about when being all brave in front of his father.

Water.

CHAPTER TWENTY-FOUR

THE HEAT RADIATED up from the sand. Angus wished he could hide in his own shadow. His skin was hot and red. He was burned... and still burning. The sand was in his mouth and up his nose. He was going to die of thirst before the sunburn became a real problem. Was he any closer to the mountain? Possibly. He squinted, trying to work out how far the tents and oasis were. Too far was the short answer.

He glanced behind him to see if he could see how far he'd come, but his footsteps became lost in the heat shimmer over the sand. He blinked. Did the sand just move?

He blinked again and lifted both hands to shade his eyes. The sand rippled closer. He jumped and nearly fell over. His breath lodged in his throat as he realized that it was moving and it was coming toward him.

He started singing again, his throat was raw, and his voice was little more than a croak. It didn't seem to matter, though, as the ripple drew closer, skewing to the side as though circling around.

Fear made his heart pound a heavy rhythm.

Then nothing. The sand stopped moving. Angus tried to run. His legs were heavy, and the sand sucked at his feet. When he clapped his hands, they stung and the noise coming out of his mouth could no longer be called singing.

Wet sand bubbled up a few paces to his left. He veered right. The thing in the sand was chasing him.

Riverwyrm... it had to be.

The ripples swept wide, then drew closer. How big was that thing?

A shadow blocked out the sun for a moment, and swooped lower. Angus ran. He knew he couldn't outrun either of the two things hunting him—and he was sure that they were hunting him—but he wasn't going to stand there and wait for them to reach him. Which would be worse—riverwyrm or the other thing? He glanced up, trying to work out what the other demon was, but the sun was in his eyes. He stumbled.

He stopped even pretending to sing and just started yelling. He didn't care who heard and what they thought. He didn't want to die like this. He would rather give his life to Saka. Die rebalancing after a marathon of sex. That would be memorable, pleasurable. If he had to die here, that was how he wanted it to be. The noise he was making must've put the riverwyrm off as it didn't come closer, but it didn't leave either. It tracked him. Pushing up mounds of sand as it burrowed through.

"Let me die in Saka's bed." He stumbled again, each breath a dry rasp. He forced himself on. If he stopped, the thing in the sand would get him. The shadow formed over him. He wanted to be relieved and to enjoy it, but claws grabbed his shoulders, and hooked under his arms and lifted him off the ground.

Angus gasped and wriggled like a fish on a hook.

"Be still, or I shall drop you into its mouth," the demon snarled.

Angus glanced down at the sand now far enough down that a fall would break him if not kill him. The riverwyrm realized its dinner was on the move and reared up out of the sand. Its scaly brown head covered in whiskers, its mouth wide open and filled with curved teeth. It wasn't big enough to swallow him whole, but it could still grab him and drag him under to drown him in the underground rivers or tear him to pieces on the surface. He had no idea how they fed, but both would be unpleasant ways to die.

He went very still.

The riverwyrm hit the sand and in seconds was gone, burrowing back into the underground rivers. The only sign it had ever been there were the dark ripples in the sand that one could make the mistake of thinking the wind had made.

His heart was beating no slower even though he'd escaped one demon. The painted tents of the tribe loomed closer. Then he was able to make out individual tents… then demons. All looking up to see what the dragon-demon had caught. In graceful circles the demon lowered until it was just above the heads of the onlookers, and then the demon dropped Angus in the center of the village. He landed on his feet, then crumpled to his knees.

When he glanced up, he realized that it was probably best to stay kneeling.

This wasn't Saka's tribe. Did his father's demon belong to this tribe? Had that been who'd saved him?

A blue-skinned demon with white hair stalked over. She crossed her arms and looked at him. "Hmm, you will make a fine gift for Lifeblood when we get there."

Angus tried to speak, but his throat was dry and cracked.

The winged demon who had rescued him stepped forward. She bowed to the mage. "This is my warlock's offspring. I smell him on the boy."

I'm not a boy. But he couldn't speak. He tried to swallow to get some moisture. But there was nothing there. He was going to die of dehydration before anyone killed him.

"All the more reason to kill him. The son can pay for the father's transgressions," the blue mage said. Angus didn't like her at all. The mage stepped closer. "Why are you here?"

Angus touched his throat and hoped that they got the idea. A demon who looked a little like Saka offered water in a wooden cup.

He took it gratefully, lowering his head for a moment in thanks. The first sip reminded him how sweet the water was here. He almost gagged, but right then, he didn't care what it tasted like. He finished the cup and handed it back. He could drink a half a dozen of them and still be thirsty.

"I don't know if you are my father's demon... but he sent me here to die."

That caused a stir.

"He seeks to rebalance?" The blue mage seemed surprised.

No one seemed to believe that. Least of all the winged demon. "It is a trap."

"I know too much about the balancing of magic and what the Warlock College is doing. He wants me dead, so I cause no trouble for him." Angus really wanted another cup of water and to get out of the sun. His skin hurt, but he wasn't sure that he felt hot anymore. Maybe they'd just let him lie down and kill him in his sleep.

He needed to see Saka. Saka wouldn't let them kill him. He looked up and opened his mouth, but the mage was glaring at him. He shut his mouth again.

Silence as the demons all considered this. They looked at their mage.

She stepped closer and squatted in front of him. Her distaste for him was clear in the curl of her lips. "And how would you know anything about magic unless you are also a warlock?"

He probably could have phrased his defense better, but adrenaline and exhaustion and sunburn were making finer thoughts hard to form.

He took a couple of breaths to buy himself a moment to get his words in order. "Mage Saka is my demon."

Conversation erupted again. Some of it was whispers; some of it was shocked gasps.

The blue mage held his gaze. She didn't blink. He did. And he swallowed, then wobbled. He needed another cup of water.

"Saka isn't here. You are mine now," she said. "I'd be doing him a favor and setting him free."

Angus undid the top few buttons of his shirt and pulled it across so she could see the mark. "He marked me. He should decide my fate."

"That matches the mark on the tree," someone said.

The blue mage glanced at the speaker. Her eyes narrowed farther as she considered Angus. Then she looked at the winged demon. "If your warlock wants him dead, perhaps he should live."

"I may be ordered to kill him."

Angus had considered this. Obviously there was no direct kill order. Perhaps his father was counting on the demons wanting blood and not asking any questions. His father wanted someone else to take the blame and do his dirty work.

"Bring him to my tent. I'll try to get Saka on the telestone." The blue mage didn't sound very happy to be having to give up a possible sacrifice, but Saka's mark had saved him... for the moment.

TOWARD DUSK, two winged demons, hunters like his father's demon, arrived to collect him and save him any more of the tribe's hospitality. They had given him water and shade, and he had slept, but he was still unwell. They hadn't wasted any magic on making him feel better. In a hammock slung between them, they flew to Lifeblood Mountain. Angus peered down at the oasis where the tree carved with Saka's mark was.

That was the oasis that his blood had made. Six young trees grew there. One for each cut Saka had made that night. His hand moved to his thigh, even though the cuts were long healed.

He wished that he'd gotten a better look at the oasis. From up here he was able to enjoy the view, and this time he wasn't terrified of dying. The sand stretched on in all directions dotted with oases that had no doubt been brought to life as the tribes had traveled. There were herds of animals wandering around, probably being stalked by scarlips. Was Terrance's scarlips down there somewhere or miles away? How big was this continent? He didn't even know if the demons measured size the way humans did.

He hoped Terrance had realized he was missing and that he hadn't stood him up. His first date since starting college and he was going to blow it.

The mountain drew closer. Even in the growing dark, Angus could see that it was magnificent. There were rivers gushing down its sides, trees, and caves. It was a piece of lushness among the dry and looked quite out of place.

Angus expected them to take him to the tribe's tents, but he was taken to the top of the mountain. He was conspicuously the only human, and it was noticed by every single demon who looked his way. He managed not to fall out of the hammock. Glass orbs were scattered around the flat mountaintop, casting soft yellow light. Demons sat in small groups, talking or they had been talking. Now there were a few murmurs and a lot of staring.

He scanned the group for Saka. He had to be here… unless it had been a trick and this was where they did the sacrifices. A horned demon broke away from his group. Saka? It was hard to tell in the odd lighting. He drew closer. Yes, it was Saka. Angus let a sigh of relief out. If he was going to die, it would at least be pleasant. After the day he'd had, that was as high as he was aiming.

Angus bowed his head, and Saka returned the gesture.

Curious.

Saka thanked the hunters, and they left. They hadn't set foot on the mountain. "This is where the mages meet. It isn't for hunters."

"Or humans?"

Saka's expression said it all. Humans came here but didn't leave. Oh…. Angus looked around. He really didn't have the energy to fight.

"The other tribe didn't hurt you?" Saka knelt so they were eye to eye.

Angus should've gotten up, but he couldn't. Everything hurt. He was sure his skin was getting tighter, and he was burned beneath his clothes. "No."

Saka touched Angus's cheek. Instead of being hot, his fingers were cool. "But they didn't heal you either. How long were you wandering the sands for?"

Angus shrugged, then winced. Mages were still watching them, and some were clearly annoyed by the delay. They scowled or snapped their teeth. Their sneers were not hidden.

"I would like the full story behind your visit, but now isn't the time."

"Will there be another time?" *Am I going to live?*

"There is no need for blood tonight. Well, not all of it. We are making delicate negotiations. Your appearance complicates things."

"You have no idea how complicated it is." His father wanted him dead. The warlocks were somehow gathering and storing magic, but in preparation for what, he wasn't sure. Angus didn't know why, but the result was still the same—no one cared if all the demons died.

Saka considered him for a moment. "I could say the same to you. Things are changing. Promises are being made." He glanced over his shoulder. "To keep it brief. The underground has agreed to send us wizards to train. It was your idea, but I brought your idea to the mages. They voted in favor."

Angus grinned, and his face felt like it was splitting in two. "That's excellent. When wizards start realizing what can be done... together, we'll be able to bring down the college."

Saka gave a single nod, but he wasn't smiling. "Angus, humans who come to these meetings aren't here to join the talks."

He knew enough about demons and magic to read between the lines. "Why have me brought here instead of your tent?"

That was where he'd been hoping to go so he could sleep and drink. He wasn't sure he could eat, but he was starting to feel a little better.

"Because word would have spread that I was keeping a human and not offering him. I can't do that. That is disrespectful to all mages, to Miniti and the greater tribe, meaning all demons."

Angus glanced around the plateau. The blue mage had wanted to sacrifice him. Was this where she would've killed him? "How many have died up here?"

"They were willing. They were sick and dying."

"There were others, though, weren't there? The underground sends traitors." He let out a snort of laughter. "My father sends traitors. Criminals and people who go missing end up here."

Saka nodded. "Be careful bringing human expectations here. You are the reason they agreed to the trial with the underground. You prove that humans can understand."

In other words, keep his mouth closed and accept that people needed to die. They were only dying because the college warlocks kept killing demons and stripping magic from Demonside without caring about the consequences.

"This is all about rebalancing."

"No, it's about magical working, leadership, and direction. We are responsible for the greater tribe. Leaders like Miniti look after only one small tribe."

Yet Miniti had acted as though she was all-powerful. Demon hierarchy was not straight up and down like the college. It was more like an all-encompassing net. It hurt to think too hard about it.

"What magic were you working tonight?"

"We want to lift the rivers around Lifeblood. Focus our efforts instead of spreading them out. The tribes will not roam as far over the coming year. You could join in if you wanted. Show them what one human can do when willing?"

Angus glanced across the gathered mages, then back at Saka. "I'm not able to do any magic tonight. I don't even know if I can stand."

"The sun has drained you that badly?" Saka put his hand on Angus's forehead and made a little noise.

Angus simply nodded. He probably had heat stroke or something. Maybe this was all a hallucination as he lay in a fevered sleep on the sand. Dehydrated and delirious.

"I... um...." He'd rather give a little blood than join in. He was too tired and weak and sore. Angus held out his hand. "If I can borrow a knife, I will give a little blood. But then I need to rest. I can do more another time."

He was on top of the demon's sacred mountain, and they were doing major magic and he was too ill to do anything. He was probably too unskilled to be of any use. They just wanted his blood.... Saka wanted a little more than that. Angus couldn't even get excited about that.

Saka drew a knife and handed it to him. "Do you know what

you're doing?"

"No. But I'm getting used to that feeling." A symbolic sacrifice was all it was. "Where do you want my blood?"

"On the stone. I could do it for you." Saka's touch lingered on his arm. Every time Saka touched him, Angus started to feel a little better. His skin hurt less, and the fear that had been lodged in his gut had shrunk down to nothing. He knew he wasn't safe here, but he felt safe. If Saka was doing some kind of magic on him, Angus wasn't going to stop him.

It was tempting to agree and let Saka do it, but if he was stuck here, the only way he was going to survive was by acting as though he wanted to be here. He wasn't going to be seen as a traitor sent here for execution. He was a warlock—a first-year student to be honest but still a warlock. He knew enough to get by, and he knew more about warlocks and humans than every mage here.

"I can do it."

Hopefully he wouldn't cut anything major.

Angus went to stand, and the mountain swayed. Saka steadied him. Where the demon's fingers clasped his arm, there was a tingle and cold traced under his skin. He could breathe without hurting. The headache had faded, and he felt fine, as though there had been nothing wrong with him all day.

"You aren't healed, but I have taken away the pain and am cooling your body. I will do more later." His horns tipped slightly to the waiting mages.

He got it. Not here. Not now. He didn't care that he was probably bright red and looked half-dead. He couldn't feel a thing. He actually felt excellent, as though being surrounded by the magic was restorative.

Saka released him. "Please don't faint or fall over. I don't want them thinking human warlocks are weak."

"I'll try not to embarrass you." Or get himself killed.

Angus walked toward the stone. The knife was warm after being near Saka's skin. Then he realized Saka hadn't mentioned going home. Was that never going to happen? He'd said that if he was going to die here, he wanted it to be in Saka's bed. That was becoming a very real possibility.

The mages were still watching him. Did they know he was Saka's warlock? How much had been said? If they did, then how he behaved would reflect on Saka. Since Saka was the reason he was alive, it was in his best interest not to screw up.

The stone was as big as a bed, but it angled toward a hole in the middle. Even in the dim light, he could see the dark stains.

Old blood.

Closer he could smell it, metallic and earthy. How deep did that hole go? Did the blood really go all the way into the mountain and feed the world? Was blood spilled here worth more than blood spilled elsewhere?

The hairs on the back of his neck prickled. Far too many demons watched him. He wasn't going to show any nerves. Fear and lust made the blood more powerful. He couldn't manage lust right then, not with everyone watching. Fear, though? Oh, that was there, and he'd got to feel it plenty today. They could have that. The terror of being chased by one of their riverwyrms. His heart beat faster thinking about it. He'd been so close to being lunch. Its teeth had been as long as his hand, big like spades but sharp and curved. His chest tightened. Those things could be anywhere beneath the sand. How did the demons sleep at night? He was never going to be able to sleep here.

He gripped the knife tighter. All eyes were on him now. Saka was watching. He needed to do it now while the fear was still making his heart dance.

Where should he make the cut? He didn't know anything about blood magic. He needed to learn. Maybe he should have let Saka do it. Nope. He was strong, and he wasn't going to let them see him as disposable.

He didn't want to bleed too much. This was a token, a polite offering. He pushed up his sleeve. Saka never cut too deep. How deep was too deep? He wasn't used to cutting. Saka had always done it. Angus drew in a breath. If he thought about it too long, he'd look indecisive. That wouldn't be good form, and it would reflect badly on Saka.

As subtly as he could, he tested the edge on the tip of his finger. Blood welled immediately. The blade was sharper than he'd expected. Before he could think about it much longer, he ran the knife over his forearm. A thin line of red formed, but no blood flowed. The cut wasn't deep enough. He hesitated. This was taking too long.

With gritted teeth he drew the blade slower and deeper down his forearm. It stung, but he kept going. He didn't know how Terrance did it on a regular basis. He didn't know how he either didn't notice or enjoyed it with Saka.

Blood splashed onto the stone and trickled toward the hole in the middle. The dark liquid seemed to catch the light and shimmer, the color darker than when it was fueled by lust. That was the magic he was returning. Barely anything. Saka had said it was about the emotion it contained. The fear he'd summoned had caused that tiny shimmer. He wasn't deathly afraid. Now if the riverwyrm had gotten him, that would've rebalanced quite a bit. In those few moments, he understood why Saka preferred lust to fear. It was more powerful.

He held his arm out for a little longer, then covered the cut with his hand to stem the flow. Apply pressure was basic first aid. If he knew a little about magical healing, he'd have given it a go. But just because he could grow a tree, didn't mean he was able to heal a cut.

Saka took the knife from him, wiped it, and put it away. He didn't heal the cut the way Angus had expected him to. Guess he couldn't stand on his own and then expect help. He lifted his hand away. It wasn't bleeding that badly.

"Your human has come to join our ritual?" one of the mages called out. The tone was almost mocking to Angus's ear.

Perhaps not all were happy about training warlocks. Angus glanced at Saka, knowing that the demon couldn't really say no without losing face. He wasn't going to let Saka take the choice from him. He'd refused to turn Saka over to his father because he believed that rebalancing the magic and saving Demonside were important. Now he had to prove it to everyone.

Angus met the vampry's gaze. "I'm a warlock. I am more than happy to join in your ritual if you think it would be beneficial. Otherwise I will not interfere with your business." Even though Saka had taken the pain from the sunburn and given him the energy to walk, there was no way he had the focus required for magic. When Saka's magic wore away, Angus wanted to be asleep.

Did the demons want a warlock watching, possibly informing, or were they more worried about the rebalancing of the magic his participation would bring? He was an in-bed, one-on-one type of guy. This was a mountaintop with a few humans and a lot of demons. He didn't even want to start counting.

"As a human you are more than welcome," the vampry said.

As a human... It was a bit late to back out now. He wasn't even sure how to do that politely. He glanced at Saka. Saka's face was set and completely blank.

Some mages were never going to let him get off this mountain without joining in. This was a test for him and Saka. It was one he couldn't fail.

He could see why wizards didn't ever want to get a demon. They were trouble. Angus pulled off his shirt. The men, and some of the women, were shirtless anyway. He dropped his shirt on the ground. Now he was just like them.

Except pasty and burned and he knew he was really going to regret this in the morning.

Saka stepped forward. "He is a warlock, my warlock, and will be treated as such. He is not one of the offerings. A formal invitation is required." Saka stared at the couple of mages who had been demanding Angus to join like the other humans.

A dark blue demon spoke. "Warlock Angus would you join us in a ritual to rebalance and raise the rivers around Lifeblood Mountain?" She finished the invitation with a small bow.

Angus glanced at Saka. He really couldn't refuse now. "I would be honored."

What was he agreeing to? The last time he'd been here, rebalancing with Saka, it had been intense, like eleven out of ten intense.

Several of the demons clapped. Guess that meant that he'd been accepted.

The blue demon spoke again. "Prepare yourselves." She gave a pointed look to Saka.

Saka drew in a breath and spoke softly. "That wasn't supposed to happen. You should have offered the blood and been allowed to leave."

"They had other plans."

"They were testing us both." Saka gave him a grim smile. "I don't know if I should be glad that you didn't back down or concerned about what is to come."

"I don't know if I can do it." He looked at his arms. Even in the soft light, he could see how red his skin was. He might not be able to feel the sting of his skin or the throb in his head but it was still there, waiting to pounce.

"It is too late for that now."

"I got that. How long will your magic last?" He didn't want to pass out. Trusting his body to these demons up here—bad idea.

Saka was silent.

"It's just sex, right?"

Saka looked at him. "With all the mages around, the energy will be like bathing in boiling water but with no escape. Once you are in, it is for the duration."

On the other side of the area, demons were untying and stripping down humans who had just arrived. "Are they going to be killed?"

"No, not tonight. They offered to be part of this. You offered."

"Not putting me in the mood." Or reassuring him.

Saka laughed. "You will be. Once the magic is churning around you, you will do things you hadn't thought of. Try not to get dragged off. There are no apprentices here, Angus."

In other words, he was out of his depth. Had he screwed up by accepting the challenge? Maybe he wasn't thinking clearly. "Was there any way I could've walked away?"

Saka considered him for a moment. "Not really. Would you have appreciated me stepping in?"

"No." Maybe. Now he was starting to get worried. Demons were stripping down. "What do I need to know?"

"Relax, sink into it. Say 'too close' if you really can't handle it, and you will be able to have a break… some mages struggle. There is no harm in taking a break and rejoining. Right now, though, get naked. The circle will be raised, and there will be a meditation to assist getting in the right frame of mind."

Nothing said "get in the mood" like naked group meditation. A half bottle of wine wouldn't have gone astray.

Angus put his hand on Saka's arm. "I know it's masked beneath your magic. But I am not well from being in the sun."

"I know." Saka placed his hand over Angus's. "And every time I touch you, I am helping your body cool. You should not be as warm as a demon. Your skin is fragile, but it will not blister. You can't feel the healing, but it is happening. Tomorrow I will do better if you are still sick from being in the sun. Tonight you have to get through this. Perhaps feeling no pain will be a good thing?"

Perhaps getting eaten by the riverwyrm would've been better.

But he didn't say that. Saka was expecting him to put aside what he was feeling—or not feeling—and do a job. How many of the mages were putting aside their doubts and fears and hopes and thinking about what needed to be done? How did anyone get in the mood for sex up here?

He nodded, and Saka released him to get undressed. Angus started to strip. He stared at his arm. The cut didn't look as fresh. Angus finished undressing and put his clothes to one side with Saka's. Then he joined the line of demons as they made a circle and walked the whole way around. Right then all he planned to do was follow Saka. It was all he could do because he had no idea what was going to happen. His stomach knotted, even though he knew he wasn't going to die.

The circle grew with each step. Blue and solid. It shimmered like sunlight on water, but there was a solidity to it that he'd never seen before. They were halfway around before he remembered that he was naked and so was everyone else, even the humans sitting in the center of the circle were watching. Some of them watched him. Angus focused on Saka's back and the play of light over his metallic-looking skin. Bet he never got burned. The sun would bounce right off him.

The circle closed, and as one, the mages and Angus sat. The rocks were still warm from the sun. He shivered, but it was from nerves not the cold. He was glad that he could feel heat and cold again. That had to be a good sign. He glanced sideways at Saka, but Saka was looking straight ahead. His breathing deep and even, lifting his chest.

The mage who seemed to be in charge talked as though expecting everyone to obey and listen. Since Angus was part of the circle, he did. He didn't want a demotion to captive in the middle. It was one thing to know it was done, but another to see them and be acutely aware of what was happening. To be a human on the side of the demons.

Where were his loyalties? Those humans had done something to warrant being sent across, but what? Were they like him, sent across because they'd annoyed the wrong person or had they been plucked out of prison, their life sentences to be served—and shortened—on Demonside?

While he tried to follow the meditation, he kept feeling that he shouldn't be there. Humans didn't join in from this side—was being on this side any different? There was going to be sex, lots of sex. It wouldn't really matter if he were demon or human. Mage or warlock or ordinary. The whole idea was to delay that moment.

Would Saka be begging by the end? It would almost be worth it to see him on his knees and desperate to let go. Saka was so much better at holding back, all the mages would be.

Ah. That's why there were no apprentices here. They were still learning.

He was still learning. He was so out of his depth.

But he didn't have to do anything except stay afloat... then it didn't matter how deep the water was. He could do that. He was more than a little excited to be part of something so big. That, coupled with his uncertainty, made his heart beat faster.

The meditation lost all words. It had become a song without words. Or maybe they were words and he didn't know them. After a while he began to feel the repetition. After a little longer, he found himself murmuring along. The air seemed thicker, his skin warmer.

He was getting hard.

That realization was enough to drop him out of the comfy zone he'd been in. He peeked beneath his lashes and saw a delicate magenta mist roiling over the ground, bubbling around the humans in the middle. They no longer looked concerned. Their eyes were bright with lust. He envied them in that moment. He was still thinking way too much.

He tried to find the song again but couldn't.

Then people were moving. Saka's tail traced up his back. Angus breathed slowly. The magic kept bubbling and swelling and ebbing within the circle. The song was still there but fading as people became caught in the moment and they fell into the magic.

Angus wasn't quite sure what to expect. He saw mages lead a human away and form a cluster, but he couldn't see what was going on because of the mist. Saka kissed him, drawing his attention away from what was going on.

"Stop thinking and relax." The demon's voice was soft. His touch was sure.

This was normal for a mage? He couldn't imagine any warlock ever doing anything like this.

While Angus felt very exposed and too naked, no one else was worried. No one else was even looking, and after a few minutes of Saka's gentle coaxing, Angus had found that place again. The place where the magic was thrumming within him and nothing else mattered.

Right up until someone else touched him. Their hand slid down his back, then along his jaw. Their lips brushed the back of his neck, and Saka pushed him back. Another horned demon caught him, and he landed in her lap. She cupped his face and caressed. Someone else was touching her lips. Angus watched, mesmerized. She wouldn't let him turn his head, but he could feel Saka's touch going lower.

It was still Saka... wasn't it? Panic leapt in his chest, and he tried to sit up. He couldn't. The woman kept caressing Angus, tracing his collarbone. The repeated motion was calming. There was nothing demanding in her touch. His breathing steadied and followed the rhythm of her touch. With each touch it became easier to give in to the magic again.

Saka's tongue flicked along Angus's shaft. He gasped, but there was nothing more. It was all touching and teasing. The woman turned her head to the other mage, kissing him deeply. Angus watched them.

And he grew braver, moving to touch someone he didn't know. When the attention was returned, a shimmer of lust burst through him. They wanted to touch him and see who this warlock was, but they were letting him make that first move.

He found himself caught up in what was happening, or not happening.

Even though no one was having sex, the mist was thickening, and growing darker. Bodies moved through it and vanished into it. Saka was never too far from his side... then Angus stopped looking.

He had fallen into the lull of lust being created.

Different demons felt different to touch. While Saka's skin was silken, some were rough, or scaly. Their lips tasted different. On more than one occasion, he found himself in the arms of a female mage. He'd never even kissed a human woman.

But at the time, it felt right. The demons were more than happy to play with him... he was a novelty. Their touch was kind and curious, much like his. He was hard but not achingly so. He was starting to have an odd kind of fun as the rest of the world ceased existing and he could barely think beyond his next breath.

Then Saka was back with him, pushing him down and moving over him, claiming his mouth and lowering his hips to grind against Angus's. "Things are about to go up. Can you feel the shift in energy?"

Angus blinked and struggled to understand the words. His brain had forgotten what they were for a moment. Now that Saka had said it, he could feel the change. There was a hunger, a need behind each touch.

"Yes."

"Touch will get more personal...." His tongue dipped into Angus's mouth. "I will find you toward the end." His nails skimmed down Angus's chest and lower, to give Angus's shaft a casual stroke.

If Angus hadn't felt the increase in tension before, he did then. He also realized that this was the bit where he was rapidly going to come unstuck and prove how inexperienced he was. Saka glanced up at whomever was behind Angus. Saka might not be with him, but he was keeping an eye on what was happening.

Angus glanced around to see who it was... the horned woman again. She smiled, and her tail flicked out and across his jaw. As he watched she licked along the length of a green cock. He turned over, intending to help her out, but a hand on his stomach, followed by a mouth, and a tongue that licked his belly held him still.

The horned woman grasped Angus's hand with her tail and guided it to her slit. He hesitated, but she didn't release him. He wasn't sure what to do. Now wasn't the time to be fussy. It was about the magic. He could make her want more without wanting her. His finger sank into her, and she eased her legs a little farther apart. Her tail remained around his wrist, guiding him.

His breathing deepened as the mouth on his shaft took him deep. Angus placed his hand on the shoulder of the demon sucking his cock. He needed a moment. The demon understood without Angus saying anything. They didn't want their ritual stuffed up. The mage, a white skinned vampry, moved, and Angus sat up. He eyed the jutting pale shaft for a moment, then gave a mental shrug. He ran his fingers along the narrow shaft, then took it in his mouth.

There were words for people like him on the other side of the void, and none of them were very flattering. The Warlock College would have him thrown out for sleeping with demons, being part of their rituals, and doing sex and blood magic. Now that the thought was there, he stalled. The lust and fun he'd been experiencing fell away. He glanced up.

The vampry smiled but pulled away. A hand landed on his lower back, and he was pushed to his stomach. Someone was on him. He tried to get up; he didn't want to be pinned down.

Lips were by his ear. "Relax... nothing that happens here matters outside of the circle." It was Saka's voice. The tips of his claws were in Angus's shoulders, grounding him in the present.

He took several breaths and tried to concentrate on the way Saka's body pressed against his. The heat of the demon's skin and the length of his hard cock between them. He'd already been thrown out of the college and left for dead. He let those thoughts go. Saka's hold eased.

This time when Angus pushed back, Saka let him turn over. The magenta mist was no longer soft. The mist had become a living thing, crackling as though lit by lightning. He didn't need to be an expert to know what was happening. Every breath he took was laced with the energy and lust, and every exhale contributed.

It was easier to stop fighting and stop thinking. Just breathe it in and be part of it. Tomorrow in daylight he could think and ask questions. He could ponder who he was, what he was becoming, and what that meant.

Saka moved against him, kissed him. *Yes.*

Every touch sparked in the crackling air. The shocks raced through his blood and made his dick throb. Angus didn't remember getting so aroused, but now he wanted release.

Saka sat up, still straddling Angus, and took an offered cock into his mouth as if it were the most natural thing in the world. Angus watched as his demon sucked another. It was desire, not jealousy, that consumed Angus. Without taking his eyes off the display, he reached down and grasped Saka's and his own cock. A shudder ran through him. He had to keep it together for a little longer, but his palm was slick with precome.

The horned woman leaned over and kissed him, distracting him just a little. Angus slid his hand down her body; her skin gleamed in the roiling storm of magic. His finger touched her slit, and then a tongue brushed his fingers—someone else was also playing with her. The magic was becoming too thick for him to see what exactly was going on.

Saka's tail wrapped around Angus's wrist, stopping him.

Angus tried to breathe, but he was drowning in the crackly magic. It was sharp like a storm, no longer soft like a breeze, and it was invading every part of him. The currents passing through him and needling his skin on the inside.

He wanted, no needed, to fuck. And at that moment, he didn't care what or who. The woman tugged his hand away. She lay down on her back and licked her lips. Angus took that as an invitation. He moved, but not far enough. Saka had caught his hips.

The woman slid under him, her tongue brushed the head of his cock. It would be so easy to sink into her mouth. Saka's tongue slid down the crease of Angus's butt as the demon gripped him. Around him, he was aware of moans and sighs, that the woman who was teasing his cock had her legs wrapped around someone else.

A tiny part of his brain warned that this was debauched. The very reason sex magic was frowned on and condemned as being cheap thrills that required no skill.

How wrong the college was.

He could've come a dozen times, if not for someone else being hyper aware of him and his low level of experience, but the time wasn't right. It was getting close now. The magic was changing in feel, in weight and texture, with every breath. Noticing the changes was helping to keep him sane, instead of going under. Did people lose their minds and never find a way out?

It seemed entirely too possible. Who would want to leave such a place when everything—even the digging in of claws—felt good?

Saka pressed the head of his cock against Angus's ass. He pushed back with a groan. That was what he wanted. But there was no frenzied fucking to the finish. Time seemed to slow. His breathing was loud in his ears. He couldn't see his own hands on the ground in front of him. Was something happening to his skin? Every time he blinked, the world seemed to have changed.

Had he died at some point?

Nothing was solid or real. It was too bright, too dark. Every sense was too alert, and then there was nothing until it all rushed back. He turned his head, not sure if he was still upright or if he'd fallen over. Never in his life had he been so disconnected from his body.

He did still have a body?

The world crashed back into him, taking his breath as though he'd slammed into the mountain from a great height. His hips jerked as he came in the mouth below him. Claws dug deep into his butt and thighs. The heat of demon come pumped into him.

He blinked, and all the magic was gone, not a trace of the mist remained. The ground seemed to shudder and sigh. He wanted to collapse, so he did. He rolled to the side and then lay on his back and looked up at the stars.

It took a while before he remembered how to breathe. He lifted his hands. They were still there, and they were still his. They were no longer lost in the magic. He wriggled his fingers. *Fingers.* They mesmerized him as he lay there. He knew he needed to ground himself, but he didn't quite have the will to move more than his fingers. He splayed his hand.

Fascinating.

Then his arm got too heavy to hold so he let it fall to the ground. He breathed deeply and tried to remember exactly what had happened, but there were only vague impressions. He shivered as his skin evoked the sensation of being touched by many all at once. He knew he'd done something he wouldn't usually do.

This whole night was something he couldn't have imagined. He knew that he'd only scratched the surface of what was possible. He'd let others do things to him. He hadn't been in control of anyone—he'd barely been in control of himself. Yet he knew that was a part of it because Saka had kept him on the edge that first time in his tent. From that first cut, there had been no relief until Saka had offered it.

That time he thought he'd try something with Jim had been a weak attempt at something powerful. He was embarrassed even to think about it.

Exhaustion weighed him down. But no one seemed to be in a rush to move. The night was warm. The rocks were warm... there was one digging into the back of his thigh, but it wasn't painful enough for him to move. Not yet anyway.

Saka lay next to him. He had one arm over his eyes, the other on his stomach.

Angus thought about reaching out, but that would require effort and moving. And in his next breath, he realized that he didn't want to be touching anyone. He wanted to be alone.

CHAPTER TWENTY-FIVE

SAKA ROLLED over and moved closer to Angus. After the late night, made later by the walk down the mountain after a short grounding ceremony of water and bread, he had no plans on getting up early. His tent was already lit, the sun was up, and people were going about their business. Tonight the mages would start initiating apprentices. One at a time. This year there were ten. Each would get a night of testing, and then they'd be admitted. The demons would spend the last few days of the gathering doing other rituals, discussing any issues that had come up between the leaders and reassigning mages to different tribes if needed. Or even making new tribes, halving big ones or merging smaller ones.

Today he would take Angus out to look at the rivers they had lifted and to talk. There hadn't been much of that last night. From what he'd gathered, Angus's father had decided that his son was a liability. That meant that his father was afraid.

He liked the idea of the college being afraid since it meant that there was still a chance to turn things around. Ideally the first lot of underground wizards would arrive before the end of the gathering.

Saka turned over again, knowing he wouldn't be able to go back to sleep even though he was tired. Angus was still asleep. It wouldn't be fair to wake him. When they'd reached the tent last night, Saka had continued the healing he'd started on top of the mountain. Angus had been asleep before he'd finished. This morning the warlock's skin was no longer red and painful looking.

Last night when the hunters had delivered Angus, Saka had thought Angus too far gone, but apparently, humans were more resilient than they looked. That would be a good thing to keep in mind when training them.

After a few more moments of deliberation, Saka got up. He'd wash and get something to eat. By the time he got back, hopefully Angus would be awake. Hopefully no one would pull Saka away and distract him with duty when he wanted some personal time.

Many people in the tribe heard that Angus was back. Some wanted to know for how long. Saka had no idea. The unspoken question was how was he going to get home? But no one was rude enough to ask.

If he had to, Saka would send him to Guda so she could return him to the right side of the void. However, that was a dilemma for another day.

Miniti stopped him in the market. "Your warlock is back."

"He is. I have yet to get the full reason, but it seems his father didn't like Angus supporting Demonside."

Miniti flicked her hand. "Who cares what his father thinks. What about his mother?"

Most demons knew who their father was, but it wasn't an issue and they had very little impact. A woman's child was a child of the tribe. "She isn't a warlock. Humans have a different structure. They mate for life."

"How odd. So the father is in charge? How does he know that the child is his?"

Saka shrugged. "I don't pretend to understand."

Miniti frowned. "I am glad Angus is here. There has been much talk already."

"So I have gathered."

"Will you be teaching him while he is here? He is the first warlock apprentice after all." Miniti was thinking how Angus could lift the status of the tribe. As long as Saka's plan worked, everything would be fine. If Demonside dried up, Saka would find himself attached to a post in the desert, waiting for death.

He'd been thinking of returning Angus as quickly as possible, but maybe it was better that he stay awhile. Saka could call him an apprentice. The trouble would be getting the scattered human apprentices home before they started to weaken or died. That was something they still needed to discuss.

"Yes. I will teach him some more. The humans need to learn."

"Be careful they do not learn enough to destroy us." She turned and swept away, her red dress brushing the sand behind her.

He wasn't off the hook yet. He'd be dangling for the next year. He had to believe that he was doing the right thing and that humans could be civilized and not selfish. Maybe Angus was the only good one.

Or Angus was his father's spy and this was all an elaborate plot.

He made his way back to his tent. The ground beneath his feet was still cool and in shadow. Later the sun would hit their tents. The lesser tribes spent the afternoon in shadow and experienced an early dark.

Saka flicked back the flap and stopped. Angus was up and dressed, but only in his pants. He was sipping water and looking at the knives that Saka vaguely remembered leaving on the table. Trekking down the mountain each night made for a very long day. Considering he'd slept most of the morning away, he couldn't really complain. After midday they'd start the walk up.

How would Angus fare with his soft feet and delicate skin?

"You slept well?" Saka put the nut cake on the table.

"Yes." There were faint scratches still visible on Angus's back.

"I should make sure you are fully healed." He had done as much as he'd dared on a sleeping patient. There was still an open wound on Angus's arm. Saka had been concentrating on taking the heat out of Angus's skin.

Angus glanced at him. "I'm… tired."

"I didn't ask for anything. But better I check it now than when you have a fever and the rot is spreading up your arm."

"When you put it like that." Angus walked over and held out his arm.

Both cuts needed cleaning. The deeper one should be healed fully. "You need to learn how to handle a knife."

Angus winced. "It's not my thing."

"If you are going to continue to associate with demons, it would behoove you to learn how not to kill yourself or others if asked to draw blood." He didn't release Angus's hand. "Bathe and eat, and then we shall talk and I shall heal the cut."

Angus looked at him. "I know there is a chance I won't be going home."

"I don't believe that. The underground will make sure you are retrieved. They are sending wizards for training, and it is something that needs to be addressed." Angus would be fine, but it also meant he could come back with the underground.

"If I go home, I will be a known rogue warlock. My name will be on police bulletins." Angus looked away. "I'm here because I refused to summon you so my father could kill you. He knew you were a mage. Someone here has been informing the college of what is going on."

"That someone will also know you are still alive and participated last night." Saka knew which mage it was. She was in a bind. Perhaps it would be best to kill her warlock, although it was useful to have mages who could report back on college activities.

"I'm screwed. I go home and I'm on Vinland's most wanted list. I stay here and I wind up dead even if I don't get killed."

"No one is going to kill you." Saka put his arm around Angus. For a moment the warlock's body was rigid, as though he didn't want to be touched. Had he been broken last night? Some humans wandered from their body and never came back. Others developed a fear of being touched. Even some mages struggled with what happened.

Angus sighed and leaned in, but his body was still tense. "I'm not safe until my father and the people he works for are stopped. Demon-side isn't safe. They want it dead so no one can have magic except what they have stored."

"How are they storing it?"

"I don't know. He didn't exactly reveal the details of his plan before tossing me through the void. Actually I chose to walk through. I didn't want to give him the satisfaction."

Just like last night. Angus had given the blood himself and offered to join in if they'd thought him worthy. Had he been there as a human or a warlock? It was something else to consider because if the mages accepted Angus as a magic user, then he wasn't really an apprentice. Apprentices weren't allowed up the mountain except for when they first took their oath to learn and then again when they were tested.

"Better to make your own choices even when your hand is forced?" Saka's hand glided over Angus's bare back. He was out of lust, but that didn't mean that he didn't like the contact.

"Something like that."

A silence formed. Saka didn't want to be the one who broke it, but he could feel the last remains of the morning sliding away and there were things that needed to be done and conversations that needed to be had. He lingered for a little longer, not wanting to be the one who pulled away. He had missed Angus. He liked talking magic and sharing what he knew. Perhaps Guda was right and it was an apprentice that he craved.

"What is this?" Angus said finally as he drew back enough that he could meet Saka's gaze.

"What?"

"Between us? I've never had a boyfriend... lover... who would quite happily watch me be with someone else. Or is there nothing and I am reading this wrong?"

"Ritual is always separate."

The frown didn't leave Angus's face. "I had sex with Terrance."

The tiniest bit of jealousy spiked in his blood. Saka didn't like the feel of it. It was jagged and caught on every thought. That affair hadn't been magic related.

When Saka didn't reply, Angus pulled away. "If I'm just a means to rebalance for you, that is fine. But I want to know."

Ah, now he saw the problem. Saka could've been equally wounded and cried that he was just a conduit for magic and that Angus was using him, but this wasn't about magic as much as it was Angus feeling cut off, alone and unsure of the ground he was standing on.

"No, you are more. You are my apprentice, my friend. I would be lying if I said I did not enjoy your company. When you first came here, you opened yourself up to the experience, and I admire that. You have also saved my life by coming here instead of summoning me. We can save Demonside and your world." With others. "We will always have a connection that no one else will have."

"So you don't care?"

"I care about you. Not who you are with. If you were to start getting close to another mage, we would have problems, because you are mine."

"Except for during rituals." Angus crossed his arms.

Saka was still not getting what Angus wanted. "Yes. If I had thought that you would be hurt or that you wouldn't be able to handle it, I would have said something. I would have lived with that. While you are here, you are my responsibility." As he looked at the human man, he began to wonder if he had let Angus go too far too soon. "Maybe you weren't ready for last night."

"I'm fine."

"Physically. But not here." Saka tapped his chest and then his head. "Or here."

Angus rubbed a hand over his face, then stopped to look at his fingers. He frowned. There was dried blood around his nails. He winced as though the memory hurt, then looked at the wound on his arm. "I'm going to clean up."

"I will wait to eat with you."

Angus groaned. "Why do you treat me like a lover when I'm here?"

"You are my warlock, my guest, and my lover, but I don't mind if you have human lovers. Would you be upset if I had a demon lover?"

"I don't know...." But Angus nodded.

And that was the problem. "Humans only have one at a time."

"Yes."

Saka thought for a moment. "Well, you have one in Demonside and another across the void. When I get another lover, they will not mind that I also have a human lover. With more mages taking on underground wizards, it will become something that has to be adapted to. It's not a normal teacher-apprentice relationship."

"What is normal?"

"When you are here, that is normal. We eat together, talk. Everything is a possible teaching moment. There are no set lessons or times. Those who want to learn sex magic need to practice." Saka smiled. "An apprentice may be tested when it is agreed they are ready. You will have to get used to living on both sides of the void if you want to study magic here."

"You are assuming I am going home." Angus walked out of the tent.

For a moment Saka was tempted to go after him to show him where the showers were, but he didn't. Angus could ask for directions. He needed to be able to make his way around the tribe's area without getting lost like a child that should still be living on Lifeblood Mountain. More importantly the tribe needed to see Angus as someone with standing despite being human.

The keeping of human slaves wouldn't help that change in perspective.

One human was valuable and the other was something to be used. How should they differentiate?

Another point to ponder.

IT WAS three days later when the underground opened up the void. Saka had been spending the morning teaching Angus how to use a knife safely—there was a long way to go—and also a bit more about the history of Demonside and warlocks from the demons' point of view. They had also been walking along the rivers, watching, and encouraging the growth. There was no point in wasting the blood spilled during knife training.

The mages allowed Angus up the mountain to watch the testing and initiation of new mages. He'd managed the walk without trouble. On the surface Angus seemed fine, but there was still something lurking beneath. It was there when they were in bed, when they kissed.

He'd also started holding back, as though he were afraid of making mistakes. That was never a good thing. Better to make the mistake and learn.

Saka paused. They had been heading back to the tribe to get ready for the trek up Lifeblood, but Guda was coming toward them.

Saka started walking a little quicker, and Angus followed. He bowed when he reached his old teacher. "You've come a long way."

"I was told you were out here." Her mouth opened in a smile. "This is how I remember Demonside as a child."

"You always said to not to waste an offering." That was even more true. Everything that could be gained out of a single drop had to be poured back into Demonside. It was also pleasant to sit under trees and watch them grow as Angus learned. There was the added important point of being seen.

Angus hung back, as though he wasn't sure he should be part of the conversation.

"Step forward, warlock. Do not hide behind your demon," Guda said with concern in her voice.

"Sorry." Angus took a few steps forward.

Guda fixed Saka with such a glare he felt like he'd made a major mistake. Guda put her hand on Angus's shoulder and led him far enough away that, while Saka had no idea what they were saying, he knew it was about him. Did Guda think he was hurting Angus?

Saka was horrified at the idea. Did everyone see the warlock's melancholy and blame him?

Guda laughed, and Angus gave her a fragile smile. It was the first one Saka had seen in days. She beckoned Saka to join them—he knew there would be words later.

"I have been in contact with the underground. Terrance reported Angus missing almost straight away. Ellis needed to be very careful about what she did next. Since we have been talking about the trainees—that's what the underground is calling them—I also let her know that Angus was with us and very much alive. You can go home tomorrow if you want. They will be opening the void at dawn, and ten wizards are going to get mages."

"Have you worked out how to get them home when they are scattered?" Saka was really asking on Angus's behalf.

"No. We may have to leave ten mages here. More debate tonight." She lifted her hands as though she was over it already. Saka knew she loved the debates.

Both demons turned to Angus. It would probably be best if he went home. His heart wasn't in it at the moment. But he had no home anymore. He was a hunted outcast.

Angus looked at his toes as they dug into the sand. "I don't know... I like seeing the magic and learning. I want to learn how to heal... I've always wanted that."

"You cannot rush learning," Guda said.

"You can always come back." Saka smiled. Angus didn't return it. There was that something.

"You want me gone." Angus looked down.

"Do you want to be here? I can feel something isn't right." Saka couldn't fix whatever was going on. Angus had to work through it.

"I want to be here, but people watch me. They are waiting for me to make a mistake. I don't want to embarrass you. I've heard how hard you pushed to stop the bloodshed. I also know you voted for human slaves."

"Almost everyone did. We had to, or we would all be dead before the next gathering. That is how desperate things are." Saka thought that they had been around this argument already. It wasn't ideal, but it was a temporary solution.

"The humans will be well looked after. Either the underground or the college gave them to us. We haven't taken any." Guda's voice was level and firm.

"I know. But you are keeping them like, like cattle for blood and soul but also for sex." He grimaced and half turned away. Then he shook his head. "What would you say... the idea isn't ready to be shared? I shouldn't have said anything until I had the words?"

Saka wanted to reach out but didn't. Angus didn't need to say anymore. He understood what the problem was. And why Angus had been so withdrawn. He'd been attending the meetings on Lifeblood and hearing the inner workings of the tribes as they talked about humans for the most part, as if they were an annoyance or something to study. Some mages had volunteered to teach to satisfy their own curiosity.

"You think your position can change in a blink, and you are unsure of your status. That is my fault for not making it clear." Saka glanced at Guda, but she was staying silent. This was his mess to fix; the teacher never stopped learning.

"You, and any warlock or wizard training with us, would be considered an apprentice. Here, becoming a mage isn't something to take lightly as it means always putting the tribe first. I volunteered to get a warlock because of the strife Demonside was in. I knew the dangers. But I got you, someone who saw and understood. Who knew already that something wasn't right. Your use of magic gives you status, and no one can take that away." He put his hand on Angus's lower back. "You are more than blood or sex. You are a friend."

"I want to believe that… and I know we have to work together. I like working together. Is that wrong that I like it?" Angus was frowning. He'd gained more freckles since living here, but he'd also changed. There was a hardness in his eyes that had been missing the first time they'd met.

"No. It would be wrong if you didn't and yet I made you participate. That is why demons have specialties. Did you notice that not all had sex? Many won't kill. I don't like to."

"But you do."

Saka nodded. "I have done. And will do it again. Until the magic is rebalanced, there will be more death. There will be blood rituals based on fear, not desire. I choose not to be part of them. But that is the fate of those sent to us."

"I was sent to you by the college." Angus's voice was flat.

Saka stepped back as he realized the full implication of those few words. "That is a very good point." He turned to Guda. "We need to

217

evaluate the people who get sent to us by the college, who we take as slaves."

"Some are criminals," she cautioned.

"I am a criminal in the eyes of the college," Angus said.

Saka was silent for a moment. They had always taken the humans sent across without asking because they needed to rebalance. "We will have to raise it tonight."

"I concur. Thank you for raising the issue, Angus. You see the human nuance we don't." Guda inclined her head. With every passing day, Angus was gaining respect from the other demons. In part that was because of his unflinching resolve to be part of the rituals, not as a victim but as a warlock... a mage.

Angus managed another weak smile. "I want to go home, but I also want to stay."

"I would like you to stay." He liked having Angus around, but he knew this wasn't the warlock's home. It couldn't be. Demonside would slowly drain him.

"Go home for the day, but be back by dusk so you don't miss a meeting. Then you can go home with the underground trainees after their first six days of training," Guda suggested.

Saka hoped Angus would come back.

Angus nodded. "I'll do that. But I don't know what I'm going home to."

CHAPTER TWENTY-SIX

ANGUS HAD SPENT the rest of the day with Saka. While his future was uncertain, he felt more settled. His place in Demonside wasn't as precarious as he'd thought. When they were alone, when Saka was explaining some detail of demon culture that Angus had overlooked or hadn't realized had so much meaning, there were the little touches again. They had stopped after the orgy.

But perhaps that had been because he had pulled away. Unsure about his own feelings about that night.

He was still a little unsure.

He had feelings for Saka that he wasn't sure he could voice or that could be returned. People didn't marry and make families here. Yet there seemed to be couples. And Saka had plainly said that ritual was a separate thing. He probably shouldn't feel anything at all for Saka, but it was hard when Saka was smiling at him and they were sharing a bed. Had he ever been so close to anyone?

Angus had spent most of the night on Lifeblood mulling over his own thoughts and dilemmas, not really listening to the mages speak. Watching an apprentice fail had been shocking. And more than a little terrifying. That could be him, eventually. He'd leaned forward, wondering what would happen to the apprentice mage.

He wasn't the only person to be shocked. Many of the mages were equally stunned. Then the teacher had apologized for failing the student.

Angus couldn't imagine one of his warlock lecturers ever doing that. They didn't even like to be questioned.

Mages seemed to like being questioned. They liked debating, even if no agreement was reached. The sharing of knowledge and skills was prized. It was why he was sitting here. He knew he'd have failed any test they gave him. He wasn't worthy to be in the circle, so he sat outside it, answering questions thrown his way about the way humans used magic or the way they lived or whatever random thing they deemed it necessary to know.

The sky was turning gray, and he was fighting not to yawn. The mages were standing up and stretching, the official part was over. Many would leave now to trek down the mountain, but some would stay to see the wizards get their mages. Some mages wondered if teaching humans would be successful.

Saka put his hand on his leg. "I will miss you while you are gone."

Angus put his hand over Saka's. "I'll miss you too." There was more that he wanted to say, but here wasn't place. "I have made another decision."

Saka's eyes widened.

"I don't belong up here with the mages. When I come back, I will be a trainee like the others." That would take the pressure off him, so he didn't feel the need to not screw up and make Saka look bad.

"No one here would make you leave."

"But some would be thinking it." He'd rather not have people eagerly waiting for him to prove himself unworthy.

"They wouldn't say it. Your participation in raising the rivers guaranteed that."

Angus nodded. "I know. That was the best choice I could make at the time. I don't regret it, but I don't think I was ready either. You know that."

Saka glanced down and didn't say anything.

"I don't blame you." He didn't want Saka thinking that he was failing as a teacher. "I would make the same choice again. How do I back down without causing offense or trouble for you?"

"Are you sure that is what you want? Because the next time you come up here, it would have to be for initiation."

Angus had thought about that too, particularly after watching tonight's failure. "Yes."

Saka nodded. "I understand your reasons. I would rather you be happy than stressed."

Angus leaned over and embraced him. "I will try not to be jealous when you come up here for rituals."

"And I when you are across the void." Saka kissed him. "You will need to stand and declare your intention. We will vote in your absence as would be correct. You wouldn't be the first mage to want to step down."

"I'm not a mage." He would always be a warlock.

"You are where it counts." Saka touched Angus's chest.

For a heartbeat Angus wanted Saka to talk him out of it, but he didn't. Saka knew that he was undertrained. That he hadn't been ready for the role that had been thrust at him.

Saka stood and tugged Angus up. "You will have to pick a specialty of course."

"I already have." He smiled. He also knew that if he was going to be properly trained as a mage he would have to learn to kill and cut even if he didn't want to use those skills. In the underground he might need to kill to survive.

Saka led him over to a knot of mages. There were a few nods of acknowledgment. Angus told them that he was going home for a day and night and would come back as a trainee where he belonged. That got bows for him and Saka. Claims of rare wisdom for a human. That they would visit him at his tribe if they needed to speak with him. That they would miss him on the night of the final ritual.

Of course they would. A willing warlock could rebalance a whole lot of energy when aroused. Angus blushed, and Saka put his arm around Angus's shoulder in a casual display of ownership. No one would be getting near him without Saka's permission, and Saka didn't volunteer him for the ritual.

Maybe next year. There would come a time when he'd have to be ready to practice. How did apprentices practice for that kind of thing? Mages must do smaller rituals all the time.

As Saka had said, the mages would vote that night.

When the void opened in front of Guda, Angus didn't know if his eyes were prickling with tears at leaving Demonside or because he was going home, knowing that his father had tried to kill him and had very nearly been successful.

The ten mages that had volunteered stepped up. They stood still as they waited.

Guda beckoned him forward.

Angus released Saka's hand and approached.

"I look forward to your return," she said.

Angus nodded. He took a final glance at Saka and then crossed the void.

In a large room, there were the ten underground wizards, including Jim and Lizzie.

There were several masked people too. College Warlocks who were part of the underground? He was sure one would be Ellis.

"Hi." Angus smiled.

The wizards gave him nervous smiles.

"The mages are ready."

The wizards were still staring at him. They'd volunteered for this, and yet they still looked anxious.

"Angus, we're glad you're alive. We'll talk later. You know the mages who have volunteered?" one of the masked warlocks said.

He nodded. He had spoken at length with them while the other mages had listened, often asking their own questions. Others were now interested in the process, but this was a trial.

"When you are ready, cross the void. We will open it for you in six days," another masked warlock said to the waiting wizards.

The young wizards were putting their faith in that promise. They were all hoping to live. Angus had always gone to Demonside expecting to die. That he was still alive was a pleasant surprise.

One by one the wizards stepped across. Angus would join them in the morning—as a trainee and not on Lifeblood. The void closed. Angus hoped the trainees knew what they were getting into. It wasn't like going to college. It wasn't like anything he'd ever done before.

Then it was just Angus and the masked warlocks. There was a shift of attention, a sharpening of intent. Maybe he should've stayed in Demonside.

"You look well."

He'd been getting less burned and more brown, although that could be his freckles joining. He was dressed in demon-style pants and shirt with bare feet. The room was chilly. "I am well. I needed to come back. What is the maximum time that it is safe to stay across the void?"

A woman shrugged. "There is no firm data. We're hoping to determine that over this yearlong trial."

"Your father knows you are alive," said another warlock.

"The mages know that there is a spy among them." They knew who it was too. The demon had offered to die, but that was vetoed. It was better to know. "My father won't know that I'm here. I want to see my mother before I go back. I want to continue my training over there."

"Guda has said that is what they would like too. You have left an impression."

His cheeks burned. He hoped Guda had left out the naked bits.

One of the warlocks nodded. "You can see your mother."

He hadn't been asking for permission.

"You should know that your name and picture have been issued to the police. You are a rogue warlock, in league with demons."

"I expected that." But it still hurt far more than any of the cuts Saka had made on his skin. It meant that seeing his mother would be that much more dangerous.

There was a pause before the woman who seemed to be in charge spoke. "To prove your commitment to the underground, we would like you to banish your father."

Angus blinked. Demonside had taught him to keep his mouth closed until he'd figured out what to say. "The college will retrieve him."

"Will they? Or will he be killed on the spot?"

When the mages knew who he was, they'd question him and let his blood coat the bloodstone. They would use fear to rebalance the magic that he had stolen. They could learn the names of those who were corrupting magic. But could he send his father to his death?

"He's still my father."

"Who sent you to die without a backward glance. Who, on learning that you survived, turned your name over to the police."

Angus stared at the floor. That was true. Why should he protect his father?

What if the killing of demons went higher than his father? Maybe it was a department of defense project. How would they ever stop that if it was government sanctioned?

One step at a time, that was how. Making sure that magic was rebalanced. Training others, supporting the underground.

"Your father went after your associates when he learned you were alive." The speaker motioned to another masked figure by the door. Someone was let in.

Terrance. He'd obviously been beaten. Angus was halfway across the room before he stopped to think that maybe Terrance didn't want to see him because he was the cause of the problem. He shouldn't have worried.

Terrance put his arms around him. "I'm so glad you're alive. That bastard. He's going to pay."

"What happened to you?"

"He and a couple of friends wanted to know what we'd been doing. I told them that we were either studying or fucking. It was almost the truth. I don't think he believed me, but there wasn't much else he could do. My demon can't talk so that got them nowhere." His lips turned down. "They killed Aqua."

"I'm sorry." She might have been a scarlips, but she'd been friendly and she'd been Terrance's demon for three years. They'd had a connection.

"They saw the cuts I made to feed her, and I got kicked out of college."

"This is my fault...." Angus stopped. It wasn't his fault. "This is my father's doing." He frowned and drew back. Someone had healed Terrance, but there were still small cuts and bruising. The underground wanted him to see what his father was capable of. Did they realize that they were just as bad in banishing his father across the void?

Angus turned back to the masked warlocks. "If you take my father, they will close ranks."

And the battle would really begin, and those warlocks involved had been storing magic.

"We know. But if we apply pressure, they will start to make mistakes."

"Perhaps there will be an opening for one of us to fill," a masked warlock said.

These warlocks had obviously been thinking about this and had worked out every possible answer. "And what about the storing of magic?"

"We are investigating. This is bigger than Vinland."

Was the underground really global? How many magic users were there? Angus knew some countries banned all magic, and it was a criminal offense to practice. They called it demon worship. Some believed in a god and priests working miracles instead of calling it magic.

Now that he was home, all he wanted to do was eat and sleep. He'd been up all night. Terrance's arms were warm around him. It would be easy to lie down with him and forget about everything else that was going on.

He closed his eyes for a moment. But only a moment, in case he didn't open them again and fell asleep on his feet. "And if I refuse to send my father over?"

"We will not be able to protect you from the police." The warlock's voice remained even, but the threat was clear.

If he didn't agree to send his father to Demonside, the underground would turn him over to the police. The underground would keep working, trying to stop the college and rebalance the magic. Someone else would send his father across. And Angus would rot in jail—they wouldn't risk sending him to Demonside as a sacrifice.

Ever since this had begun, the only person who had asked what he'd wanted... or had even worried about his happiness was Saka. A demon. Someone he wasn't supposed to care about.

What did Angus want?

Not to be rotting in prison.

In Demonside he had a place and a purpose, even if it was only rebalancing magic and learning. That was what he wanted. To know the intricacies that humans had forgotten or had banned. He wanted to stop the ice age and save Demonside. He wanted Saka when he was there. Terrance hadn't let him go. He was familiar and strong. Angus was torn between two worlds.

But he had to have a place here, to be able to come back and forth.

Terrance drew back. "Angus? They won't help you if you don't help them."

"I know." He understood Saka's hesitation when it came to killing. It was a weight that had to be lived with, even though he wouldn't be holding the knife. "Would you be able to do it? Would you be able to look at me if I had readily agreed?"

Terrance lowered his gaze. His embrace loosened. "He wanted to kill you."

"I know." But he wasn't angry. He was hurt. Lashing out as his father wouldn't heal that wound. Only time would. Maybe. Unraveling his father's destructive work would help. "I will do it," he said loud enough for the warlocks to hear. "But I need to rest first."

One of the masked warlocks nodded. "You can have six hours. Then we will take you to your mother's house. I am sure that it won't take long for your father to show up."

They had planned this, no doubt from the moment that they'd

discovered that he was alive.

Terrance showed him to a small bedroom with an even smaller bathroom. He had no idea where he was. He actually didn't care. It was obviously a building that was used by the underground, and they were used to having people stay.

Terrance stood in the doorway. "I can go."

"Stay." He might not want to stay later when he realized what was actually going on. Angus wasn't sure that he wanted to have that conversation now, but if he didn't, then it would be on his mind, and he didn't know when there would be another chance.

It was clear that something had to be said from the way Terrance had reacted when he'd seen Angus. The way Angus had reacted. He liked Terrance. He didn't want to see him get hurt. Although after looking at the fading bruises, that was already too late.

The room filled with silence.

Angus didn't know what to say. "I'm sorry that knowing me has caused you grief."

"I chose the underground… meeting you was a result of that. I had hoped to finish college, though." Terrance shrugged. "I knew the risks."

"You didn't volunteer for the training?"

"No. I'm not ready for another demon. I don't know if I will be." He leaned against the door, arms folded. "Certainly not a mage."

Angus studied the mottled blue carpet. "You can learn a lot from the mages."

"I can see that. You're different this time."

"Frecklier?" Could Terrance tell what he'd been up to?

Terrance gave him a half smile. "That too. I saw the way Saka was with you, and I knew that wasn't what I wanted. I would've been happy being a wizard, but I got a scholarship to play rugby. The kind of magic you do isn't for everyone. Maybe the college needs to screen people better. Then we wouldn't be in this mess."

Not everyone who had the ability should be encouraged. Saka had said mages had to put the greater tribe before themselves. The warlocks in charge were putting themselves first.

"True." Angus paused. "I plan on going back to Demonside."

"I know. You stood me up."

"Yeah." And he felt bad about that. "I wanted to be there."

Terrance nodded. "Do you love him? The demon?"

Angus frowned. "I don't know. I feel like I'm trying to live two lives at the same time. No matter where I am, I'm letting someone down. Or hurting someone."

"Does he love you?"

"I don't even know if that is possible. Demons have a different society. I guess they do love. They seem to care more about each other than humans do. He has to look after me because I am his student. I thought of you while I was there." His toes curled against the carpet. "Maybe I shouldn't be starting anything with anyone. Magic will come first. It has to come first." He sounded just like a mage. The realization didn't make him smile. "I can be honest with you, but never faithful. I can't promise to be around when you want me. But I can't walk away either and say that I don't want to see what happens."

Terrance deserved better.

"I could feel what is between you and your mage like static."

He was glad that he didn't have to admit to the orgy. Terrance might be able to accept that he occasionally slept with one demon... but many? "It's...." He still wasn't sure what it was. "It's a relationship but not like the ones on this side of the void."

Terrance held his gaze for a moment and then looked away. "You don't need to dabble with a human. And now you don't need to worry about passing your exams...."

Angus shook his head. No, the exam he would have to pass in Demonside would eclipse anything the college wanted. "I want more than rituals and magic. I need something that doesn't have a bigger purpose. That just is. But I can't ask that of you or anyone because I wouldn't want to date me."

Terrance held his gaze. "You could've lied about everything, and I wouldn't have known."

"You would've suspected, and that would've been worse. I'm giving you an out. We never got that first date. We were just seeing what might happen." Angus still wanted to know what might have happened. They had talked magic, about movies and normal stuff. There had been simple lust that could be acted on without any elaboration or requirement.

"I'd still like that chance... I don't know how I feel knowing that when you're over there you're intimate with him."

Saying it was just ritual wasn't going to mean anything. That Saka had admitted he got jealous had shifted what was happening. Was it just ritual? They kissed outside of magic. There had been moments when it seemed like more. But every time they slept together in Demonside, Angus was aware that magic was being rebalanced—it was hard to ignore when the room lit up.

If they dated, Terrance would get hurt. "Run and don't look back." It was the best advice Angus had for Terrance.

Terrance shook his head. "No. I still want that first date. I want to know what would've happened. I don't want to run. But a lot has happened and I need to process."

"Yeah. Maybe after I've seen my mother, we can get some takeout and watch TV." Something completely normal. His life was never going to be normal. He could see that, and he didn't know how to deal with it. He didn't even know what he was going to say to his mother. Sorry wasn't right because he wasn't sorry about what was happening. He was sorry about the hurt he was causing her, though, and *would* cause her when he sent his father across the void. He wasn't sure he could do that. He obviously wasn't the same as his father.

"That sound's good. You look tired."

"I was up all night." As the words left his mouth, he knew what it sounded like, even though that hadn't happened. He wanted to explain, but he saw the look on Terrance's face.

It was better that he just shut up and let Terrance sort out how he was feeling.

Angus had no idea how he was feeling. Was he trying to hold on to the almost nothing he had with Terrance because he was desperately seeking a reason to come back here?

Mages didn't have family; the whole tribe was their family. But he

TJ NICHOLS

wasn't a mage. Or a demon. He was human, and he didn't want to be alone with just his magic and studies.

"I'm going to go." Terrance took a step back. "I'll see if there's any winter clothes around for you."

Angus wanted to ask him to stay, but that wouldn't be fair. He watched him leave the room. Angus closed the door with a click. In another life he'd have been dating Terrance to see if there was something worth exploring. In this one he was letting him go because he knew that anyone he got close to would get hurt.

Too soon, the masked warlock from the underground woke Angus. Then someone drove him to see his mother. He was still wearing his demon clothing under a borrowed jacket and shoes.

It was a reminder that he didn't belong in either world.

He hadn't seen Terrance since that morning. Maybe he'd be back this evening so they could spend the night together before Angus went back to Demonside. Was it wrong to hope?

The car stopped at the curb in front of the house, and Angus got out. The whole trip had been silent, and Angus hadn't bothered to break it. The car disappeared around the corner. If things went badly, he'd be escaping to Demonside.

Snow dusted the sidewalk even though it was only autumn. He scuffed his foot in the stuff, sketching out an A like he used to when he was a kid. Then he erased it and stared at the house he'd grown up in. He shivered, the light pants from Demonside not keeping him warm at all. Heatstroke, then hypothermia. Did neither world like him?

He made his way up the path and knocked on the door, not sure if his mother was even home. His heart was beating hard. What if she didn't want to see him because his father had poisoned her mind? How fast would she ring the cops or his father?

The door opened, and there she was. She looked as though she'd been crying. Her hair was pulled back in to its usual bun, but bits were sliding out.

Her eyes widened, and she covered her mouth with her hand. "Angus? I thought you were gone for good this time."

"No, Mom." Angus hugged her and shut the door. "I'm not that easy to get rid of."

She squeezed him harder. "Your demon should be killed for continually snatching you. It shouldn't be allowed."

Ah, so that was the explanation being given. He closed his eyes. She was crying again. He didn't want to join in, but he knew this might be the last time he saw her. She might never want to see him again after this.

There had to be another way.

He had no idea what it was. The underground wouldn't help him if he didn't help them. The college was never going to help him, and the police would arrest him. He needed the underground. They were the only ones who could bring him back from Demonside. Demonside would drain him eventually, taking the magic in his blood and then his soul even if he didn't participate in any rituals.

She released him. "I should never have let you go to Warlock College. You never wanted to go."

"I like magic." Angus tried to give her a reassuring smile. It faltered for a moment. He couldn't let her believe that it was Saka's fault. She needed to know it had been his father. "Mom, my demon didn't snatch me. Dad sent me over."

"What? That makes no sense. Why would he do that?" She stepped away from him. "He was so proud that you were finally a warlock."

He hadn't told Angus that. His father had offered him a way out of the Warlock College—hand over Saka and get a mind wipe. If he'd taken that option, his life would've been easier. Would he have realized that something was wrong every time he listened to the news and saw the spreading icecaps or a demon in the streets? Or would the mind wipe have been so thorough he wouldn't have realized anything was amiss? That was a chilling idea. He'd have been like everyone else, looking to the warlocks for help without realizing they were the cause.

"Dad wanted me to hand over my demon so he could take Saka's magic."

His mother stared at him as though he'd been speaking another language. "Why didn't you? Your father knows about these matters. Your demon snatched you. He should be killed. I'm sure your father would've made good use of that magic. They need all they can get to stop these brutal winters."

Angus sighed. She wasn't going to listen to him. He couldn't convince her that demons were people too, and she would never side with the underground. He closed his eyes and drew in a breath. He needed to walk away. Maybe one day when things were better, he'd be able to stop by and see her.

"I came to say good-bye, Mom. It's not safe for me to visit you. The police want me. I'm accused of being a rogue warlock." He wanted to make sure that she didn't look for him, but he couldn't lie and say that he was safe. Nothing he was doing these days was safe or sensible or anything like the way he'd imagined his life or even studies going.

"Your father can fix that. I'm sure it's a misunderstanding."

"He caused it." He smiled sadly at her. "Whatever they say about me, I am trying to stop the ice from overtaking the world. I am trying to be a good person and help others, the way you always told me to. I'm going to become a healer."

"Angus, I think you are confused. Let me call your father. We can talk this through. Fix it up. You've obviously been through a lot and are upset." She touched his cheek as though he was a child in need of calming. "Maybe you need a rest."

Her life was going to be ruined. He'd be gone. Her husband would be gone.

A car pulled into the driveway. She didn't need to ring his father. The people who had dropped him off had obviously called his father to tip him off. The car door slammed. He was running out of time with his mother.

"I'm sorry, Mom." Not for being who he was, but for the pain he was going to cause.

The front door opened. Angus knew who it was before his father walked into the room.

"You made it back." His father didn't seem happy that his son was alive.

Angus faced his father. "I'm hard to kill."

"Tell him this is all a mistake, dear." His mother looked at her husband.

"Angus has been consorting with demons. He has joined the underground. He is no son of mine." His father pulled a knife.

Angus had nothing. He didn't know where the knife that Saka had given him was, or any of his other things. The underground hadn't given him any weapons—but then who would expect a father to pull a knife on his son? His gaze flicked to the blade. That was a knife made for stabbing and killing, not the fine little blade that Saka liked to use to draw blood.

"No." His mother stepped between them.

Angus moved from behind her, he didn't want her caught in the middle.

"Stay out of this. Call the police and tell them that we have Angus in custody." His father ordered his mother in a way Angus had never heard before.

She hesitated, then backed away to obey, her gaze darting between her husband and her son.

"There is no escape this time. I cannot send you back since your underground friends will just retrieve you."

"You could let me leave. We don't have to do this."

"You have broken too many laws." His father held the knife loosely.

"So have you. The unwritten rules were supposed to protect demons and humans." Behind him, Angus felt the shimmer as his father opened the void. Angus still needed to walk the circle, and it took him time to pluck apart the void. His father was much more powerful—but then he'd killed plenty of demons to get that way.

Angus knew how this was going to happen now. He knew why the car hadn't waited.

"The unwritten rules were created by weak warlocks who couldn't see a different future."

Someone moved behind him, a demon. He could feel the cold of the void but at the same time, the scent of Demonside, dry and spicy. He longed for the heat and the noise of the tribe. The singing to keep away the riverwyrms.

Angus didn't argue with his father. There was no point. His father believed in what he was doing, that somehow the world would be better if it was colder and magic was locked up by a select few. It would take a very long time for the magic to trickle back across the void and for the world to warm. It would be too late for a barren Demonside.

"Don't let him through," his father ordered his demon. "What I want to know is how you got a mage. A demon bursting with power. We would all like to know."

Angus smiled. "I have no idea... maybe because I never believed that a demon should be used as a means to an end." He was lying now, but there was no way that he was going to share the truth. If his father or the college knew that mages could select, then they would find a way to manipulate it.

"All you had to do was follow in my footsteps, and you could have had everything you ever wanted."

"I have everything I need." He spread his hands and stepped back. He glanced over his shoulder. His father's demon, the one who had saved him from the riverwyrm, was waiting. "Do you want me to fight? Cry or beg? What would ease your mind?"

Sirens were coming up the street. His mother had called the cops, and they weren't wasting any time. He glanced to where she had been standing, but she was gone, hiding.

His father rushed him. The knife sank into Angus's stomach. Angus grasped his father's hand. Instead of catching Angus and taking him across, the demon turned. Angus and his father tumbled across the void.

Angus's back hit the hot midday sand of Demonside. Pain radiated through his body, each breath was short. He stared at the knife is disbelief. His father had stabbed him.

Angus's hands slipped on the blood, and he let go of his father.

His father pulled the knife free and raised it to stab again. Angus gritted his teeth but didn't close his eyes. He'd make the bastard look at him. He pressed his hand to the wound, blood wept between his fingers. He wasn't a doctor, but he knew it was too much.

"You couldn't even die properly. You've dragged me to this demon-riddled desert. You were a failure as a warlock and a son."

Angus would've said that he was a failure as a father, but he was struggling to breathe.

The winged demon caught his father's hand before he could bring the knife down. The wrist snapped.

His father screamed and dropped the knife. "Release me. I command you."

"You command no one here."

"You can't harm me. The unwritten rules forbid it." The words died on his father's lips as he realized what he was putting his faith in.

The demon forced Angus's father to his knees. "You will apologize to Angus."

"Never. I will be retrieved."

The heat seeping from the sand was nice. Angus was cold. He'd never felt cold in Demonside before. His fingers were slick and warm where they covered the wound. His blood was wetting the sand. This wasn't supposed to be how he died in Demonside.

"Saka." His voice was little more than a whisper.

He could hear shouting. Demons didn't shout, or at least he'd never heard them shout.

A vampry knelt beside him.

Angus flinched. He wasn't ready to give up his soul. He turned his head away. "No."

"Hush." The vampry placed her hand over the wound.

Another demon appeared and added his hand. "We can't wait."

A circle went up around the three of them.

Angus wanted to move, to argue, but he'd run out of energy. The vampry placed her other hand on his forehead, and his eyes became heavy. Something moved within him, a tearing heat. He might have screamed.

CHAPTER TWENTY-SEVEN

SAKA PACED HIS TENT. An entirely useless activity but there was nothing else that he could do. It was dusk. He should be up the mountain, but he wasn't. No one had expected him to go. He wouldn't have been able to concentrate anyway.

He'd arrived too late to do anything but stare in horror at the dark stain in the sand around Angus's body. Saka had wanted to lash out with magic at the old warlock who was Angus's father for doing this. Someone had held him back. Several someones. They had stopped him from doing something he would regret, though no one would've blamed him. Loss could temporarily break a mind.

The ache he'd felt when Kitu had vanished was nothing like the fragmentation of his entire world he'd felt when he'd heard his name being shouted out across the sand.

He forced himself to stand still and be calm. It was for the best he wasn't up on Lifeblood. He'd want to hold the knife and spill the blood, but a ritual was best done with a cool head and a calm heart. His was still beating too hard.

Saka paced to his bed and swept the curtain aside. Angus hadn't woken.

Most people thought magical healing was neat and easy. It wasn't.

But it was effective. The mages who had attended Angus both knew what they were doing. He wouldn't have been able to focus, but he could've lent energy or at least held Angus.

The tent grew dark, and Saka lit a single orb. He didn't want to leave. People had left food, or clothing, or items that Angus would need to live, as if they could entice him to stay in his body. His body would be healing... but there was still a chance that he wouldn't wake if the shock had been too great.

Was this one too many?

He remembered Angus's smile as he'd decided to go home and see how things were.

Saka wanted to keep him here forever and safe from the humans who would hurt him. If he didn't wake tomorrow, he would have to go home. Maybe being there would help. Maybe the underground could do something.

They had let him get stabbed—by his father.

An angry snarl escaped as the rage bubbled back up. He wasn't used to feeling so helpless or useless. He needed to do something. Anything.

So he went back to pacing.

Green light rippled across the sky, illuminating the tent for a moment before fading. Saka inhaled and then exhaled slowly. The warlock was dead. Saka expected that the warlock had hated every bit of rebalancing he'd been forced to participate in. That brought him a small amount of satisfaction. Which was very petty of him.

He hoped that the magic helped lift the rivers and strengthen Demonside.

That was a better thought. One that was more worthy of his status.

Someone stood at the flap of his tent. Saka walked over. The woman bowed and held out her gift. He didn't know her; she wasn't from his tribe.

"For the human mage from Guda's tribe."

"Thank you." Saka returned her bow and then unwrapped the bundle. It was a set of knives in a red leather wrist sheath. The handles were white bone. They were a very valuable set of knives. He had been planning on trading for a full set for Angus to use while he was here.

"You are pleased?" She smiled uncertainly.

"Yes." How could he not be pleased? Even if he wasn't, turning away a gift would be rude... worse, it might encourage Angus's spirit to leave because he wasn't valued.

Usually demons would want the human to give up their soul. But not this time. Saka hadn't realized that anyone else, or any other tribe, had really cared about Angus. He thought they'd healed Angus because they knew that was what he'd want. And maybe because Angus was not a bad human, but one who was trying to help. He saw now it was more than that. The greater tribe wanted him to live.

"Thank you. I am sure that he will use these well." *If he wakes up.*

"If you ever need knives, I would gladly trade with you." She bowed again and disappeared into the night.

Saka carefully rewrapped the knives. In the morning he would have to speak to the trainees. They knew what had happened to Angus and would want to know what had happened to his father, but they had been kept out of it. No doubt they would be shaken.

Putting himself out of the situation for a moment helped, but not for long.

He put the knives with the other items spread over his main room. Angus had managed to accumulate a life in half a day. Quite an achievement for a human warlock in training. Saka smiled. There was enough here to tempt him to wake up and rejoin his body.

He stood by the curtain, watching Angus sleep. "You have work to do, warlock. I am not done with you. You will wake up."

He willed Angus to blink or stir. Nothing.

Pacing all night wasn't going to help. He needed rest too. Although he wasn't sure that sleep would actually happen. He lay down on the bed, and the warm breeze skimmed over his skin. Outside the tent there was soft singing and talking. The usual sounds of life.

Saka turned over to watch Angus. He was breathing.

He put his hand out so he could feel the human's heart beating. His fingers traced the mark he'd carved there. He leaned over and kissed it. Angus had a good heart. He'd known that from the first time he'd seen him.

"I don't want another warlock."

Angus's chest stilled for a moment before resuming the even breaths. Saka propped himself up. He kept his hand over Angus's heart. "I don't want another warlock. I want you."

There was a definite reaction this time. Angus blinked a few times as if trying to focus. He went to move, but Saka kept him down.

"Rest. You are still healing." How far had Angus's spirit drifted away?

Angus closed his eyes, then reopened them. "It wasn't a dream, then." His voice was quiet and rough.

"No." How much should he say?

"Is it done?"

"Yes."

Angus closed his eyes again. "Don't leave."

"I haven't. I won't."

"You weren't there."

"I tried to get there. They had started...." There had been too much blood. "I thought I was going to lose you."

Angus's lips curved, but he didn't open his eyes again. "You're my demon. We have too much to do."

"You are my warlock, my apprentice, and my lover." Saka kissed him. "The tribes brought you gifts to help you wake. They all know you. You have a place here." He wanted to say home, but they both knew that Angus would always be moving between the two worlds.

Angus opened his eyes. "You really think we can fix Demonside?"

The death of Angus's father had healed a hole in Demonside, and not just in the returning of magic but in the demons. They had seen that those in positions of power could be brought down.

"Yes. We can rebalance both worlds. But we can plan our next step tomorrow."

Tomorrow would come whether they wanted it or not. Saka lay down, his hand still on Angus. For the moment it was enough that

Angus was alive and the rivers had been raised. He knew enough to take the quiet moment and enjoy it for what it was.

Angus moved closer. "What's the longest a human has lived here?"

Saka wasn't sure. "I will ask. Some of the older mages will know. You can go back with the trainees as you need. I was thinking you might have to go back after…after getting injured."

"Stabbed. No, I want to stay until the trainees go back. I need to learn. I need to be able to defend myself. I need to know how to fight." An edge had formed in his voice. The uncertain young man who Saka had dragged across the void had died out on the sand, and in his place was a warlock who knew what he wanted.

READ on for an excerpt from book 2, Rogue in the Making

EXCERPT

ROGUE IN THE MAKING (STUDIES IN DEMONOLOGY 2)

WHILE THE WOUND had been healed with magic, the new skin was tight, and the memory was raw. Angus Donohue kept his hand over the scar on his abdomen as though he expected his skin to tear open. He knew it wouldn't, and it didn't stop the pain, but he couldn't drop his hand and walk easily either.

The red sand was warm against the soles of his feet, and the bells around his ankle jangled as he left the shade of Lifeblood Mountain. For the first few days of his recovery, he'd stayed close to the tents of Saka's tribe. When he wanted to go out, Saka was with him. Each day a little more magic was worked to make sure all of his intestines were properly repaired. His body was healing fine.

But when he was going to sleep, he felt the blade of the knife thrusting into his stomach, twisting and tearing. He was so used to Saka's sharp knives and the way they cut skin with no whisper of resistance. The knife his father had used wasn't designed for magic or ritual. It was a knife for killing.

Angus walked and sang softly to himself, even though dizziness darkened the edges of his vision. He would get there and back on his own. He was tired of being trapped in the tent and having people—demons—thinking him a fragile human. He lifted his gaze. The orange sun was low but crawling its way up the cloudless violet sky. He had plenty of time to return to Saka's tent before the intense heat of midday. If he fell over, he was sure someone would be watching him anyway.

Someone was always watching him. He wasn't a human trainee sent across the void by the underground. He was Angus, the human apprentice mage—which was something else entirely. Though no one had actually explained the difference, he seemed to be an honorary demon.

His father would've been horrified.

Angus's lips twisted into a bitter smile. His father died knowing that all his stolen magic was being returned to Demonside with every drop of blood and smothered scream. Maybe he didn't bother to hold back his cries. Maybe he yelled and threatened until his voice was hoarse. Yes, that was more like his father.

Angus stopped three yards from a small cairn that marked his father's grave. It was well away from the river, the mountain, and the area where the tribes camped. Their tents were colorful blocks in the distance. His chest tightened. Was he too far away?

He scanned the sand for telltale ripples and increased the volume of his singing—a human pop song that blended seamlessly into a demon ballad. It didn't matter what he sang, only that he made noise to keep the riverwyrms away. The bells around his ankle were another simple deterrent. After one near brush, he had no desire to have a closer look at how many spade-like teeth the creature had for tearing off limbs and dragging its victims beneath the sand to the underground rivers.

He shuddered, not sure which was a worse way to die—bleeding to death, suffocating in sand, or drowning? He'd come so close to finding out.

The demon-style loose pants and shirt fluttered around him in the warm breeze, and the sky stubbornly remained cloudless. His father's death had lifted a river, but it had sunk just as quickly. Everyone was waiting for rain, hoping that clouds would gather after the next ritual.

He dug his toes into the sand and tried to suck up the heat, but the cold in his bones remained.

If there was no rain, Demonside would die. It was already on the edge. For Demonside to live, the magic trapped across the void had to be returned. Human blood would be spilled that night in the hope of rebalancing some of what had been taken.

He closed the last three yards and knocked the top stone off his father's cairn. "Because of you."

He shoved another and another off. They rolled down the sides and landed softly in the sand.

"Because of warlocks like you." He picked up a rock and threw it. The fresh pink skin of his scar tugged. He pressed his hand harder to his stomach, but the pain wasn't in his gut. His gut was healed but tender. His heart was torn open, and no magic could heal that wound.

"You don't deserve a marker." He used the ball off his foot to kick off another rock. "You stabbed me. You tried to kill me."

His father had almost succeeded.

"I hope your death hurt. I hope you regretted everything you'd ever done in your life." His mother had lost her husband, and her son was a wanted criminal for siding with the underground and refusing to turn Saka over to be killed by the college. His father had told the college that Angus was a rogue warlock. He'd never be able to live in Vinland without looking over his shoulder. His mother would be heartbroken.

Tears welled, and he didn't brush them away. "What was so important that you had to kill me? Or was it just that you hated me?"

A breeze tugged at his clothes, and the bells added their tune. There was no other reply. All Angus had needed to do to please his father was graduate from the Warlock College and become a warlock of standing, just like him. He shuddered. The idea of being anything like his father was abhorrent.

He'd tried to avoid going to college. Then he tried to get kicked out. He couldn't even do that right, because that was the day he met Saka, and Saka had brought him to Demonside.

In one day he'd seen the destruction the warlocks were causing with their quest for power—the way they manipulated the media to blame the demons for the cooling of their world and the increasing rampages.

There was only one flaw with their spin—no one could open a tear in the void from Demonside, not even a human. The void could only be opened from Humanside. A warlock had let the demons through, let them cause fear, and then killed them for their magic.

Too much magic taken and not enough rebalanced. His father's blood had barely wet the bottom of the dry riverbed.

Angus picked up the rocks he'd knocked off and rebuilt the cairn. The anger was there, but he'd get no answers from a week-old corpse.

Fast footsteps on the sand made him look up.

It wasn't a demon, but a human.

He lifted his hand and squinted. If it was one of the humans being kept for rebalancing, there was nowhere for them to go. Running would only bring their deaths sooner. He didn't like the squirming sensation caused by the idea of humans being treated like cattle. But without them, Demonside would die before there was any chance of saving it. If Demonside died, Humanside would freeze over. Ice ages didn't sound like a whole lot of fun, and already the winters were longer and colder, and crops were failing.

He dropped the rock in his hand. Two worlds were dying so a few could control all the magic. The demons should have thrown his father's body to the scavengers....

The running human came toward him—not a sacrifice but a trainee.

"I wanted to talk to you before you went back to the camp." Jim huffed out the words and put his hands on his knees.

"Town... it's a town, not a camp." A town that could be packed up and moved to wherever the water was, which left few options these days. Saka had told him how all the land around Lifeblood had once been green and littered with trees. Now it was hard to see even the twisted dead trunks. Many of the tribes were going to stay close to Lifeblood instead of breaking away like they usually would. Fear was in the air and whispered on the breeze.

If Jim wanted to talk to him out here, then it was something he didn't want to say around demons.

"You didn't have to run to catch me alone. I'm not speedy at the moment." Angus patted his stomach. It could've been him buried in the sand with no one to mourn his passing. That wasn't entirely true. Saka would be saddened. He picked up the rock and placed it back on the cairn. He was a better man than his father.

Jim pushed his hair back as he stood. "Yeah. How is that?"

"Fine." He wasn't in the mood for chatting with his ex. It hadn't been long enough for the little flip to stop when he saw Jim smile, but Jim had moved on. He was dating another underground trainee, Lizzie.

Jim picked up the other rock Angus had thrown. He tossed it from hand to hand as he walked back. "How is it really going here? With Saka?"

Ah, so that was what Jim really wanted to know. Angus held out his hand for the rock, and Jim gave it to him. "Good."

The word fell from his tongue without thought. Saka had been with him, healing him, helping him. Some days they were closer than mage and apprentice. Some days it felt like they were lovers playing with magic the way he and Jim once had, although the amount of magic that he and Saka played with was very different from his early fumblings with Jim.

"Back to rebalancing?" Jim's eyebrow twitched upward.

Angus swallowed, but his throat was dry. He untied the waterskin from his waist and took a sip. It was warm, but enough. He offered it to Jim, who hadn't brought water—a foolish thing to do in a desert.

There'd been no talk of rebalancing with blood or sex. The third kind of rebalancing required soul. His father had paid in blood and soul for his magic. Angus doubted the ritual would've made a dent in the amount his father owed.

"No, I haven't been doing much but healing." And learning about how it was done. That was what he was interested in. He'd wanted to be a doctor, not a warlock.

Jim didn't have a demon. He had no bond with Demonside, and he

245

couldn't draw magic via a demon. He was, in Angus's father's words, "a know-nothing wizard and not worth wasting your time with."

"The college will know he's dead." Jim handed back the water skin.

Angus had no doubt it had been reported. Everyone knew the demon who spied for the college under duress. What Ruri told her warlock was carefully discussed with the other mages—enough to keep the college happy but not enough to give them any ideas. His father's death wasn't a secret that could be kept.

Dead. It was so final, so unreal, even though he was standing at the cairn. He waited for sorrow or even remorse to kick in. When his father stabbed him, Angus made the snap decision to drag his father to Demonside with him. He knew his father would die there, and it hadn't stopped him. He might as well have held the blade that took his father's life.

But he didn't regret bringing his father there. Beneath the anger was the lightness of relief. His father would never hurt anyone, human or demon, again.

"I know. The Warlock College will blame me for not having the decency to die alone." He was making a habit of not doing what they wanted. What lies would the college tell his mother this time?

Jim drew in a breath. "You aren't to blame. He made his own choices. We all did."

"What do you mean? You regret coming here?" The wizards who volunteered to come to Demonside to learn magic were in a unique situation. They learned from the mages as though they were apprentices, and they learned how to pay for their magic to keep the balance, but they had no bond with their demon. The bonus was that magic was visible in Demonside. It made learning so much easier.

Jim shook his head. "It's weird, but it's good to know how to use natural magic, how to be strong without a demon...."

Angus was learning that too. He didn't want to be reliant on Saka for power. The underground was made up of rogue warlocks and wizards who resented the stranglehold the college had on magic. It was an uneasy alliance, made only because they had a common enemy.

Jim shoved his hands into the pockets of his pants. He wasn't wearing demon-style clothing. None of the trainees did. "He's dead, so you should know the truth."

Angus went still. "About what?"

For a moment nothing moved. Even the breeze and the endless sand were still. It was too quiet, too unnerving. Angus stamped his feet a few times to hear the bells.

Jim scowled. "He paid me to break up with you. I couldn't say anything because he threatened me. The college versus a wizard—it was never going to end well."

"So you took the money and ran." Angus bit out the words. *Give him a chance to explain.*

Jim looked at his feet. "I didn't have a choice."

The rage bubbled up and threatened to suck him under. *There's always a choice. You took the easy one.*

Angus pressed his fingernails into the tender skin on his belly. The pain grounded him. If he pressed harder, he might draw blood, and then he'd be able to open the sand beneath Jim's feet and let him vanish the way he had months before. He relaxed his fingers and pulled together a fragile calm. He didn't care why Jim had taken the bribe, but that didn't make it all right. "Sometimes it seems like we have no choice because the alternative is too terrifying."

He sounded like Saka. Maybe he was spending too much time around mages.

Jim looked up, and hope lit his eyes. "So you understand?"

Angus blinked and assessed his former lover. The man who had first introduced him to sex magic—they had tried and failed at it. The man who had introduced him to the teachings of the underground and made him question the college. He nodded because he didn't want to put what he really felt into words.

Betrayed by someone he thought he loved and who he thought loved him.

He wouldn't let it happen again.

He liked Saka for his magic and for the sex, but a human couldn't love a demon, and demons couldn't love humans. No matter how

247

much he wanted more from Saka, he was never going to get it. He shouldn't want it either. Humans were destroying Saka's world. Their alliance was so delicate that Angus wasn't sure how it would survive.

Jim smiled.

That time there was no stirring or fondness to the memory of what they'd had.

His father and the college weren't done trying to ruin his life. Some days it would be easier to be demon.

AFTERWORD

Thank you for buying Warlock in Training. Get a free copy of A Wolf's Resistance when you join my newsletter.

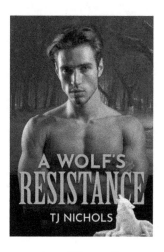

A gay shifter novella

Join Now

OTHER BOOKS BY TJ NICHOLS

Studies in Demonology trilogy
Warlock in Training
Rogue in the Making
Blood for the Spilling

Mytho series
Lust and other Drugs
Greed and other Dangers

Familiar Mates
The Witch's Familiar
The Vampire's Familiar
The Rock Star's Familiar

Holiday novellas
Elf on the Beach
The Vampire's Dinner
Poison Marked
The Legend of Gentleman John
Silver and Solstice

A Summer of Smoke and Sin

A Wolf's Resistance

Olivier (an Order of the Black Knights novel)

Hood and the Highwaymen

Writing as Toby J Nichols

Ice Cave

ABOUT THE AUTHOR

Urban fantasy where the hero always gets his man

TJ Nichols is an avid runner and martial arts enthusiast who first started writing as child. Many years later while working as a civil designer, TJ decided to pick up a pen and start writing again. Having grown up reading thrillers and fantasy novels, it's no surprise that mixing danger and magic comes so easily. Writing urban fantasy allows TJ to bring magic to the every day. TJ is the author of the Studies in Demonology trilogy and the Mytho urban fantasy series.

TJ has gone from designing roads to building worlds and wouldn't have it any other way. After traveling all over the world TJ now lives in Perth, Western Australia.

TJ also writes action/horror as Toby J Nichols.

You can connect with TJ at:

Newsletter

Patreon